Forest
for the
Trees

Diane Pelkey

ISBN 978-1-0980-8856-9 (paperback)
ISBN 978-1-0980-8857-6 (digital)

Christian Faith Publishing, Inc.
832 Park Avenue
Meadville, PA 16335
www.christianfaithpublishing.com

Printed in the United States of America

MY NAME IS TANNER TRUMP, no relation to the Donald. I'm seventy-nine years old, have been told I look scads older, but could care less. My days of chasing skirts came to a screeching halt on that fateful day when I began to drink, eat, and sleep journalism; when I was the shark; and when I began consuming newsroom guppies like ET popped Skittles. My mind is as sharp as it was the day that I left the Big Apple, New York Yankees, and haute cuisine. I suffer from lack of sleep, fallen arches, and a gastric, ulcerated stomach. I bailed out and went in search of my own personal Bali Hi. To coin a sixties phrase, "I had to find myself, man."

My eyesight's lacking because I refuse to permit some snotty-nosed, pimple-ass surgeon to remove the festering cottage cheese that they refer to as cataracts or pin back a set of drooping eyelids that would make an old coon dog proud. I could go on forever, however, I imagine that it is of little interest to the reader that events such as one good BM, one good poop in a twenty-four-hour period is cause for celebration or that two bottles of my favorite brew are sufficient to give me a late-afternoon buzz and enough gas to transform my bathtub into a Jacuzzi for a minimum of five seconds.

I'm not perched before the Dell, with my cheeks supported by what the polite medical community calls a doughnut, intent on creating the great American novel or a volume worthy of the *New York Times*'s roster of best sellers. I intend to say it plain. If you are put off by semi-off-color colloquialisms; words such as hell, damn, crap, screw, or ass, to name a few, I apologize. Let's be real, folks. My pocked digits flatly refuse to form phrases the likes of "poo-poo," "grunty buns," or the ever popular "number two." Rest assured that no matter how ornery or agitated I become, I never ever use the f-word. I don't believe in taking linguistic license that far. So what's the bottom line? I'm not out to offend anyone's sensibilities, and I will not be upset if you decide to use this text to line the birdcage or as tinder for the hearth. After all, you paid for this book.

After high school, I earned an engineering degree, tested the waters, and walked away from a lucrative profession for reasons I won't share because they are tiresome. I purchased a second-rate laptop, beat-up printer, and two reams of paper; and then I set out to make a name for myself as a freelance writer. I chased ambulances and interviewed street dwellers and tramps that rode boxcars from one end of the country and back again. I forged credentials to gain entrance to political debates, press conferences, and any other venue that required formal identification. I kicked, bit, clawed, and stepped over bodies on my way to the top. I had no social life, had few friends, and eventually had secured the position of reporter for a large newspaper located in a cosmopolitan city on the East Coast. I've won more damn awards than I care to count. It's not necessarily that I wanted the dust magnets but primarily that I didn't want anyone else to have them. I am fatigued and tired of the cut and chase as young men and women pass me on the right. I decided to resign my post shortly after a weekend trip to Pittsburgh, New Hampshire. It was by far one of the most tranquil, beautiful places that I had ever been.

I purchased a ten-acre section of wooded land just off Route 3 and, with the help of a nearby realtor, met with an architect who was able to design a retirement home fit for my purposes. For an additional fee, he agreed to oversee the construction while I settled my affairs back in New York. Within six weeks, my single-story woodland home was complete, and I moved in the day after the local furniture chain delivered a selection of furniture purchased with the intention of minimalizing the use of floor space, while maximizing comfort.

One morning, after a lengthy thunderstorm cleared, I set out to purchase several staples, intent on filling the cupboards and fridge. There was a nearby general store that proclaimed, "If you need it, we have it."

Several of the town elders sat on a nearby stoop as I made a couple of trips, lugging multiple sacks of necessities and a nice thick ham sub for dinner to my SUV. That damned early-morning shower had transformed the unpaved parking lot into a murky mess. On my final trip to the car, with an armful of paper bags, I offered brief pleasantries to the men outside; and when I stepped off of the stoop, I misjudged my step. I tripped, slipped, and stumbled ass over teakettle into a murky puddle. Cussing softly, I gathered my soggy goods, huffing and puffing. I chanced a glance at the old coots, and they appeared to be taking this in stride as if it were a common occurrence.

I returned home, began unloading the soggy mess, and realized that I was tracking mud-encrusted feet from the doorway through the living room to the open kitchen, and I had inadvertently left the door open. I'd allowed my stumble in front of those men to occupy my mind as I stored the canned goods into the cabinets. I swore continuously; I needed to vent. I had been a shark for a very long time, but today I felt like an insignificant guppy when I took that tumble in the presence of the elders. This brought about a string of epitaphs that would have made those lumberjacks blush.

"People have burned in hell for far less, sir. Curb that tongue. There's a lady present."

This scolding took me off guard at a moment when I was still in a rage. "Don't you people around here knock?" I bent to retrieve the can of peas that I'd dropped. "Can't you see that I'm busy?" I lashed out, not in anger but embarrassment.

"I have come from a bit of a distance. If you would please allow me entrance. I shall rest these weary bones while you complete your chore." She traipsed through the front door and settled comfortably in my favorite recliner. "There are several cruets out on the porch. They are a newcomer's gift."

The least that she could have done was to sit at the kitchen table. I was, after all, in that room. But no! She went and sat in my recliner. My favorite spot in this entire house, *My Recliner*!

"Does this chaise possess some sentimental value?" She remained seated. "It appears so new."

"You wouldn't understand."

"A cool glass of water, Tanner Trump? I prefer to take my libations in a glass receptacle, please. Plastic taints purity."

"You have me at a disadvantage. You are?"

"Miriam."

"Miriam who?"

"Simply Miriam shall do."

"Fine! I'll get the damned water, but as soon as you've finished it, leave." I knew that my behavior was rude, but I didn't care for the fact that I'd been caught in the middle of a mess and wasn't in the mood for company. Particularly when a visitor simply waltzed into my home unannounced. "Here. Knock yourself out."

"Thank you, sir." She set the tumbler aside and walked out to the porch, returning with the cruets.

"What's in those things? Hemlock?" I was in true form.

"You'll know. Everyone knows." She set them on the kitchen table.

"Where are you from?" I couldn't quite place the accent.

"Hereabouts. Born and raised." She assessed the living area. "Very nice. You will enjoy sunrise and sunset at this angle."

"Hereabouts? Half a mile from my home? Quarter a mile to the east? Here in Pittsburgh?"

"Nearby."

"Okay, I give up!"

Now this senior had to be eighty if she was a day. She sat proud, straight as a rod, and clasped diminutive hands at the waist. Her hair was abundant, shone silver, and was enshrouded by a multicolored snood that appeared handmade. The five-footer smiled, displaying rows of snow-white teeth that were as even as my nephew Joe's, and he'd sported braces for six consecutive years. Her figure was slight, unassuming. Her face bespoke of a woman of many years, wrinkled yet soft. Faded azure eyes sparkled with mischief. When I paid her little attention, she rose from my chair.

"You, Tanner Trump, must open your heart and mind if you are to live hereabouts. This is a very special place. You shall see."

"Thank you for the gifts. I'm certain that they will come in handy."

"You are welcome. I shall return on the morrow at first light."

"For what purpose? I certainly don't expect you to prepare breakfast." I slipped unnoticed into my comfort zone and surprised myself.

"Ah, levity. You should practice it more often. It suits you." She made for the door. "I will have broken fast prior to my visit. However, a glass of cool water will do nicely."

"Of course." I was about to make mention of the one that remained untouched, forming a damp circle on the mahogany table.

"Dry the area fully and then apply a touch of bee's wax. That is in the second cruet to your left. We've an abundance of the busy critters this year."

"Oh." I convinced my practical side that she'd followed my gaze, nothing more. No mind reading here. "Thank you."

I walked her to the door and stood there watching until she reached the farthest tree line and disappeared from view. I approached the counter and glared at the neat line of earthen jars. I did not want to subliminally or intuitively recognize their contents, as Miriam had insisted that I would. The root of my irritation sprung from an intense certainty that she'd omitted titling on purpose. She had done so in order to annoy me. I dismissed this stupid train of thought as a childish offshoot of my grumpy mood.

I vigorously applied bee's wax to the water stain and then crept into bed with the intention of taking a late-afternoon snooze. I awoke at dawn the next day, cursing the sunlight that seeped into my bedroom, revealing a hoard of dust mites that were bound to annoy my sinuses.

I am uncertain if it was the quality or quantity of shut-eye that transformed this night owl into a quasi-approachable host long before I had the opportunity to polish off two cups of coffee. As I reached for the second half of a cream-cheese slathered cinnamon-raisin bagel, there was a light knock at my door. Wiping my mouth with a sheet of paper towel, I prepared myself to encounter whoever chose to visit this early in the day.

"You look fit today. I suppose you slept well."

Miriam. I'd forgotten that she had promised to return this morning. I schooled my slightly irritated reaction, intent on not letting her ruin my day.

"I did. You want to come in? I'm eating breakfast." I strolled nonchalantly into the kitchen in hopes that she wouldn't sit in my recliner.

"Yes, thank you." And there she went! Without hesitation, she smoothly slipped her posterior on the beautiful red leather. I forgot myself and groaned.

"This chair has special meaning to you? Perhaps a fond memory or an attachment of some kind?"

I proceeded without preamble to offer a truthful response. "A man quickly becomes attached to some of his possessions, particularly when he lives alone."

"I understand."

I wanted to say, "No, you don't" because she remained seated in my chair.

"It soon shall be time for us to leave, Tanner Trump. I wish to introduce you to The Well."

"Really?" I huffed. "Do you mind if I finish my coffee and bagel first? As a matter of fact, if you'd like, you can go right out back. That is where they drilled my well."

"Not that well, sir. The Well of Dreams."

"Of course!" I smacked my forehead for emphasis. "How silly of me!"

"You are many things, Tanner Trump, but silly is not one."

"Would you please stop addressing me as Tanner Trump?"

"That is your name."

"Call me Tanner, call me Trump, call me foolish and feeble-minded, but for the love of gawd, quit using the two in tandem. It's annoying the hell out of me."

"I will remember this."

She rose with the effortless grace of a woman half her age, putting me to shame.

"This is a good time to begin our walk."

"If you're planning on a lengthy nature walk, count me out. These knees are too far gone." I was not overly fond of any kind of exercise.

"What we seek is nearby. Do not fret."

"Then let's get this over with. I have a date with a good book."

Miriam sought an ill-traveled path. The pucker-bush was so dense; we had to proceed single file, and then suddenly, the daylight burst with such force that it caused my eyes to close. I should have brought along a pair of sun glasses.

"We have arrived, Tanner."

I then found myself standing amidst low-hanging boughs; a domed retreat lit by shards of sunbeams that caromed off early-morning dewdrops. The initial effect was awe-inspiring. We crossed a spongy moss-carpeted area, so unlike the firm forest floor that jarred my lower joints.

"This is not a bad place, my friend." Miriam grasped my hand and guided me forward and stopped before The Well of Dreams.

Its circular boundary was made of beautiful granite slabs. The intricate workmanship and carvings came into view as we neared the rim. An ingenious craftsman had carved four sections that joined to form a perfect circle. I have no idea how far they sat beneath the verdant floor; however, the exposed portion stood at approximately three feet.

"I am fond of this place, Tanner."

"It's unearthly." I whispered.

"You are observant."

"No flies on me." An anxious chuckle escaped.

"I will explain. You shall be reassured."

"Really?"

"Yes, look here." She pointed to each section individually. "These four outer barriers represent north, south, east, and west. The granite sections that form the surface depict winter, spring, summer, and fall. Look at these markings."

I was able to interpret a few of the rudimentary carvings, while others left me baffled.

"I am west, you are east, Neris is north, and the warrior is south."

"I still don't understand. How am I supposed to be anything, unless the person or persons who built this knew me?"

"There are unknown factors that, for lack of a better explanation, simply are."

"I think that you are making this up as you go and that you and those other people are trying to pull my leg. I'm no innocent, gullible person. I've been around the block a few times, and I am not that easy to dupe. That said, what is your true purpose in dragging me out into no man's land?"

"Are you so jaded that you no longer believe that there are things yet to be explored, experienced?"

"Call it what you will, but a spade is still a spade. This is a well, albeit a very beautiful one, I'll admit. Probably set in someone's front yard in appreciation of some talented mason." I was making this up as I went on, convinced that it was making sense. "They are long gone, their property went to seed, and this is all that's left."

"Ah, do you truly believe that?" She raised a hand. "No, do not answer that. Will you humor me for a moment?"

"What have I got to lose? I'm out here. May as well rest for a bit." I crossed my arms, affecting a no-nonsense-pose.

"Very well. As I explained, you are west. This section, if you please. Place your right hand over your heart, and your left upon your ledge."

"What is that supposed to prove? Is there someone in the woods taking a picture of the city schmuck falling for your antics?"

"We two are alone, I assure you. Now please do as I ask. I shall remain at your side until you are finished."

"All right!" I placed my right hand over the old ticker. "Here goes looking up your address!" I touched the cool stone with the opposite paw.

No longer was I the old man, the retired newspaper reporter, nor was I standing beside The Well of Dreams. I was, in fact, somewhere very, very far away. I was in a different time. As my eyes, very keen eyes, perused the immediate area in front of me, I saw a wondrous array of highlanders, sporting plaids of various colors and squares.

They were boisterous, hearty men who had apparently set aside their chores in order to attend the games.

A fragrant, brisk breeze assaulted my senses and yes, made its way up my skirt. No, not a skirt, a kilt! How invigorating was the feeling of total freedom, of release from my usual garb. A giant of a man approached me, and while he was quite large, I was yet a half a head taller. As he was about to call my name, his voice changed.

"Tanner! Tanner Trump? Miriam! Tanner Trump? Please step away!" Her voice was sharp yet as gentle as the hand that she placed upon my shoulder.

"What the?" Had I not grabbed the lip of the well, I would have toppled to the verdant forest floor. "What the hell was that? Where did that come from?" I was shaken.

"Calm yourself, good sir. I shall explain, if you will?"

I brushed her hand aside and peered down into the cavern, thinking for a moment that there may have been a movie camera within. Stupid, but I wasn't able to explain exactly what had transpired.

"I am afraid that you are far too upset for me to carry on. Let us return to your home, and I will cool your brow with damp cloths."

"No!" I didn't want a cool brow. That sudden outburst made me realize that whatever had happened, I wanted more! And more! And more! "I, um, I, how can I explain it? I really felt like I was in Scotland. I felt the cool breeze go up my damned kilt! I saw me dressed just like men throwing stones, cabers, and well…; and well, I smelled that sweet, fresh air. I saw children running around, playing happily…"

"I am not privy to what it is that you experience. It is your past, not mine."

"What do you mean, my past? This is getting too weird!" I was hooked, but I had no idea what to. "Okay, please tell me what is going on here. I need to know that it wasn't the result of you dropping some type of hallucinogen into my morning coffee."

"If that is what you wish, I shall proceed."

"You have my undivided attention." And she did. By all that's holy, I was prepared to keep an open mind.

"I am not privy to time frames, only to say that it was a long time ago that a young Italian immigrant joined a group of his peers who were building a magnificent church in the southernmost area of our state. He met a lovely young woman by the name of Antionette. They became quite infatuated with each other and began what was to become a deep, loving relationship. They shared dreams of a life together, a life of wedded bliss, a home of their own, and of course, children."

"Don't tell me that this is a love story." She pressed a finger to my lips, quieting me instantly.

"Do not interrupt, Tanner. Now, may I continue?"

I nodded my head and vowed to be patient.

"Time passed quickly for Antonio and Antionette. He continued to work as a stone mason, and she was gainfully employed by a local shoe manufacturer. They set aside their hard-earned money with the intention of purchasing a home of their own. Now Antionette had, the previous year, visited our beautiful Pittsburgh and had been determined since to make this her home. Consequently, when she regaled Antonio with bits and pieces of its beauty, Antonio was hard-pressed to rob her of this dream." She paused for a brief moment. "If you wish, I will continue this tale as we return to your home, I do not wish to overtax you."

"No, let's get this done with, please." I remained steady, still leaning with my left hand on the Well.

"They were wed, and he moved into her apartment with her, sharing the expenses and pooling their savings. One Saturday morning, he left the apartment complex in which they lived and went to work. They labored for a few hours when, all of a sudden, the man closest to Antonio commented that he surely smelled smoke in the air. As they raised their heads in search of the source, they saw billows of smoke towering into the sky. With dread and fear, Antonio ran from the worksite, certain that the fire was coming from the vicinity of the apartment house where he and his Antionette lived. He ran as if the hounds of hell were on his tail. By the time that he reached the building, it was fully engulfed. Constructed completely of wood and decades old, the flames greedily consumed each floor. His Antionette hung halfway out of a window, calling for help."

"How high was their apartment? Was she not able to jump to safety?"

"Alas no, it was six-stories high. Her love called out from below, and she pleaded with him to come to her rescue. He laid caution to the wind and ran headlong into the structure. A weakened ceiling collapsed. A beam struck him in the head, knocking him unconscious. Another man who had followed in his wake removed debris from atop Antonio who was then transported to a nearby hospital. Sadly, Antionette perished in the fire. While her love lay abed in a questionable state, her family set her remains to rest in a nearby cemetery, for they were no longer able to delay this ceremony awaiting her betrothed's recovery. When Antonio regained cognition and was told that Antionette had died, he was beside himself with grief. In addition, he had been rendered blind by the near-fatal blow to his head. He was inconsolable. After recovery, the doctor sent him off with a cousin who promised to watch over him. Some feared that he would take his own life. One night, according to what Antonio told his family, his beloved came to him in a dream. She asked that he go on with his life and insisted that he move forward with their plans to purchase a section of land up north."

"So that's how he came to live in Pittsburgh? Surely, he couldn't get here on his own." I wanted, not needed to try this contraption again, and hoped that there would soon be an end to this saga.

"His second cousin drove him here, assisted with the purchase of this small lot and a small motor home." Miriam turned, gesturing with an open hand. "What you see before you, this open, grassy area, consists of his entire property with the exception of the immediately surrounding trees. The cousin stayed long enough to clear the area. However, he was unable to remain any longer."

"He couldn't just up and leave Antonio alone, that man was blind for heaven's sake!"

"Ah, but he did. Arrangements were made with the local men and women. They would see to it that his larder was filled and his motor home cleaned, and they offered any other assistance as needed.

The residents who occupied this area were, and still remain, a caring lot. Now I have forgotten a very important part of this narration, lengthy though it may seem. Antionette had an affinity for wells. She collected as much memorabilia as she could find, but sadly, even that perished in the fire. When two of the local men visited him, he requested that they fetch a goodly amount of granite. They asked why, and he said that he wanted to build a well, not a functioning fixture but a tribute to his wife who had come to him in a dream and asked him to undertake this project."

"He couldn't possibly have built this by himself."

"But he did. These men offered their help. 'No, thank you,' he said. 'I, and only I, must do this.' It took the better part of spring, summer, and fall for him to complete, and his visitors would attest to its progress, unaided. With tender, loving care, he scribed the uppermost ledges and then placed them in proper order. As you can see, it was not only a labor of love but also a beautiful monument. His love, he said, came to him one final time and praised him for his efforts. Additionally, she said that throughout the years, this would be a place where special people would visit, where they could enjoy their fondest memories. Should they forget from whence they came, this would stir up recollection, for nothing meant more to her than the footprints that her ancestors left. I believe that is the gist of it. However, my wording may not be precise."

"Do you believe that she had a hand in transforming this ordinary collection of stones into something akin to a time machine?"

"Not quite, because our recall is solely a time past. Not present or future. At least I have never experienced prophecies."

"What happened to Antonio?" I was interested.

"He perished shortly after. The doctors believe that it was a brain aneurism that took his life. Possibly additional damage from the blow to his head. Nevertheless, he was interred beside his wife. May they rest in peace." She made a sign of the cross, and I, without thought, emulated her.

"That's a nice story. However, I find it hard to believe that he did this all by himself." I removed my left hand from the rim and was about to continue when I noticed the rendering that was under my palm. "Oh no! No, no, no!" I bent to look closer. "This is not what I think it is!"

"What do you see, Tanner?" Miriam moved closer in order to observe what it was that had caught my attention.

"See here? This carving in the stone? I carved that into a tree when I was in high school. The girl that I was dating broke up with me, she'd met another guy when on vacation with her family and fallen in love. I carved this broken, inverted heart, our initials on either side, and then decided that I didn't want any of my friends to see it. It took me longer to chisel it out of the tree than it did to carve it in the first place. No one but me knows that.

"I cannot imagine how you returned to your home in such a state."

I detected a deep sorrow in Miriam's tone. Not pity, I would never have tolerated pity.

"This." I pointed the slab. "This is what I carved."

Miriam perused the sketch, nodded, but remained silent.

"When I was finished, I felt strong enough to go home, get past my mother, and spent the remainder of the afternoon and evening in my room. My mother was a wonderful woman. She was also very intuitive. Mom could read my moods and keep my father at bay when I needed time to myself. And yes, I wept. Once the tears began, it was like opening a floodgate. But I was stubborn and thickheaded. I never wore my heart on my sleeve. So the next day, I got up, joined my parents at the breakfast table, and went to work with my dad. He never asked me about Kirstie. That had to be my mother's doing."

"She possessed a beautiful soul."

"Yes, she did. And life goes on. I attended college, and well, the rest is history. Oh, and on a final note, she divorced Grey shortly after their first wedding anniversary. He had a heavy hand. I never saw her again, but my mother did. During one of our weekly moth-er-son calls, I was told that that once beautiful face, the face I'd seen in many a dream, was damaged beyond recognition." I turned to Miriam. "Why do women let men do that to them?"

"Low self-esteem, fear, and even love, I suppose."

"That may be, but I never, ever would have treated her like that. My father would have kicked my ass from her to kingdom come had I laid a hand on a woman. It just was not done."

"Ah, both a handsome and wise father!" She smiled.

"You obviously haven't met my dad! I get my good looks and charm from my mother!" It felt good to smile, to move on.

"So Tanner Trump. Do you now believe that this portion of the well was meant for you?"

"I am baffled! How in the name of Zeus did he know? I don't believe in the supernatural, but this really gives me the creeps, this Roman Numeral. You see it here?"

"I do. What is the significance?"

"You add up the numbers, a stupid thing that I did as a kid. I added all the numbers of my birthday. Then when someone asked me for my date of birth, I told them 'MCMLXIV.' I thought that the Roman Numeral thing was quite clever."

"August 31, 1925." She blurted out the date so quickly that I was startled.

"How did you? Oh, never mind." I wasn't about to go there! I was very close to an emotional overload. "Look here, they're carved in stone, of all things. The entire surface was well and evenly worn. It didn't look like someone had carved my personal information recently.

"Nothing here surprises me, Tanner. After all, I brought you here today in order to introduce you to this wonderful creation. You may pose before it and see lives past, your past. Once in position, right hand over your heart and left on 'your' stone. You may also depart with many wonderful dreams, but no more than one for each visit. There is no evil here, please rest assured. Sometimes, there are magnificent gifts left behind for those who are deserving."

"I can't imagine what I possibly could have done to be 'deserving'."

"Perhaps, you have yet to 'do it'." She smiled.

"Humph! What are those nine circles over there?" I pointed to the opposite side.

"Yes, on my stone. They represent my life cycles."

I laughed. "You would have me believe that you have lived nine lives?"

"Yes, Tanner. Do you believe in reincarnation?"

"I don't know what I believe anymore. My head is spinning."

"Let us return to your home. I am parched."

"I'd prefer to stay and investigate this Well further."

"You may return at your leisure. However, enough for today." She turned and began to walk along the pathway. "I shall elaborate on the subject of rebirth."

I couldn't let her leave alone. The path wasn't easy to navigate, and I didn't want her to fall along the way. "Please do."

"There are a select few who are blessed with the gift to reincarnate. Do I understand the why and wherefore? No, the answer evades me. Those whom I have met during the in-between stages have had no explanation. I've been told to focus on the skills that I would need to adapt to my future life on earth."

"I hate to sound like a 'Doubting Thomas,' but even with the experience that I had back there, I don't believe in reincarnation." We entered the clearing, the noon-day sun shining on my porch. "Sorry!"

"It is a difficult concept to understand. However, those whom you will meet during your in-between may have answers that you can accept."

I held the door open for her, and then went directly to the kitchen. As she sat in the recliner, I prepared a cold glass of water. I would think on this later and wonder at how easily we slip into a pattern so quickly.

"You said, 'my in-between.' Are you telling me that I am going to be reincarnated?"

"After this life-cycle, yes."

"Please continue. I'm going to have lunch in the interim."

"Very well. However, I have just now realized that I failed to explain why there are four sections encircling the lip of the Well of Dreams. As I said, you are east, I am west, Neris is north, and the champion is south."

"Why four? Why not six, seven, or eight?" I brought my lunch and set it on the coffee table. "Let me guess, you don't know."

"I am not privy of what Antonio was about. I can only impart what I know. That he was a seer, a wizard, or a witch, I know not. However, I am convinced that there were far more powerful beings that played a hand in this."

"For the time being, I guess that'll have to do. I need to chew on this sandwich, and then I'll chew on all this information later."

"A wise decision. Neris and her warrior are destined to meet. Their lives shall be intertwined, they will form a bond that will last a lifetime. You and I are cut from a similar cloth. However, we are destined solely to acquaint in this life cycle and will meet again in the next."

"Okay, then! That only adds more questions to the hopper." I sighed, feeling exhausted all of a sudden. "Let's set this reincarnation crap aside for now. Who the hell is Neris and this champion?"

"Patience, Tanner. I fear that I have overwhelmed you this morning. Perhaps I should curtail our discussion and continue on the morrow."

She was about to leave the comfort of her perch when I shouted, "Oh no, you don't! You're not going anywhere!" I slapped the table firmly for emphasis. "Sorry. I didn't mean to raise my voice to you. I really need to finish our talk today."

Miriam relaxed. "I shall offer an abbreviated response to your question. Neris is a lovely young woman who resides not very far from here. She was born and raised in these woods. You will meet her soon enough, for she loves the forest and can wander for hours when she sets her mind to it. You may hear her before she comes into view. She possesses a lovely voice and raises it often to announce her presence, for she does not wish to frighten the forest creatures. She is a bit timid at first but warms fairly quickly. She is unable to speak though."

"She's speech impaired? How is it that she can she sing but can't talk?"

"It is the way of things, and someday soon, you will come to understand her plight." Miriam raised a hand to deter me from speaking. "Please, Tanner. I am tired."

"Sorry. I'll accept what you have to offer today, but we are definitely going to talk more about Neris and about reincarnation. Agreed?"

"Agreed." Miriam gradually rose to her feet.

"Can I walk you home?" I truly wanted to know where she lived and was hoping to see the place.

"No, thank you." She glided to the door. Yes, that's what I said, glided! "We shall visit again soon."

"When might that be?"

"Soon, Tanner Trump. Soon." With that, she walked to the tree line, turned, and waved.

Once the remnants of lunch were put away, I decided to go into town. I needed a few things, including an alarm clock. If Miriam was going to visit often, I wanted to make sure that I was up and dressed. I also needed a good pair of hiking boots if I was going to be traipsing through the woods.

On the return trip, I pulled into a small market that claimed to make the best subs around. I left there with a yummy dinner consisting of a roast beef sub with all the fixings except hot peppers, a pint of potato salad, a pint of coleslaw, and three bottles of root beer.

When I entered the cabin, I experienced a slight twinge of loneliness. It looked too neat and organized for a bachelor pad. Setting aside the food, I went into the bedroom and programmed one of the two alarm clocks that I'd purchased. The second went on the table by my recliner in the event that I should fall asleep there. That done, the waterproof hiking boots along with the socks that the store clerk had recommended went onto the floor of my closet. As I placed them there, I wondered if I had it in me to visit the Well of Dreams alone. I was still feeling the aftereffects from our trek there this morning, and frankly, I'd been rattled. I closed the door and went to the kitchen, suddenly feeling ravenous.

Everything was delicious. I'd ordered a medium-sized sub. The woman behind the counter was preparing one for another customer and stuffed the darned thing with mounds of meat, and I knew that I'd only be able to eat a small or medium and treated myself to the latter. Not only did I polish off the sandwich but, I also consumed about three-quarters of the salad and slaw. I was full to bursting, but even as I made my way to the recliner, I vowed to make that trip again.

With root beer in hand, I went into the living room, fell onto my chair, and settled in for a night of movie binging. Well, frankly, the most that I could get in before nodding off was about one and a half flicks.

The alarm scared the ever-loving hell out of me! I knocked over the empty bottle, almost knocked the lamp over, and cussed repeatedly. I didn't like getting startled. It was one o'clock in the morning. I don't know why I set it so late. After reprogramming the damned thing for an earlier time, I went to bed.

Ladies and gentlemen, I had the most vivid, awesome dream that I'd ever had in my life! The highlander, yours truly, was the featured character, and we, sorry, I participated in the games. I was the returning champion and victor in each challenge. Have you ever had a dream that was so powerful, so pleasing, that you didn't want to wake up? Well, that was the case for me. The incessant buzzing in my ear got louder and louder by the second. It was the alarm! I'd programmed it to do just that because I wasn't confident that I'd hear it. Like the wisp of a butterfly's wings, the dream was gone. It was gone!

I reluctantly shuffled into the kitchen, set the coffee to brew, and took the bagel and cream cheese out of the fridge. I preferred my morning meal at room temperature.

After a quick shower, I sat down to eat my breakfast and had no sooner brought the bagel to my lips when there was a knock at my door. I set it down and went to greet my morning visitor. It seemed strange that I slipped into this routine without thought or reservation.

"Good morning to you, Tanner Trump." She handed me a warm loaf of dark bread. "I baked this morning and thought that you might enjoy some." She strolled by me and, as was her custom now, settled in. "Did you sleep well, good sir?"

"No, I mean yes." I put the bread on the counter but gave it a sniff before doing so.

"A touch of fresh honey adds to the flavor." She shifted into a comfortable position. "A cool glass of water, please?"

"Of course." I curbed my tongue. "Thanks for the bread. It smells great."

"You appeared confused when I inquired about your sleep. Did something keep you awake?"

"No. Actually, I slept very well. I had a pleasant dream and awoke quite refreshed. Do you mind if I finish my breakfast?"

"Not at all. Please eat." She smiled. "Boiled dough?"

"Yes, boiled dough." I chuckled. "It could be worse."

"How so?"

"I could be eating chocolate-frosted, dipped doughnuts from Krispy Kreme!"

"Perish the thought!" She feigned a swoon.

"What? They have to be the best doughnuts ever invented by man!" I laughed, thinking that perhaps this was going to be a good day after all.

"Perhaps they are. I haven't much of a sweet tooth, with the exception of honey, that is."

I took a sip of coffee and then raised half of the bagel. "Here's lookin' at ya!" It tasted exceptionally delicious. "So what's on the agenda today? Are we staying in?"

"Yes, we are. I was thinking that we would discuss rebirth, and then if you are able to get past that, Neris."

She had yet to take a drink of water, again leaving it untouched, but the morning was still young.

"Your choice. I'm going to move this stuff over to the coffee table where I can get comfortable." And I did.

"Very well. May I first ask your position on the subject of rebirth?"

"If you're talking about reincarnation, I've given it some thought and came to the conclusion that some people just need something to believe in; but in reality, it doesn't exist, doesn't happen."

"Then should I move on to Neris?"

She didn't appear to be upset that I'd taken that stance, but in reality, I was curious. "No. Just because I don't, at this moment in time, believe, that doesn't mean that I'm not curious. Please share your take on the subject."

"I have enjoyed nine lives and shall walk into the sun very shortly. As I told you yesterday."

"Does east or west have a significant meaning?"

"Yes. At the end of my time here on earth, I shall walk into the setting sun. You, on the other hand, will depart into the rising sun."

"Why the difference?"

"When you were born, that is the direction in which you entered this world."

"Same entrance and exit. Interesting." It really wasn't, but what the hell.

"I sense ridicule in your speech. I shall not tolerate insolence."

Oops! I'd have to school my tone and responses if I wanted her to stay. "Sorry, Miriam. I truly do want to hear what you have to say. Forgive me."

"Very well." She sighed audibly. "As I said, we both shall end our time on earth in such a manner. I am preparing myself to do just that in a matter of weeks."

"You're leaving so soon?" I was quite surprised by my reaction to this news. It was troubling, to say the least. "But we're just getting to know each other. If I've done something to push you away, I should at least get the opportunity to make it up to you! I don't understand!"

"Calm yourself, Tanner Trump. This was preordained. Nothing that you have done could change that, and an apology is unnecessary."

"Damn it, Miriam! This news has come just at a time that I was getting used to your company!"

"I apologize for the inopportune timing. However, it is what it is. But fear not. We shall meet again in our next life and enjoy countless moments together."

"You can 'walk into the sun' believing that, which may make it easier for you, but I can't bring myself to believe in rebirth."

"There is nothing that I can do to help you." She paused for a minute and then looked directly into my eyes. "If you wish, you may walk with me a portion of the way."

"And what happens to me then?"

"You will not be alone, Tanner. You are meant to be with Neris through her upcoming ordeals, and her Champion shall offer male companionship."

"How am I going to help Neris? I have yet to meet her and don't even know if I'm going to like her. As far as her 'ordeals.' I'm not the man for the job. Let this 'champion' fellow take care of her."

"Tanner Trump! Shame on you! The least you can do is allow me to share her tale with you. Perhaps this is not a good time." She stood, back straight, chin raised, and held a hand out. "I offer you my hand, Tanner. Take it."

I complied. It was calloused yet as soft as down. We shared a silent moment, and then she spoke quietly, just above a whisper. "We must believe in each other. For without that, we are nothing."

I looked deeply into her beautiful eyes, and at that moment, if she had told me that the moon was made of cheese, I would have believed her.

"Until tomorrow?" I simply couldn't think of anything else to say. I was at a loss for words.

She nodded, released my hands, and waltzed out the door.

I stood on the porch until she reached the edge of the forest and disappeared from sight. I don't think that there was any malice on her part. She truly believed what she was trying to sell. I, on the other hand, required good, hard evidence in order to accept that, which I had no personal experience.

I gathered the remains of my lunch and washed the dishes, all the while rehashing our conversation. When my chore was complete, I still had the afternoon and evening ahead of me. I was unable to stay here for such a lengthy period of time. Grabbing my keys from the hook, I hopped in the car and drove south.

It was a beautiful day, and I found myself beginning to quiet down. I passed the little grocery store on the left and made a mental note to stop there on the return trip. I kept my eye out for moose.

You couldn't take chances. After all, this wasn't called Moose Alley for nothing. At any given time, you could come across a bull standing astride the white line as if he owned the place. When he was prepared to saunter off, he would but only at his leisure. I've also seen them from afar as they exited the woods behind a person's backyard, picked up steam, and rushed headlong onto the roadway. Cows were accustomed to drinking from puddles aside this route. They liked the murky salt water, which helped with milk production. Those mamas needed to feed their young ones in order for them to grow to be big and strong like their dad.

I had been on the road for about a half hour and decided to head back. As I was driving north, I saw a pickup truck parked aside the road by a quick-moving stream. I pulled up behind it, shut off the motor, and exited the SUV. There was a man standing approximately midway, fly-fishing. It was a delightful sight to see this person in the water wearing hip boots. He stood steady as the water flowed past him, creating small whitecaps. In one hand, he held the lengthy pliable rod; and in the other, he constantly controlled the tension in his line. I often wondered at the leg strength that it took to remain in place without being swept away because the movement of the water appeared almost too swift at times.

As I was leaning against my vehicle and enjoying the moment, I was startled by a metal-crunching sound behind me. I turned in time to see a midsize car, a Toyota Celica, roll to a stop. Lying atop the damaged hood and partially into the windshield was a lanky-legged moose.

I ran full tilt into the roadway, around to the driver's side, and paused. I was unable to see into the car because the window was covered with blood. I removed my shirt and began to wipe it clean as best as I could. I didn't want to open the door for fear of jostling the driver. As I tended to the glass, the sound of that animal registered. It's lowing broke my heart. That poor thing was still alive.

A firm but gentle hand came to rest on my shoulder. Although he had attempted not to startle me, he did so all the same. I hadn't realized that I was in tears until the vision of that police officer standing before me wavered. I let them run their course and couldn't dry my face because my hands were covered with blood.

"Sir? Thank you for trying to help. You can let us take over from here." He took me by the arm and escorted me off of the tarmac. "I have some bottled water in my cruiser. Come with me." We walked past another officer, and a bevy of emergency-response people pull up. "Did you witness this accident, sir?

"No. I didn't." I extended my arms as he poured cool water over them. "I was watching a young man fly-fishing. All of a sudden, there was a loud crash, and I turned to see what was going on." My voice trembled. "Do you think that the person driving is okay? I couldn't see through the window. And the moose! Oh, dear God in heaven! That sound will stay with me forever!"

"Here, take this one." He opened the last bottle of water and passed it to me. "You go ahead and take a good pull from that bottle. It's good and cold. Do you need to sit? I can put you in the back seat if you want?"

"No. Thank you just the same. I still have quite a bit of blood on me, and I don't want to make a mess in your cruiser."

"Nothing that can't be cleaned. If you're feeling better, I'd like to get your name, address, and telephone number. It's for the reports, nothing more. Your driver's license, please?"

"Sure." He followed me to the car, blocking my view of the tragedy as much as possible. "Here you go, sir." I dropped the ID; I was so startled by the shot. Evidently, someone had discharged their weapon, putting that magnificent creature out of its misery. "My God!"

"Yeah, I know, it's never easy for a ranger to have to do that, but he had to put that poor animal out of its misery."

"What about the driver? Are those people going to be all right? I didn't want to open their door for fear of causing them more harm."

"I can't answer that right now. Let me get your information, and then you can be on your way." He wrote the necessary data from my license, and I gave him my telephone number. "That's it, sir. Again, I'm sorry that this had to happen. There's no winner when a car hits a moose. Keep that in mind when you drive this road. Their legs are so long that when hit, they fly toward the vehicle, and we see accidents like this more often than you'd think. Now can I do anything else for you today?"

"No, thank you, officer. You've been a great help. I think that I'll head back home now."

"You drive carefully now, you hear?"

"Oh, I will." With that said, I prepared to leave the scene when a thought suddenly occurred to me. "Officer? What will happen with that moose?"

"It'll be butchered, and then the meat will be given to the local food kitchen. They'll appreciate the sacrifice that this bull made in order to feed the disadvantaged."

"That's good to hear. Thanks again, sir." I shook his steady hand and marveled at the duties that these men, and women undertook every day.

I passed on the grocers, and the thought of food was unappetizing. When I got home, I turned the vehicle off and sat there for a few moments. With eyes closed, I rested my head and marveled at the frailty of life. The person in that car had probably set out to do some errands just like me. Now they would accomplish nothing. I hadn't seen nor heard an ambulance leaving the scene. No jaws of life hard at work to free the injured. "That could have been me." I barely recognized my own voice.

Once I felt steady enough to stand, I made my way back to the cabin, glancing at the wooded area where I'd last seen Miriam. At that moment, I decided that if I was going to die, which was really not an "if" but a "when," then I may as well do it Miriam's way. At least I could hang on to the hope that she was right.

I showered until I'd exhausted the contents of the water heater. It was dinnertime, and although I felt a twinge of hunger, I just couldn't eat anything for dinner either. The picture of that poor animal remained in my mind, and I thanked my lucky stars that no matter how I rubbed that driver's side window, I hadn't been able to see them. I think that would have put me over the edge. I opened the fridge and grabbed a nice cold beer.

Television had nothing decent to offer, so I opted to play some mindless games on my tablet. One beer became two, and then three, right on until there were six bottles to donate to the recycle bin. I fell asleep with the kindle in hand and all of the lights on. If I dreamt, I wasn't aware of it. The alarm clock woke me with a start. My tablet went sailing across the room and knocked over the bottle that sat unfinished on the side table. My throat felt gritty, my stomach felt like it was going to erupt, and my head felt like it was about to implode. I was not a drinker. Although I enjoyed a beer or two on a hot summer's day, I'd never drunk to excess. The events of the previous day had affected me deeply.

I forced myself to leave that chair and made my home as well as myself presentable. I paid dearly for every move and found that bending over was out of the question. When Miriam knocked at the door, I did a quick once-over, making sure that everything was in order, and then went to welcome her in.

"Good…Tanner! What is it? Are you ill?"

When she reached for my forehead, I leaned away. "I'm okay, Miriam. Just a little headache. It'll go away soon enough. Now are you going to stay out there, or are you coming in?"

"I shall enter although I am inclined to fetch some herbs that might help."

"Not necessary. I took three Tylenol. They should kick in soon." I guided her into the house, and she immediately sat in the recliner. She leaned toward the right and saw a label on the floor. Evidently, I'd peeled it from one of the half-dozen bottles that I'd consumed.

"Tanner? Was my visit yesterday so troubling that you sought comfort in the consumption of alcohol?"

"No, Miriam." I sat on the couch because I was still a little off-kilter. "I happened to be at the site of a serious motor-vehicle accident and found it to be very unsettling."

"You are not injured?"

"No, I wasn't involved. Let me get you a glass of water, and I'll share the details, then we can move on. I need to get past it and concentrate on something else. Perhaps Neris?"

"No water today, Tanner. Please tell me what happened?"

And I did, right down to waking up in my chair this morning. She hung on my every word and was kind enough to allow me to narrate without interruption. When I finished, I got up. "I need a coke. Are you sure that you don't want any water?"

"None, thank you."

She waited patiently as I filled a large tumbler with ice and then poured my soda.

"What a terrible experience! Sadly, no matter how many vehicles operate on that roadway, the moose never seem to become accustomed to sharing it with humans. It does not bode well for the people behind the wheel. Often times, both suffer the consequences."

"Well, enough about that, please. What can you tell me about this Neris woman?" I sat back, relaxed, and gave her my undivided attention.

"The telling takes us back to her grandfather Jacob. He was an unassuming man who had inherited an acre of land from his father. A lumberjack by trade, he was pious, humble, dependable, and hardworking. On weekends, he, along with a neighbor, constructed a small abode. He attended services at a nearby church. In his twenty-fifth year, he met Isabell. She was a cousin to one of the church members and was there to stay at the behest of her dying mother. Jacob was smitten, and the two enjoyed a weekly stroll after services. That year, the congregation decided that it would be wonderful if its followers were to join together in celebration of Thanksgiving. Jacob and a few of the men volunteered to hunt for the turkeys, and each of the women agreed on a dish that would round out the fare. It was a happy time for them."

"I can just imagine how delicious that meal had been. Fresh turkey, not frozen. And oh! Pies! They must have had a slew of home-baked goods."

"Ah, pies are not my specialty, breads, now those I bake weekly."

"I've been eating the one that you gave me by the slice. Every time I pass by the bread box, I grab one."

"I am pleased that you have been enjoying it. Now where was I? Oh, yes! It was at that gathering that Jacob asked for Isabell's hand in marriage. Her uncle agreed to the union, and they were wed two months later."

"Just in time for Christmas!"

"Christmas Eve to be precise. It was a beautiful ceremony, and the celebration following was talked about for years to come. The next January, Isabell took special care in preparing Jacob's favorite fare for dinner; and when he came home to such a wondrous meal, he suspected that something was up. Nevertheless, he awaited his wife's explanation for such a lavish meal. When he arose from the table, sated and content, he took his beautiful wife into his embrace and asked her what he had ever done to deserve her love. Why was he so blessed with the perfect wife? After a loving kiss, she told her husband that she was with child, and they would be expecting in September. Jacob wept as Isabell embraced him lovingly in her arms."

"So far it's a great love story." Having been a news reporter, I understood how things could change and not for the better.

"When Isabella's due date was drawing near, a local midwife explained the birthing process, for Isabelle would give birth at home. When her water broke, Jacob ran to their neighbor's home, and soon there were three women supervising. It was a difficult labor. With little room to move about, Jacob was forced to wait outside; the midwife's husband was there for support. Eventually Mara's screams subsided, and a newborn's cries rang out. Jacob rushed inside to witness one woman swaddling his newborn daughter, another gathering blood-soaked linen, and the third drawing a sheet to cover Isabell's face. He shoved his way past them, pulled the shroud from his wife's face, and released a horrific cry. He went to his knees. His despair drained him of the ability to remain standing. Jacob crept onto their bed, took Isabell into his arms, and wept. He was inconsolable."

"What did the women do with the baby while all this was going on?"

"The midwife brought the babe to her home, and one of the nearby women who had given birth the week prior offered her mother's milk. Jacob remained in his home, and attempts by the good people to remove Isabell's remains were thwarted. Finally, with a constable at the lead, she was taken forcibly. He never once asked for his daughter, nor did he care. Mara, as she was christened, was the name that Isabell had chosen for their child. Jacob left his home long enough to venture into town to purchase several bottles of liquor. He returned home and began consuming the vile stuff. While in his cups, he cursed the God that allowed this to happen to him and vowed to make a pact with the devil in return for his wife's resurrection. At midnight, so it is told, a sinister being appeared, offering just that in return for his soul. He carried with him a decanter of vile, putrid liquid that Jacob agreed to consume as long as he was reassured that his wishes were met. And so he spat venom, cursing the child that he believed was responsible. As he swung the decanter about, spilling some, consuming more, he bade the fiendish apparition; curse his daughter and her offspring.

"That's frightening, Miriam! How could he do that?"

"It was the devil that was urging him on. Jacob was no longer in control of his words or actions, for he had sipped from a flagon that contained a disease of the mind. So when the demon offered a malediction in exchange for Jacob's soul, he agreed. The demon insisted that this man must take his own life, sealing the bargain. However, Jacob would have none of it until he was told what this curse entailed. So the evil vow was as follows; should Mara procreate and produce a female offspring, her life would end at the moment of birth just as her mother's had. Furthermore, this would apply to any subsequent female offspring. The demon attacked women as lacking virtue. 'Whoars of Babylon,' he cried! It became more complex as they schemed. Sons were welcomed and required their mother's milk; therefore, female descendants bearing male babes were permitted to live."

"This is insane, Miriam! Was Jacob that deranged?"

"Unfortunately, yes. For each female offspring was also robbed the power of speech, and in their twisted mind, more ill will was to be doled out. They devised two more edicts. One, these women would not be able to get with child until after their thirtieth birthday, and while they were supposedly born mute, they would be allowed to raise their voice in song. Not words, a sort of humming and cooing.

This, they laughed, would mimic the mythical Sirens who were the downfall of all men who could not resist the sound."

"Don't tell me! Neris is Mara's daughter?"

"She is. One in the same."

"Do you know how old she is? You've heard her. Is her song that tempting?"

"She is now thirty-one years of age, and she creates the most beautiful sounds that I have ever heard."

"Should I wear earplugs when I venture out?"

"Not necessary. It is the undertone that draws young men, not the sounds that you and I hear. This demon and Jacob wanted these women to tempt men of their own age, men who would suffer similar anguish as he had. If Neris's love song attracts men and makes them fall in love with her, then they, too, will have the woman that they love taken from them at childbirth."

"Only if the babe is a girl, am I right?"

"Yes. I realize that all this is very complex and difficult to fathom. Those who do not believe in this tale are far more in number than we who have witnessed these events firsthand. However, it was important to both Neris and myself that you understand her fate. You needn't believe it, but I am asking that you look in on her occasionally, particularly when men of her age are about. She will croon, as it is the way of things. Women tempt men, and men succumb to their wiles. I have known her since her birth. I was present when Mara passed away. It was I who promised to care for Neris. I have done so. However, she has grown and wishes to have a life of her own, which is fine. She now enjoys the freedom of adulthood and the life that she desires. Now that the time has come for me to leave my life behind, I fear for her safety. Please, Tanner? Will you help her if she is in need?"

"Miriam, I'm a bachelor and a cranky one at that. I know nothing of young women's needs! It'd be different had I married and had children of my own, but holy gawd! I can't see myself making a promise like that. I don't want to hear about you dying and this 'walking into the sun' business either."

31

I stood and began to pace, and then it occurred to me. Isn't that what we men do? Pace? Walk away from some of the responsibilities of raising children? I loved my mother and was a very observant child. I understood, by the time that I was twelve years old, that my mother ruled the roost, dealt with all the family trauma, and wrapped my father around her little finger. My father went to work, earned a good living, and then came home, and sat in his recliner; and that was it. That was the end of his duty to his family. Yeah, sure. He'd discipline us, but only after my mother asked him to.

"She is self-sufficient, Tanner Trump. My concerns are few. I do not want men to take advantage of her. It is dangerous, both for her and them."

"How so? There's more, isn't there?" I returned to the couch. I preferred receiving bad news when I was sitting down.

"Yes. The consequences of Neris mating with a young man can be dangerous. Have you seen fallen birch trees in your travels, in your own front yard?"

"I have."

"In the area where Neris resides, there are two in particular that are different from the rest. She has shared her bed with two young men. She is not promiscuous, but passionate. It is in her nature to procreate. That wretched curse does affect not only her life but also those who will bed her. If they do not leave her with child, they are intertwined among the roots of the birch. Once cocooned therein. They supply oxygen and nutrition to the young men. Neither shall perish until Neris gives birth. Should her offspring be female, it dooms ill for the men. They will die. If she carries a male child, they will be set free. I fear that loved ones will follow their travels here in an attempt to find them. Should that occur, it would not bode well for all three. Neris must not be taken away from this forest until the curse is broken; otherwise, she will die as would the two young men."

"Now that is insane, Miriam! I can't believe that you, an intelligent woman, can believe any of this to be true. I certainly don't."

"Perhaps, I have shared too much in one morning, the day after you consumed several beers."

"It has nothing to do with a hangover!"

"And what of the Well of Dreams? You have been there and have experienced its wonder. Are you not willing to believe that there are other possibilities for uncommon circumstances to present themselves?"

"I'm not sure that I understand what happened the other day when you took me there. I don't understand how that Italian mason could have known anything about me! I don't know anything anymore!"

"Perhaps I should give you some time…"

"No. If you want me to believe you and you expect me to help this Neris, the least that you can do is make sure that I understand the rules of the game!"

"This is not a game, Tanner Trump."

"Okay! Let's see. Mara, Neris's mother, died after birthing because her child was a girl. Correct?"

"Yes."

"The same thing will happen to Neris if she delivers a girl."

"True."

"If she has a boy, then she will live."

"Yes."

"Now one of the conditions of this curse is that she is speech impaired with the exception of humming and cooing oohs and aahs."

"You are correct."

"She is forbidden to have sexual relations until she is thirty. And if a man is to have sexual relations with her and does not impregnate her, he is cursed as well. He is then taken to the woods where a birch tree will topple over, wrap its roots around the man, and he is there to stay until such a time as some other man gets her pregnant. And she gives birth to either a boy. If a girl, both she and that poor guy or guys hanging out in the backyard will all die. I assume that there is no limit to how many men can get entrapped?"

"None."

"If she gives birth to a son, she and those men get to live happily ever after. The prisoners, who have been kept alive and nourished by these white sentinels, are free to go with no recollection of their time in the forest."

"Yes."

"So, let's break this down to the simple facts. Neris loses her virginity at the age of thirty. She has slept with two men. They are hanging out in the yard, entwined in tree roots. More men will perish until some guy comes along and gets her with child. Come time to have the kid. If it's a girl, everyone except the baby and the kid's father die. If it's a boy, cause for celebration, Jacob! Everyone lives, no one is worse for the wear, and life goes on."

"I do not care for your tone. It is disrespectful."

"Then accept my apologies. I am attempting to keep an open mind, Miriam. I wouldn't even be listening to all this mumbo jumbo if it wasn't for you. I do believe that there is something otherworldly happening with the Well, because I can't quite put my finger on a rational explanation. I'm also shifting through some ideas that I have regarding the baby's gender. It could be a heredity thing, and some women do die when delivering a child. I need some time to make sense of it all. But I will tell you one thing. I don't believe a word about birch trees latching onto young men, keeping them in a state of suspended animation for who knows how long."

"You are entitled to form your own conclusions, Tanner. I have told you these things so that, should you decide to look in on Neris occasionally, you will be prepared. That I have mentioned them to you is enough to ensure that any event will not take you unawares. Do you understand this?"

"Forewarned is forearmed?"

"Exactly."

"I definitely don't want any of this to interfere with our friendship. If, as you say, you have only a few weeks left to live, I certainly don't want to spend them arguing. You want me to peek in on Neris once a week or so, I'll do that if it is important to you."

"It is, which is why I spoke with her yesterday. She has agreed to a short visit in the early afternoon today. Will you come with me?"

"Moving right along, hun?" I guess it couldn't hurt. Any particular attire required?"

"No. You may come as you are, but I would recommend that you wear shoes." She smiled. "I believe that I shall await you outside. It is a marvelous day!"

That said, she left me sitting on the couch and wondering if I should wear my sneakers or walking boots. Just like that, she got her way. Cunningly, but without ill intent. My Miriam! Now when had she become MY Miriam? The day was getting stranger and stranger with many new revelations. I set that aside and decided to wear the boots. They needed breaking in, and I was planning to visit the Well either this afternoon or after dinner. When I joined Miriam on the porch, she smiled.

"An excellent choice in apparel, good sir."

She slipped a hand onto my arm, and we walked toward the woods where I'd seen her disappear the day before. It felt good to take a nature walk.

The temperature changed when we moved from the sunny brush into a densely lined path. It was well-worn, having been used many times over the years. Forest creatures called out to one another, some scampering nearby. A handsome oriole flew directly in front of us, his mate a short distance behind. The male of that species was a wonderful shade of red, while the female blended nicely within the trees. Perhaps it was because she nested and was protected from prey due to her camouflage? I did not know.

We made it to the clearing, I'd say, in fifteen minutes. I heard Neris long before I saw her. Miriam had been right. This woman's tunes were both angelic and appealing at the same time. She was sitting on a small stool, feeding bread crumbs to all who approached. Birds, squirrels, and chipmunks alike scurried frantically, collecting food for the larder. She laughed silently, and I sobered at the sight. I'd never given much thought to how simple, easy and natural we laughed. *How many other things do we take for granted?* I wondered? Well, that was for another time and place.

Miriam whistled a tune as we approached, and Neris turned her head toward where we stood. As we moved closer, I came to appreciate Neris's beauty. Yes, there was the physical wonder of her, but I vow that woman exuded pure joy.

"We have come, Tanner and I." They embraced. "You look lovely. I love the circlet of flowers that you have worn today, my dear." Miriam touched the buds, causing a few petals to dislodge and settle in the woman's thick wavy hair. "May we join you on the stoop? A short rest after our trek through the forest."

I followed them to a rough-hewn cottage that was approximately twenty-by-twenty feet square. The entrance was a bit low, so I bent in order to avoid a good rap to the forehead. It was a simple place with many touches that only a woman can imagine. Some herbs hanging here, a small pot of fresh flowers there. One wall featured a large fireplace, some pegs for drying clothing, and such miscellanea. To my left, the sole windowpane shined clean and bright. Straight ahead, there was a pallet built into the wall. It appeared to be four-foot long, and the bedding looked to be handmade and warm. I imagine that the woodpile to the side of the home was much needed fodder for the winter months and deduced that some nearby friend volunteered his time to maintain a good supply. No privy to be seen inside, so I deduced that it was around to the back.

Neris and Miriam each took a stool in hand and began to walk past me. I came to my wits and offered to assist, but they passed me by.

"Here we are, Tanner. Please sit. We shall return momentarily."

My posterior overhung that stool with good measure, and I chuckled at the thought of my weight turning into tinder and picking splinters out of my arse for days.

"Here we are, Tanner. Neris was anxious to surprise us with gifts that she made yesterday. But before she presents them to you and I, we must make the formal introductions." She stepped aside. "Neris? I am most pleased to introduce you to my dear friend Tanner."

She curtsied, of all things, and held forth the gift. I nodded, for to bend a knee would have looked silly. "The pleasure is all mine."

Neris's relief was apparent. Did she fear that I would be unreceptive? Perhaps, but she gestured for us to sit. Once the two women were comfortable, or as comfortable as was possible atop these small stools, I myself sat.

"Let's see. What have we here?" I made a production of examining the small round basket that she had, no doubt, woven herself. Each detail was beautiful. She had blended in a few wildflowers. The adornment was a nice touch. Within were several yellow strips of some sort of treat, I supposed. "This is not only thoughtful, but also beautiful, Neris. I thank you and regret that I have nothing to offer you."

She smiled and turned to Miriam for confirmation. Evidently, each shared some rudimentary hand signals that only they knew. As I watched, my appreciation for the gift was imparted, and she soon turned to me beaming. I was tempted to touch her hand; however, I wasn't sure if it would cause her to fear me.

"Neris is so pleased that you like the gift. She prepared those honey strips in hope that you have a sweet tooth. You may lick them as you would a pop or break off sections to add to your tea."

I looked directly at our hostess as I spoke. "I am thankful that you have shared these sweets. Thank you."

Miriam turned toward me to speak, obviously for the purpose of blocking Neris's view. "You have made her very happy, Tanner. It was wise of you to refrain from touching her. It takes a bit of time and trust before she has contact with someone new."

Was there anything that this woman missed? "No problem. She appears to be quite cunning and eager to please. That she is a real beauty should go without saying. My sole concern is that I can't sign. What are we to do with our time?" I whispered the latter.

"Fear not. You will learn quickly. She is eager to please and will see to it that her manner of communicating is understood. Now if you would, please join us in the side yard. It is there that the two fallen birches lie."

"And what do you think that will accomplish? Is it going to make any difference in my acceptance of your tale if I see two trees that have fallen over? The damned things have shallow root beds and are prone to toppling in severe weather."

"True. However, these are the exception. Please, Tanner?"

"If we must. It would appear that your insistence has stirred my curiosity. Let's be done with it." I stood, placed the small basket atop the stool, and waited until Miriam communicated with Neris. I immediately recognized a change in our hostess's demeanor, and she looked to me for confirmation. I nodded.

Without preamble, we three walked around the cottage, and I was able to see the trees in question. They bordered a copse of other trees and appeared to be healthy considering their plight. Perhaps they had just recently toppled over. We all three stood to within approximately three yards. Neris, who had held Miriam's arm along the way, disengaged from her trusted friend. She walked over to my side and just stood there.

"Tanner, please do not cross your arms so. She must hold one of your hands in order for you to see."

"I can see those two trees from here!"

Miriam placed a hand on my arm, speaking in a gentle yet firm tone. "Do not get stubborn with me. Please? This is not the time for you to dig your heels in." She stood firm.

"Oh, all right! If you insist. I'm only doing this to pacify you. You are aware of that, aren't you?"

"Of course, I am. Nevertheless, you agreed to this excursion, and as much as I dread these things, sometimes it takes a bit of a push for people to see with their own eyes where the line between reality and fiction is delineated." She removed her hand. "Now, please?"

I complied. No sooner had my hands rested at my sides. Neris took hold, and I glanced straight ahead. Those damned trees wavered before my eyes, and I witnessed the impossible. Both were identical with the exception of its captive. Each root bed cradled what appeared to be a young man curled into a fetal position. Each gnarly tendon pulsated as if delivering life-sustaining fluid. It was by far the most disturbing sight that I have ever seen in my life. I've witnessed a myriad of tragedies, car accidents, plane crashes, murders, and as early as yesterday afternoon, a bull moose and vehicle collision. But none of them made me want to run away. None of them made me feel this sick to my stomach. None of them had made me question my sanity!

I pulled my hand away violently, turned, and started for home. Pride had escaped me as I hid the tears that poured freely. Gift forgotten, Miriam forgotten, I felt an immediate hatred for Neris. How could I not? It was she who had put those young men there after all. But that meant that I had to believe in Jacob's curse, and I didn't want to. At the cost of my own sanity, I would not go there! Oh, no! Oh no! Such a panic overtook me that I began to run. I thanked my stars that I was close to home. My heart couldn't survive the stress.

When I reached my doorstep, huffing and gasping for air, I chanced a moment to look from whence I came. There stood Miriam, soothing the weeping Neris, with the most dejected look on her face. Her motherly posture broke my heart. Was this the end of our friendship? Was this the last time that I would see Miriam? With only a few weeks left, I would lose the woman that I loved. This revelation sent me barging into my home and bolting my door. For the first time since I'd taken occupancy of this place, I locked the damned door! How telling was that? I was scared half to death and of whom? Miriam? Neris? I didn't know. I did realize one thing; there was evil in this world, and not of man's making. What could be worse?

I paced, stopped, and then paced some more. Was there some way around Jacob's curse? Oh, yes! I now believed that it existed. I went to the small roll top desk that was in my bedroom and removed a notepad and pen. Returning to the kitchen, I leaned over the counter and began to write. Did Neris know what the consequences of her sexual encounters with men entailed? Why did she not refuse any other advances? Why were her activities not supervised? Why didn't Miriam forewarn any suitors? Why wasn't Neris institutionalized? Had she murdered those young men?

It was almost dusk, so I walked through the cabin, closing the blinds. I'd never once done this before, so they too, were a bit stiff. I had to protect myself against the night. As I passed a light switch, I decided that closing the blinds was not enough. On went every light.

That done, I returned to each window, having forgotten to check and make certain that they, too, were locked. I couldn't think of any other measures that would ensure my safety. When one lives in the forest, we come to realize how pitch-dark it can be out there. You can't see anything except the stars and the moon as long as it is a clear night. They are a magnificent sight to see, almost larger than life. When it's overcast, forget about wandering out without a strong flashlight because you'll find yourself lost and scared.

I reviewed the list of questions once more, and then a thought occurred to me. If Miriam was done with me, who was going to answer them? Was there anyone else nearby who was knowledgeable enough to help me out? I sat at the kitchen table, rubbed the back of my neck, then placed my trembling hands over my face. The headache returned with a vengeance. I thought that maybe I'd live with it. Maybe it would keep me awake through the night until sunrise. I saw a small sticky spot where I'd spilled something, began picking at it, and concentrated so hard that I easily slipped into a daze. I remained that way for the better part of an hour. Wherever I went consisted of a place where there was nothing. There was no fear, no magic, no pain, no sadness, nothing! Reluctantly, I returned, disappointed that I had to face my demons, or better yet, Neris's demon.

I paced, I fretted, I feared, and I reviewed the brief list. Night sounds interfered with my thoughts. Insects chattered, owls hooted, and the cacophony was continuous. Forest dwellers who felt safe coming closer to my cabin scurried around, playing or worse yet hunting their prey. I hadn't had trouble with bears, deer, or moose; but there was no guarantee from day to day that they'd attempt to pay me a nocturnal visit. It seemed like every possible insecurity rose to the surface, intent on robbing me of even the slightest scrap of sanity.

I went to the cupboard, then to the icebox and filled a tumbler with cubes. There were a couple of cokes left, so I made a mental note to purchase more the next time that I went shopping. Returning to my seat at the table, I poured a glassful, immediately drinking half.

What was I doing to myself? It came to me that every possible fear that I hadn't experienced in my lifetime had come forward now until my very sanity was shattered. I'd never let things like this bother me. Even when I was a child, things that went bump in the night were mere challenges for whatever superhero I was on that particular day. Other kids feared the monsters under their bed or in a closet, while I grasped my bow and arrow, or sword, or whatever praying for an evening adventure.

I passed the remainder of the night speaking to those voices in my head. I dashed each misnomer or fantasy to smithereens and breathed a sigh of relief when the blackness outside began to fade. I was tempted to go to bed, but Miriam would be arriving for her daily visit in approximately two hours. I had, thankfully, survived with my mind intact. A confident stroll through the house, opening drapes and blinds, occupied little time. The safety bar across my door was now secured under the couch.

With one and a half hour remaining, I brewed a pot of coffee, retrieved the last piece of Miriam's bread, and sat down to this humble breakfast. The bread was a bit dry and hard in places, but otherwise quite delicious. Reviewing the list that I'd compiled last night, it appeared that all were in order. Then when the time was right, I poured a glass of water and set it on the table aside my recliner. Confident that I had everything in place, I helped myself to another cup of java.

I sat on the couch as the time passed. No Miriam. She was always punctual, but not today. As doubt crept its way into my mind, I feared the worse. She wasn't coming! I strode to the front window and searched the tree line, no signs of activity.

Two hours later, I emptied the water into the sink and began to get angry. Wasn't I the one who had suffered mental and emotional trauma when Neris revealed her captives? Wasn't it I who had been ill prepared, and at who's fault? Wasn't it I who needed reassurance? Had she not covered the list of questions that I'd taken my precious time to compile during a stressful night? All these questions fueled the anger, the upset that turned to rage, directed at her? Well, I wouldn't wait for her any longer. I slipped into my sneakers, grabbed the car keys, and left. Surely, I could seek entertainment somewhere?

I didn't allow my testy mood full reign, for to do that could be a dangerous thing. Inattention along these roads was unwise. Randomly turning here and there, I detected what looked like a sandy clearing up ahead. Sure enough, to my right was an unpaved parking lot, and at its center, a rough-hewn building. A sports bar, of all things. I pulled in, parked my SUV, and climbed the stairs. It was a great place, a bar directly ahead, pool tables to the right, casual dining tables in the center, and a stage to the left. I worked my way to the bar and sat three stools down from two men who were in a heated, but friendly argument about baseball. I wasn't trying to be unsocial but wished to let them have as much privacy as could be afforded in a place such as this.

"Afternoon, mister! What can I get you?" A large man dressed in a red plaid shirt, jeans, and an apron around his narrow waist sauntered over. His build was sufficient to deter any physical confrontation between the other men whose discussion became more heated. "George! Harry! You two settle down now. We have a newcomer come visiting."

"Sorry, Bobby! You know how much George likes to push my buttons!" Harry turned toward me. "So sorry. I'm Harry. This here is George."

"Pleased to meet you both." I got off my perch, went over to them, and shook their meaty paws. "I'm Tanner. New to the area. I live in Pittsburgh."

"Well, now so do we. As a matter of fact, you're still in the Pitt. We're brothers. Came to live here a couple of years ago. Got tired of the city life and left Boston behind in our dust but can't seem to shake loose of love for the Red Sox. Isn't that right, bro?"

George, who had been sneaking peeks at the huge television set on the wall, nodded.

"He's not the social one. Anyway, let me buy you a beer."

Bobby approached, placed a menu in front of me, and asked me what kind of beer I wanted. I opted to let him pick a brew that he thought I'd like and began to review the menu. Not having eaten since yesterday morning, I found my appetite. I ordered curly fries, onion strings, and a patty melt. The brothers resumed their prattle while I enjoyed being out of the cabin, with a few men as company, and the game of the week on an enormous TV.

I tell you, that was, by far, the largest patty melt that I have ever had; burger, cheese, and fried onions slathered with their special sauce. I bathed in the stuff! With a never-ending supply of napkins at my disposal, I was able to limit the mess to three spots on my favorite blue shirt. And the hand-cut onion strings were seasoned to perfection. The curly fries, well, I know that you can only do so much with those, but they, too, deserved a round of applause. Unable to do the servings justice, I requested a box to go, all the while applauding the quality of Bobby's fare. In passing, he had revealed that he was the proprietor. He had attended culinary school but, upon graduation, discovered that there was a limited demand for his talents. He strode into a bank with a design for this place, a business plan including future expansions, and a wealthy brother who believed in Bobby's dreams.

"Are you content with your decision? And how can you survive this far into this neck of the woods? If you don't mind me asking, of course."

"It's quiet in here right now, but come dinner time, it fills to overflowing. In the evening, guys come in to have a few beers and to play pool. On weekends, a band plays and the locals get the chance to stomp their feet. I couldn't be happier. Now how was your food?"

"Incredible! That sandwich was out of this world! I'll be back again soon. Maybe check the place out on a Saturday night." I offered him my right hand. "It's been a pleasure, Bobby!"

"Likewise, Tanner. Don't be a stranger."

I paid the tab, which was very reasonable considering the quality and quantity of the fare, and left him a hearty tip. He may have been the owner, but he worked hard to earn a gratuity.

I had a very good sense of direction and found my way home without incident. When I approached the door, I looked for evidence that Miriam had visited. A note, perhaps. But nothing. The place had that feel of loss. Not emptiness but loss. I couldn't explain it.

I put the keys back on the hook, kicked off my sneakers, and decided to lie in bed for a while. Believe it or not, it was a good thing that I emptied my bladder before doing so, because I slept straight through the night. The alarm screeched, and I swatted it off the nightstand. But then as conscious thought set in, I sat on the side of the bed. No sooner had I done so, mother nature called. By the time that I finished and sprayed the room, a soft knock at my door set me in action. I sprayed one last time and dashed to the front room. I inhaled deeply and received my visitor.

"Miriam? What brings you here today?" Wrong, wrong, stupid! I wasn't getting off to a good start sounding pissed. "Please come in. Can I get you a glass of water?"

"That would be nice. How have you been, Tanner?" She sat in the recliner as was her habit.

"Frankly? May I be honest with you, Miriam?"

"I would appreciate that. Please do."

"Here's your water. I had a miserable night after you brought me over to Neris's, and yesterday sucked. You could have at least come over to see how I was doing after witnessing that horror show. I couldn't even seek your comfort by going to you, because I don't know where you live!" I poured my heart out. "I don't know what the hell to believe anymore, and you were the only person who could clear anything up, Miriam. You weren't here for *me*!"

"I have been at Neris's side from the moment that you departed until today. You are not the only person who was in need of me. She was inconsolable, Tanner. I have explained that she is a gentle soul and innocent of all wrongdoing."

"You call her innocent? She's at least thirty years old and sexually promiscuous!"

"That is not so. Promiscuity? You will have her running a brothel? Do not be so cruel! She is capable of a deep abiding love and only seeks companionship as do you and I. If you continue in this vein, I shall leave!"

"Please stay. At least long enough to answer some questions that I have."

"Such as?" Her posture was rigid, and I knew that if I wasn't careful, I'd never see her again.

"I shall answer them as long as they are reasonable and appropriate."

"Okay, I have a short list that I compiled last night." I went to the kitchen and returned with notepad in hand. "Why haven't she or you, for that matter, warned these men of the consequences of their actions? I know that she can't speak, but the least she could do is pass them a note."

"First of all, she is unable to write. Try as I may, throughout her life. I have attempted to school her in the art of reading and writing. However, it has been in vain. From an early age, she began to form her own sort of sign language. She and I would enjoy communicating in that form. It pleased her, and we have continued to this day. Mind you, she is not ignorant, and I do not know if this is a result of the curse or not. Secondly, if I were to interfere in any way, I would suffer the same fate."

"Are you telling me that you'd spend eternity entwined in one of those root beds?"

"Yes, as would Neris if she were to somehow make them privy to their fate."

"Then why not abstain? Surely, she could say no and walk away."

"Her destiny is prearranged, Tanner. She has no choice. She must either procreate or miss out on the opportunity to break the curse for future generations. It is her load to bear."

"Don't you think that it's selfish of her to copulate with any Tom, Dick, or Harry when she could just push them away and send them packing? Someone has to take responsibility for her actions. Shouldn't she be in an institution? Shouldn't she be in prison for doing that to them?"

"Jacob sealed Mara's fate. Jacob sealed Neris's fate. She is unable to refuse. It is not a matter of choice. She has not, at least, yet taken their lives. There is still a chance that they will survive. If she is removed from the forest, she will die. If she consumes prepared food, she will either become severely ill or die as a result." Miriam leaned forward. "Tanner, there is no 'out' as you would say."

"Keep her secluded, Miriam. Hide her deeper into the forest where she can't get into any trouble. Get some help from someone so that she has twenty-four-hour supervision."

"I have tried that. Don't you think that I'd rather see her suffered complete seclusion than to have to bear the consequences of what she is capable of, or in this case, what she has done? I have garnered assistance from our nearby neighbors, women whom I reluctantly led to believe that she was ill and required care and supervision twenty-four hours a day." She trembled visibly. "Jacob's demon has interfered with my efforts. I scheduled others for daytime duty, while I assumed twelve hours during the night. The other volunteers found her to be a joy and taught her to cook, sew, and knit. They wondered at her quick mind and ability to learn in such a short time. She was shown how to grow her own vegetables, which she may consume without ill effects. Nevertheless, that fiend, that hellhound, has been thwarting my attempts. He intervenes by causing these women to fall into a deep slumber if a man comes along, that is a man interested in Neris. And then she is unable to refuse their advances. Again, I cannot emphasize enough, she is compelled to lie with them. She sees nothing wrong with this, as it comes natural to her, and she is happy to please." Miriam's voice shook, her emotions getting the better of her. "We have visited together, Tanner. Do you think that I would, for one moment, condone a behavior that would cause any harm to someone, stranger or not?"

She had me there. I was confident that Miriam was a good, honest, and loving person. I know, without a doubt that she loves Neris and that she loved Mara, the girl's mother. There wasn't a mean bone in her body, and she wouldn't condone a murderous act. "Why didn't you tell me all of this the day before yesterday? Why did you hold out on me?"

"You were being unreceptive. It was quite obvious that you would refuse to believe me. I curtailed our discussion so that I could bring you to meet Neris and, most of all, so that she could show you evidence. That is why."

"Okay, okay! That's water under the bridge. You've apparently answered my questions and done so honestly. Do I believe that you've done everything that you can to intervene, to stop this horror from ruining Neris's life? Yes, I do believe that you have done her a great service, and Mara would be overly pleased. As far as some evil entity hovering about? I'll need to chew on that one for a while. All that mumbo jumbo stuff is foreign to me. And before you bring it up, I do believe that the Well of Dreams has a magical quality to it, good magic. I don't know how it was done, and I don't want to know. As long as I can make use of it, and I know that it isn't causing me any harm, I'll continue to visit there when I can."

"I am pleased to hear this."

I continued before she could go any further. "Last night seemed different to me. I've never had the urge to secure this place, but after dark, I locked it up tight. The night sounds troubled me, and I felt unsafe to the point that I wished I had a firearm. I don't even believe in bearing arms, although I don't decry a person's right to. Even the sounds out there were intensified as if the night creatures were all worked up over something. This is insane! It has to be all in my mind."

"We, too, have been aware of this for the past few evenings. I have thought this over thoroughly and believe that this evil entity senses that someone may foil its plan. This may be causing it to stir. Animals do sense danger, which can make them skittish."

"Your visit today has brought new light to this entire debacle. If Jacob were still alive, I'd shoot him myself!"

Miriam breathed a sigh of relief. At least Tanner believed her. Neris had finally settled down yesterday, in late afternoon. She refused to leave the young woman's side. With the time growing short for her departure from this life, she didn't want to walk into the sun leaving Neris unprotected. She knew in her heart that the champion would soon arrive, but until then if Tanner would be willing to check on Neris, that would have to do.

"Since neither you nor I shall be given that opportunity, it is important for we three to keep tabs on one another. I will be leaving at the end of next week, Tanner. I beg of you to at least walk over there once a day. Vary the times so that you are not setting a pattern. Otherwise, she may be more vulnerable."

"You can't just up and leave! I won't have it, Miriam!" I stood so abruptly that I almost knocked over the coffee table.

"It has been preordained, Tanner. I have no say in the matter. At least I do know that my humble life will be rewarded. We, you and I, shall be reborn again. We shall be rejoined in the future, and that is enough for me." She, too, stood.

"I wish that I could believe that."

She walked over and took my hands in hers. "You have believed everything that I have disclosed so far. Why not this too?" She raised one of my pockmarked hands to her lips and bestowed a gentle buss on the ancient paw.

"Where there is love, there is always hope."

The next couple of days were peaceful. Miriam and I fell into a routine. Visiting, walking, and enjoying each other's company. She'd occupied her afternoons with Neris and tried her best to convince the young woman that I was a good man and, most of all, harmless. She also had to prepare that poor woman for her departure. Miriam was the only mother whom Neris knew, which made matters worse. The day prior to Miriam's death, she brought me back, hoping that I could try again.

"I don't know if this is going to work, Miriam. If she's still afraid of me, what are we going to do?"

"Have faith, sir."

It was a beautiful morning. As we approached the woods, squirrels scattered, leaving their bounty by a tree so that they could return for their treasure.

"It is a moot point, Tanner. She has no choice in the matter. I refuse to leave her alone without companionship of some sort. I've explained that you will not interfere with her life, her routine. That you are simply going to make certain that she comes to no harm."

"And her stand as of yesterday?"

"She was still unconvinced that you have her best interest at heart."

"Then we will just have to convince her, or if she full-out rejects my friendship, I'll have to try other tactics. And before you misunderstand my meaning, I will watch her from afar. The only problem is that if she needs something, I won't be able to help her out from a distance."

"Ah! Here we are, Tanner." She checked my attire, brushed a few crumbs off of my chest, and smiled.

"Did I pass muster?" I grinned when she swatted my arm.

"You behave now. And try to speak in soft tones and do not stand too close."

"Okay, all ready! Let's move along, please?"

When we entered the clearing, it appeared that it was laundry day at Neris's. She toiled over an old-fashioned scrubbing board while humming away. Frankly, I don't think that I'd be that happy washing my stuff like that. Miriam whistled a welcoming tune, and I thought that she should teach it to me so that I wouldn't startle Neris in the future.

"Neris, my love! We have come to visit. I see that you are busy with your chores today, so we will not keep you. A simple hello and a brief sit before we continue our stroll. It is such a marvelous day!"

The woman was pleased to see her friend, all smiles. She was about to run over, but then changed her mind when she saw me. I felt guilty. I hadn't truly understood how my behavior had affected her. She was afraid of me, and I hated it. "Good morning, young lady. I pray that you are enjoying all of this sun. It's a great day to hang your laundry to dry. Isn't it, Miriam?"

"It certainly is. Now come here, my dear. Give this old woman a hug!"

They embraced each other, and as they enjoyed an intimate moment, I walked over to the bucket. I noticed that there was a small pile of wet clothes sitting in another, its contents ready for hanging.

"Can I be of assistance, Neris? I'd be happy to empty this wash water. Just show me where you dispose of it." I waited patiently for her approval. After silently consulting with Miriam, she nodded and then pointed to a copse of trees. This was a step in the right direction. "You got it!"

When I returned, I found the two women sitting on stools in front of the cabin, and Neris had something in her lap. As I approached, I realized that it was another basket, only larger. Miriam had managed to position the young woman in the middle so that I sat to her left. She got up when I took my place, curtsied, and gave me the gift. Her smile was reserved, and she immediately returned to her perch.

I made a fuss over the small tomatoes, two cucumbers, and honey treats. I thought it best not to mention the previous gift that I'd forgotten in my rush to leave. As I sat there silently, the two conversed, and occasionally Miriam told me what they were talking about. When I got the cue to stand, Miriam embraced her. I nodded my head then waved. Neris waved back, and then we were off.

Neither one of us spoke until we were a few steps into the woods. It was I who broke the silence. "I think that went well, don't you?"

"I do. She has accepted the fact that you will be visiting her more often. However, she will not accept that I am going to walk into the sun day after tomorrow. At least, she has agreed to join us for this fortuitous event. She is aware that she must remain behind with you when I take those final steps."

I still refused to believe that her life was going to end that way but accepted the invitation graciously. "We'll have to spend some extra time with each other today and tomorrow. When do we leave day after tomorrow, and how long will it take to get there?"

"I shall visit with you in the morning. Come noon, Neris is expecting me to join her for lunch, and we plan to stroll about here and there until dusk. She and I have been together since her birth. When she was old enough, some friends constructed that cabin for her; and as all young women are wont to do, she began to set up housekeeping. Like I explained when we were at the Well of Dreams, I am west. Therefore, it is at sunset that I shall move on in preparation for my next, my tenth, life."

"I want you to know that I am not taking this well. I am behaving because you want me to. I thought that I would move to this place, lead a solitary life, and then die in peace. You and Neris certainly put a kibosh on that. I haven't eaten much but went to the store yesterday and came back with two sacks of junk food, the local newspaper, and four twelve packs of coke. I won't be needing any more of that for at least three weeks. I can't concentrate long enough to read, television sucks, and the games on my tablet are a bore." I stopped walking when my cabin came into view and placed my hands on her shoulder. "I can't function knowing that you won't be here each morning. I can't eat because my stomach rejects everything, and I can't sleep. Do you understand how difficult this is for me?"

"Of course, I do, Tanner. I, too, have lost loved ones. Far too many, I'm afraid. Nevertheless, it is out of our hands. I am not able to plead for more time. My purpose in life is complete."

"And what purpose is that? May I ask?"

"You may. First and foremost, the care and protection of Neris to her thirtieth birthday and making your acquaintance. As I told you, we are destined to rejoin in our new lives, and..." She winked. "I wanted a sneak peek!"

"Why the sassy seductress all of a sudden!" Without forethought, I slipped my hands around her waist and kissed her. It's a gentle buss. "Just making sure that your sneak peek is sealed with a kiss!"

"You are a sweet man, my Tanner Trump. All rough on the outside, but a romantic at heart." She gently worked her way out of my embrace. "I shall wait here until you enter your home."

"Until tomorrow then." Without preamble, I stepped away. I didn't turn around until my hand touched the doorknob. "Until tomorrow, my love!" She then disappeared into the woods.

The tears began slowly at first as I unlocked my door, then flowed more freely as I looked about the cabin. I had to do something to keep my mind occupied, or I'd lose it for sure. Two ideas formed in my mind: the first was a much-needed trip to the Well of Dreams, and the second was a silly idea, but I'd decided on what I would give Miriam as a parting gift.

The well didn't disappoint. This was a memoire worth revisiting. When I was ten, my friend Jack's father decided to take him on a bus tour to Boston. It was all inclusive; hotel room for Friday and Saturday nights and New York vs. Boston at Fenway Park, one of the oldest baseball parks in the States. We sat in the third row, along the third base line. The Yankee's dugout, which was directly across from the Red Sox, was almost within reach. They had to have the longest rivalry in the history of baseball. And the kicker? I was invited along! Nothing could have been more exciting for two ten-year-old kids. My father balked, but my mother took up my cause. She understood how important this was and how much it meant to me. Of all of Jack's buddies, I was the chosen. In the end, she won out. We took the subway into the heart of the city so that she could buy me a couple of new shirts and a pair of jeans. Now that I think of it, that in itself was a special day. We had lunch at Faneuil Hall and walked to the waterfront before returning home with my new clothes. The

Well of Dreams took me back to that day, and I vow that everything was so realistic as it took me through one of the most memorable experiences of my childhood.

Time passed by quickly when 'I was surfing the Well,' as I liked to call it. When I left that day, it was almost dusk, so I hurried along but was careful not to trip and break my neck.

After I got home, I washed my hands and grabbed a coke and some club crackers. These I set on the kitchen table, and went into my bedroom closet to retrieve the box that I required to prepare Miriam's gift. It was intended for girls six to ten due to the nature of its contents. It took me three hours to see the job done. These things were meant for petite hands, and I fumbled more often than not. Upon completion, I rummaged through several drawers, looking for a box that I could put it in. My old Bulova watch box was the best that I could find.

I went to bed shortly after and wondered if I was the only man across the space-and-time continuum who gave a woman about to die a personal gift? On that note, I closed my eyes and didn't wake up until early morning. I'll admit one thing: I wouldn't miss that dang alarm.

We skipped our visit to see Neris because I wanted the morning entirely alone with Miriam. I was pleased that there were no preparations for her departure tomorrow. I would have thought that morbid. She loved that pink, purple, and orange beaded necklace and the matching bracelet, which consisted mostly of faux crystal. I guessed at its length, recalling that Miriam's wrists were petite. She made such a fuss over them that I beamed. As I secured them, I thought how nice a beautiful set of pearls would have been in lieu of a children's baubles. A coworker had gifted me this toy as a joke. Miriam played along, modeling each and beaming with joy.

"I absolutely love my gifts, Tanner Trump! I vow that you will have me in tears!"

I kissed her hand. "The pleasure is all mine, sweet lady. I only regret that I didn't think of buying you the real McCoy."

"These are far more precious than any store-bought trinkets, and the fact that you gave much attention and time arranging each bauble warms my heart. Thank you again. Now you know that I must leave. Neris is, no doubt, wondering where I am."

"Miriam?" I stepped forward, slipped my arms around her waist, and remained silent for a minute or two. I wanted to memorize every line of that beautiful face so that it would be imprinted in my mind forever. "You know that I love you and that tomorrow will be a difficult day for all of us. I've poured my heart out, making you sit there while I shared a summation of my pitifully lonely life. I've insisted that you search for a way to stay, and I've accepted the reality of your walk into the sun. However, I can't imagine how it works. Are you certain that you can't spend tomorrow with Neris and me? I wouldn't mind sharing you with her."

"Oh, Tanner. I am so sorry. I must prepare myself spiritually. This requires deep meditation without distraction or interruption." She reached up and tenderly cupped my face in her hands. "This is our final visit." She kissed my lips softly and then stepped away. "Neris and I shall see you tomorrow shortly before sunset. Although I've impressed upon her that she may not interfere, I am uncertain that she understands the full impact of my final day on earth. Please, Tanner. If you must detain her, do so. Her composure may give way to hysterics."

"And who's going to hold me back?" I brushed an errant curl from her cheek. "I may turn into a blubbering fool myself."

"Be strong enough for all of us. That is all I can ask." She stepped away. "Until tomorrow, Tanner Trump."

"I love you, Miriam!" I called out as she walked away. "You remember that when you're meditating! You take that with you tomorrow, Miriam!" I could hear her whistle as she raised the hand wearing my bracelet.

I'm not going to bore you with the events of the next twenty-four-some-odd hours because I can't expect you to sit there and listen to my emotional distress. Suffice it to say that they were pure and unadulterated hell.

By the time that Miriam, with Neris in tow, arrived at my doorstep, all it would have taken was the slightest nudge to put me over the edge. Miriam was a vision. She was dressed in a flowing white outfit consisting of a billowy blouse and tapered pants. She wore sandals with a complex web of straps. She and her charge were smiling as if they were enjoying a lovely walk in the park. Both waved, and I'll admit that the sight lightened my mood some.

"Tanner! I see that you are prepared to continue on with us."

"I am. You both look stunning today." The only adornment that she wore was the necklace and bracelet that I'd given her the day before and a crown of flowers, which I am certain that Neris weaved because she, too, wore one. "If you don't mind, I'll sandwich myself between the two of you. A thorn between two roses."

She gestured to Neris, who immediately widened the distance between her and her surrogate mother. This simple act struck me a deep, painful blow. My tumultuous emotions had to be insignificant in comparison to Neris's. She would, after all, be parting with the woman who had loved her from cradle to womanhood. For all intents and purposes, Miriam was her mother. She was about to suffer an emotional event that would leave her alone in these woods to fend for herself. I was surprised at my reaction to this, for I immediately wanted to offer both my companionship and protection. When they wove their hand into my arms, I smiled. We were connected, we three, and this posturing was symbolic of that, at least for me.

"Very well then. Let us be off." She directed us west, which wasn't at all complicated. The sun was sinking lower on the horizon. It was a clear day. An albino buck crossed our path. He paused momentarily, then leaped quickly, continuing on.

"That was amazing, Miriam! Have you ever seen an albino deer before? He was huge!"

"They are quite rare. However, I have seen one other in my lifetime. Beautiful, was he not?"

"Incredible!" I winked. "And dressed perfectly enough to join our procession."

"I think that he has a date with a very lucky doe."

"More than likely."

Just ahead was an area that I, on first glance, thought had been decimated by a forest fire. But then, on closer inspection, the huge area was denuded of trees, with only an array of stumps remaining. I commented on this, telling Miriam that it appeared as if a group of poachers had snuck in and taken their bounty.

"It does appear otherworldly."

Her choice of words was fortuitous, for after we entered this quiet spot, I had the feeling that we must whisper as we proceeded reverently amid an array of corpses.

"This is far enough. If we move any farther, I will be unable to witness the sun's descent into its position over the horizon." She disengaged from me, and all of a sudden, Neris's hand clenched, her grasp felt almost painful.

It was time to say farewell. Suddenly Neris threw herself into Miriam's arms and began to weep. I don't know the why or the wherefore of it, but witnessing a soundless cry seemed very troubling. She didn't object when they parted and then stood aside so that I, too, was able to bid my love fare-thee-well.

"Tanner, I must hurry. There is no time for a lengthy adieu." She came to my open arms, laid her head on my shoulder for a moment, and tilted her head back. "Until we meet again, Tanner Trump." We shared a soft peck on the lips, and then she turned away without another word. I can't tell you if she had shed a tear or not. I simply can't remember.

Neris stepped to my side, taking my hand. This is how we remained.

Miriam's progress ended abruptly. There was nothing out of the ordinary further out. There was no heavenly host singing, no parting of the celestial clouds. I don't know what I expected.

She raised her left hand. I was just able to make out the faux-crystals at her wrist. She didn't turn around to acknowledge us. And as she resumed her steps, a shard of light found one of the glass trinkets, and a blinding starburst exploded before my eyes. Then she was gone. Miriam was no longer there!

I rushed forward, stopped once to look around, and then continued to the spot where I thought that she had stood. Another three-sixty proved fruitless, and as I looked down to see where her footsteps ended, something caught my eye. I bent and examined the shiny object. Much to my surprise, it was one small faux crystal.

I placed it in my palm and marveled at the sight as this tiny bead shined brightly. In the blink of an eye, it returned to its normal state. I removed a handkerchief from my back pocket and gently placed that wonderful trinket within its folds. Then I glanced back at Neris. She hadn't moved so much as an inch.

"Come along, my dear. I will walk you home."

She nodded, offered no resistance, and placed her hand on my arm. This young woman was now my responsibility. I have no doubt that my Miriam had lectured Neris as she had me. We were to watch out for each other.

I patted the pocket where my treasure was secured and felt confident that we would fare well. And when the day came that I would "walk into the sun," I would carry it with me.

The Champion

M Y NAME IS WARNER TRIDENT. I'm thirty-five years old, once divorced, no children. I am CEO and president of Trident Enterprises, a competitive long-distance carrier. My father founded the company, which I have overseen since his passing ten years ago. This tragedy reduced our family further, for my mother had perished in a plane crash when I was twenty-five and my brother, Skip, fifteen.

Dad did as best as he could to raise Skip; however, grueling hours spent at the Enterprise's helm left the boy with far too much unsupervised time. My brother has always been popular, energetic, and easygoing. Unfortunately, he lacked ambition.

Our dad envisioned us managing the Enterprise shoulder to shoulder. Skip's lack of enthusiasm was attributed to immaturity, so father gave him sufficient time to sow his oats, convinced that the boy was simply suffering from growing pains and that he required more time to mature than yours truly.

I, on the other hand, learned the family trade. My father demanded one hundred percent, and I returned one-ten.

Skip and I were devastated when father suffered a massive stroke. He was kept on life support for forty-six hours, as my brother and I struggled with the morality of pulling the plug. We were told that he was brain-dead, yet we weren't quite prepared to let him go. Ultimately, we ruled that dad's dignity took precedence.

My brother decided to pursue a career in biotech and pledged to apply to medical school after enjoying a summer of relaxation joined by his best friend, Clare. I returned to the office, confident that Skip would then be ready to grow up.

I don't care to share my personal affairs. Sorry, but I am, by nature, a private man. Nevertheless, I vow to reveal whatever details are necessary for you to understand who I am.

My brother and his friend suddenly disappeared. Their communications stopped abruptly. I hired a private investigator to follow their trail, which led to Pittsburgh, New Hampshire, and suddenly ended there. I just wasn't the type to stand around and delegate such an important matter to someone else. He recommended that I talk to Tanner Trump, a retired newspaper reporter. In addition, my brother's best friend, Clare, had phoned his mother raving about a local Pittsburgh beauty that he meant to take as his wife. This all occurred two months after we buried Dad.

I borrowed a travel trailer from a friend, hooked it up to my Ram-Charger, and drove north, leaving the company in the reliable hands of our CFO and operations manager, Will Farley. He was a reliable man whose business savvy rivaled my own. To be honest, I was in such an impressive financial position that I could retire whenever I pleased. I don't mean to blow my own horn, but it is a fact. Between business revenue, stock portfolios, and inheritance, I could live a life of leisure if I so desired.

I left early on a Tuesday morning in order to avoid commuter traffic. I traveled along Route 95 and picked up Route 3 heading north. I found it interesting that I'd lived my entire life in Boston, Massachusetts, and had never once visited the famed Moose Alley, which bordered on Canada. The drive was uneventful, but it seemed like it took me forever to get there.

I came across a sports bar owned and operated by a guy named Bobby. He and the other patrons were very friendly, and the food was excellent.

I struck up a conversation with a man named Hal, who seemed to know everyone in the area. When I inquired about Tanner Trump, I was told that he was a nice-enough guy for an ex-newspaper reporter. He admitted to only seeing the man a couple of times as he watched him and others fly-fishing in a nearby stream. He'd offered to let Trump give it a try, but the man begged off, stating that his equilibrium wasn't that great. As to where he lived? No one was able to say exactly where.

While I was eating, the owner received a FedEx package. I told Bobby that I wasn't finished eating, said I had to go out to my truck to get my meds, and caught up with the delivery man just as he was about to leave the lot. After some deliberation, he did recall Trump's address, having made a delivery there the week before. He quickly drew a map on a scrap of paper and said that he had to leave because he was on a tight schedule. Thanking him, I returned to finish my meal.

By the time that I'd finished eating, it was too late to do anything more than find an area, or a park where I could spend the night, get a little shut-eye, and head out in the morning.

I slept like a log. There was something about the northern air that made sleep seem so rejuvenating. After showering, I drove back to Bobby's place.

"Hey, Warner, good morning to you. Come for some of my famous blueberry pancakes? Have a seat. Coffee?"

"Oh, yeah! And it's a yes on the pancakes. How about some bacon with those?"

"You got it."

People came and went. I was anxious to get back out on the road, not sure of which way to begin. Bobby returned with my flapjacks. One bite and I was in pancake heaven. I was gnawing on a strip of bacon made to perfection, and there, too, was a hint of maple. As Bobby topped off my cup, he leaned forward.

"If you're wanting to speak to Tanner Trump, he just walked in the door and sat at table 3. Ah, sorry. Force of habit. He's the elderly man wearing a blue shirt and setting his Yankee's cap on the chair beside him."

"No way!" I swiveled around to take a quick peek.

"Look at me!" His tone brooked no nonsense. "That man is eighty if he's a day. He's not born and raised here but has chosen to make this his home. We don't like it when strangers aren't nice to the locals, if you catch my drift."

"I do." I, too, leaned over the bar now. "I mean him no harm. Rest assured that I will not hurt him. I've no reason to. But 'rest assured' that come push to shove, I can take pretty good care of myself." It was not my intention to stand toe to toe with anyone in the process of searching for Skip. However, I wanted to make it perfectly clear that I wouldn't be intimidated by anyone. "Are we good here?"

"We're good. Now, are you going to introduce yourself, or am I going to have to get your name off that credit card?" He smiled.

"Warner. Warner Trident." I extended my right hand. His grip was as firm as mine. "Pleased to make your acquaintance, Bobby."

I passed him a credit card, and before I signed it, I made certain that the tip was commensurate with both quality of the fare and the service as well. I left the bar, making my way toward Trump.

"Mister Trump?"

"That's me. Who's asking?" His voice was neutral.

"My name's Warner Trident." I offered a hand, which he accepted. It was dry, plump, and unassuming. "I'm visiting from Boston, Massachusetts, hoping to find my brother, Skip, and his friend Clare. He was last seen in this area. Can you help me out?"

"I'm not familiar with the names."

"I doubt that many people are. They were just passing through."

"I'm sorry. I can't help you. Maybe Bobby can. He's the owner and probably sees more people coming and going."

"I'm afraid that I have to insist that we have a chat. I was specifically told that you, sir, could be of assistance. That is, you or a young woman in the vicinity. I would have you know that I will comb every inch of these woods, if necessary, and I will not be deterred. I will not leave without my brother!"

Tanner set the menu aside. He felt every nerve in his body tensed, and was certain that sooner or later, Warner would pay him a visit. This was very shaky ground, and he wanted nothing more than to run away and hide. At this crucial moment, his future and that of Neris hung in the balance. If he made the wrong decision now, it could spell disaster. On a moment's notice, he opted for best possible scenario.

"Please follow me, sir. I have been completely forthcoming. I may be of some assistance, and I will do what I can. But I need you to follow my instructions very carefully and to a T."

"It's a start. I'm the Ram with the trailer. Lead the way."

Bobby suddenly appeared at the table. He'd caught a portion of the conversation between Tanner and the newcomer. The old man's posture was rigid, his hands trembled a bit, and he was as white as a ghost. He wouldn't abide any bullying in his place.

Warner watched the barkeep out of the corner of his eye. The man's lips thinned, and he slid the sleeves of his shirt back from wrist to elbow. Sensing trouble, he gradually inched his feet apart in order to gain his core, his center of balance. Those who knew him would recognize this as bad omen.

"Tanner, is everything okay over here? You look a little peaked."

A pair of men at a nearby table pushed their chairs out bit, and Warner took notice of that as well.

"It's okay, Bobby. I forgot to take my meds before heading out. I think that I'll pass on breakfast and head back home. Sorry for the bother."

"Seems like everybody's forgetting about taking their meds lately." That was meant for me. "You want one of the guys to follow you, make sure that you get home safely?"

"You and your friends don't have to worry about Tanner, Bobby. As a rule, I don't beat on unassuming, elderly men. Now, me and Tanner have some business to discuss, and we're going back to his place. If you or anyone else wants to check on him later, be my guest. You have my credit card information and can track me back to Boston if need be. So, you see, I couldn't get away with anything if I wanted to. Now if you'll step aside, we're wasting daylight." He reached over and placed a hand on the back of Tanner's chair in the process, gently brushing Bobby's arm. "Need some help, sir?"

"I'm okay, guys. Just give me some space, okay?" Tanner rose and made his way to the door. He hated making a spectacle of himself in front of his neighbors. "Let's go, Warner. Now, please?"

Warner followed Tanner to his vehicle. "I swear that they think I'm going to kill you and bury your remains where they'll never be found." He held the door open for a moment longer. "Am I going to want to murder you, old man?"

"Time will tell." Tanner closed the door, started his vehicle, and waited for Warner to follow. He made certain that Warner's vehicle remained in his rearview mirror. He had no intention of escaping Skip's brother. There was no sense in delaying the inevitable, but he hoped that he would have the time to talk to Neris first. He pulled over to the side of the road, left his car running, and walked over to Warner's truck.

"I have to ask that you stay right here. I'm going to continue on to my place, and ask that you give me a half-hour to forty-five minutes before you come the rest of the way."

"Need time to hide the evidence, do you?" He didn't trust the old man.

"No. I need to talk to someone." He sighed. "I'm not going to play games here. I'm too old for that shit! Now are you going to stay put, or do I head back to Bobby's place to get the cavalry?"

"I wouldn't be surprised if there was a stream of traffic this way for the rest of the day. Now listen. I mean you no harm. I'll wait here for you, forty-five minutes max. If you don't get back here, I'm going to the local police. Your choice."

"Be back soon."

Tanner drove to his place and headed directly to Neris's. He needed to prepare her for the worse.

His initial reaction to Warner's reason for being in Pittsburg was terrifying. But it didn't take him long to realize that he had two choices. The first, bring the man to his house, and tell him all about the curse. The second, bring him directly to Neris' and then fill him in. Then he remembered how he had reacted with disbelief when Miriam had told him about Jacob's curse. He didn't believe one bit of it, and he had required proof. So it came to be that Warner and Neris would meet on this day. A day that began well and then went south really quick.

Neris was humming as she stood on a small stool, cleaning the window. Her hair swayed with the motion of her hips as if she were keeping beat with a pleasant song. His shrill whistle caught her attention immediately. She stepped off of her perch and walked over to him.

"Hello, honey! My! Don't you look as bright as sunshine today!" He embraced her briefly, cutting the hug short. "We have to sit down and talk. Let's get the lawn chairs, why don't we?" She ran back to the cottage and retrieved the chairs. He'd purchased them for her the week prior because he just couldn't abide her flimsy stools. "Good girl! Now, sit down, please."

He made sure that the chairs were at an angle so that they could talk, he in the spoken word, she in sign.

"Neris, I have to ask you about those two men over there in the tree roots. I don't have a lot of time, and this is very important." He saw her tense; and reached for her hand. "It'll be okay. Now, is one of them a man named Skip?"

Without hesitation, she nodded and then ran to the rear of her home. He followed her and watched as she retrieved two backpacks from a cubby. She shook the cobwebs off and then blew dust into the air. With one hanging from each hand, she presented them to Tanner.

"Oh, Neris! My sweet Neris!" He choked back a lump that formed in his throat. "Let's go back out front, okay?"

He followed in her wake and was amazed that she hadn't run away when he'd mentioned Skip's name. Never once had he thought to ask the identity of those two, and he wondered at his stupidity. Now that he had little time to digest this earth-shattering revelation, he had to make haste.

"Let me take a look here. Neris, please sit." He quickly surveyed the contents of each and withdrew two wallets, one in each. "As I thought." His trembling words were slightly above a whisper. Neris touched his hand and leaned forward. He saw strength in her posture and resolve in her eyes.

"There is a man, back at the side of the road, waiting for me to get back to him. This man is Skip's brother, Neris. I have to go back to where he is waiting and bring him here to both your home and mine. He needs to know what has happened to his brother and that other boy. I ask that you to show him where his brother is. Then I'll take him back to my place, and I'll tell him all about Jacob's curse. Do you understand all of this?"

She sat straight, almost rigid, and nodded. With chin raised, she was preparing herself for this revelation. He understood that she'd fallen apart the day that she had shown him the evidence and had forced him to believe. Miriam had been there to console her after she'd seen his reaction and felt the hatred that ensued. Now, he was the one who would be there to pick up the pieces, but two-fold? Did he have the strength and fortitude to counsel both and maintain his own sanity? He understood that the stranger would have to hold her hand and witness their suspended state. A sudden thought came to mind. What if Warner rushes forward, intent on pulling his brother free?

"Neris? What if someone were to try to set those two young men free. You know, pull them out of there?"

She signed death.

"Good Lord! How am I supposed to stop that from happening?"

She signed again. "I shall not allow this."

"How so?" Her reply worried him even more.

Neris signed sleep.

"You can do that? You can put a person to sleep?"

She nodded 'yes'.

He checked his watch. "I have to go, honey. I'll be late. Now you put these away in the house. I'll be back in a couple of minutes with our guest. His name is Warner. He is Skip's brother. Okay?"

She stood, took hold of the backpacks, and reached up to give me a peck on the cheek. Nodding slowly, she then turned and went inside. I, on the other hand, set out to meet the man who would be the deciding factor as to whether Neris and I, for that matter, lived. For to remove her from this property would be fatal. As for myself, I simply wished for the opportunity to walk into the rising sun, and joining Miriam.

I drove up to Warner's truck to find him standing outside of it with his back to the driver's side door. He appeared to be in deep thought, arms folded, legs crossed at the ankle. How he had passed the time, I don't know, but he stood at the ready when he saw me coming. I pulled up beside him, chose to remain in my vehicle, and rolled down my window.

"Please follow me. The access road to my cabin is rather narrow, but you'll be able to navigate that thing just fine if you go slowly. There's enough room for that camper if you keep it straight and under control."

He cranked the engine and maneuvered his truck and his home on wheels so that they were in a straight line. He didn't appear to have any trouble and began to follow me. When we arrived at my place, I waved him over to my side and suggested that he park the entire kit and caboodle in my front yard.

"Well done, Warner. You handle that thing like an old pro. That's an impressive rig. Had it long?" I remained beside my car.

"It's not mine. I borrowed it from a friend. It's got all the bells and whistles and is pretty comfortable. I'm not that fond of pulling something that big behind the Ram, but I wasn't sure if the motels around here would have any vacancies. This seems like a popular place to visit."

"Yeah, although we, permanent residents, tuck ourselves far enough off of the road for that very reason. Besides, this is an off-shoot of Moose Alley, which is inundated with sight-seers morning until night. Got anything from cell phones to movie cameras taking pictures of bulls, cows, and calves. You've got to be careful about getting too close to them. They've been known to stomp people to death, people too stupid to take them seriously. I walked a path over there just last week. When I came to the end, there was a sort of large lean-to. Rangers posted a sign saying that if a moose was on your tail, you were already dead. That said, you be careful if you see one in this yard, or at the pond. Be still and don't startle them. They'll leave you alone."

"I have to admit, it's beautiful here, and that's a fine home. I've always liked log cabins. With a fireplace, of course."

"Most have one, but I don't. Can't be bothered with all of that wood, and the smoke can cause soot that covers everything."

"Okay. Now that we've shared some small talk, what can you tell me about my brother, Skip?"

"We're going over to Neris's place, and I'll do my best to explain. Keep in mind that 'believing is in the seeing'."

"You mean seeing is believing."

"I prefer the other way around. Now, we are going to a place that, as best as I can explain it, has a sort of mystical air to it. Neris has lived in these woods all of her life. She has never left the forest. While she is speech impaired, I can communicate with her for the most part."

"Never left the forest, you say?"

"That's right." I stopped for a moment. "You may want to start believing everything that I tell you, because if you don't, we're not going to get anywhere. I suggest that you save your questions for later, and I'll explain it all as we sit comfortably on my porch, sharing some beers."

"We'll see. Now can we move on?"

"As you wish. You may hear her humming or cooing. The sounds are soothing and pleasant to the ear. She lives a solitary life, with the occasional visit from locals, a lumberjack who's accidently cut something off, and of course, the wildlife. Neris has never consumed processed food, fast food, or even health food. She has a garden, grows what she needs, and lives on the simple fare. Oh, and honey. She makes the best honey candy that I've ever tasted."

"It sounds like you are very fond of her. How old is she?"

"Thirty-one this last year."

"Oh, hell! Come on, Tanner! You can't tell me that a thirty-one-year-old woman hasn't stepped foot out of this her entire life." He stopped for a moment.

"It is the truth. If you continue to question the veracity of the facts that I am disclosing, we will have a difficult time, you and I."

"Listen, I was born and raised in Boston, Massachusetts. This kind of life is foreign to me, but not at all unappealing. I get the moose thing, I get 'living in a cabin in the woods' thing, I get about half of what you're selling, but I don't buy the rest. If you want to sit down and toss back a couple of beers, fine. But don't think for one minute that you can pull anything over on me. I'm not gullible!"

"I know that you are not stupid, or easy to deceive. We are several yards away from Neris's home. Now if you want to object to anything, or everything, that's your prerogative, but this is getting us nowhere. This is deterring us from seeking enlightenment. Do we continue or not?"

"All right! Let's move on!"

"Please lower your voice, especially when you speak to her. She is not accustomed to shouting, and it frightens her. She is no coward, but dislikes discord."

Neris sat in one of the lawn chairs, weaving what appeared to be a spice of some sort. When we entered the clearing, she raised her head, acknowledged us with a nod, and rose. Neither Warner nor I spoke until we were a couple of feet away.

"Neris, my dear! This is the gentlemen who is searching for his brother, Skip. Please meet Warner Trident. Warner, this is Neris." I stood aside as she offered her hand, a casual gesture that I'd taught her. The two took a moment to assess each other and then stepped back.

"I see that you have prepared seating for the three of us, dear. May we rest our weary bones?"

Warner had yet to speak, and I prayed that the deep timber of his voice would not upset her.

"After you." He waited until she sat on the small wooden stool.

"Thank you. I won't dance around the subject. However, I wish to make it clear that both Neris and I understand your concern for your brother. That said, I ask that she return to you that, which is Skip's and Clare's."

"What?" He stood abruptly, knocking over the featherweight chair.

"Please sit! now!" He was so surprised when I raised that he obeyed.

Neris sensed the tension, but passed the two backpacks his way, and then sat between us, awaiting further instructions.

"Where'd you find these?" We did not reply immediately, giving him the opportunity to examine their contents. "This is Clare's! Here's his wallet, his passport!" Warner dropped it to the ground, and hesitated a second or two before reaching into the second pack as if its contents would cause him physical pain. "I'll be a son-of-a-bitch!" The second joined the first on the stoop as he rose in anger. "You tell me what you did with my brother!" He reached for my shirt and lifted me as if I were a sack of spuds. "What did she do to my brother?"

If not for Neris's distress, I vow that this man would soon be wearing even the minutest speck of food that was left in my stomach. The sound that emitted from that poor woman was so soulful and so full of distress that it, in itself, suffused every pore of my body. I believe that Warner had experienced the same effect, for he released me immediately.

He placed his hands over his ears and cried out, "Please make her stop!"

I will tell you right now, that the sound did not cause any physical pain as would an overly loud, or a high-pitched note. This imparted all of the anguish, in toto, that I had experienced in my lifetime! It tore at my heart so fiercely that I thought that I was about to perish from the force of too much weight upon my body! It was sadness beyond sadness. I was also subjected to both Neris and Warner's despair.

I fell to my knees, and she joined me, holding on with a ferocity of a person who was afraid to fall into a frightening pit. Immediately when she touched me, her wails subsided, transforming into great sobs as tears coursed down her lovely cheeks. Had she been so cloistered, so cocooned, in these dense wooded areas that she had not witnessed what one man is capable of doing to another? Or, was she mourning Warner's temporary loss? I did not know, but after recuperating for several minutes, she finally separated herself from me, went over to Warner who was bent over, gasping, and took his left hand.

He didn't resist but allowed her to lead him away from the cabin. Quite suddenly, I realized what she was about and followed behind. How was he to bear what he was about to witness? It would take a very strong man to walk away with his sanity.

When the two fallen birches came into view, I watched as he looked to Neris, then the tree roots, and back. He disengaged his hand from hers and realized that it was like unplugging a television set. The picture went away. He reached for her hand and, firmly, but not overly so, saw his brother and his friend. As they floated amongst the sinewy roots, he fell to his knees, released Neris's hand, placed his over his face, and began to cry. The sound of his sobs broke my heart, but what did I expect? Neris and I witnessed his despair silently, at the ready to help him any way that we could.

He rose suddenly, turning to look at us, then the trees, and then her home. He appeared confused, unable to decide something, or at a loss as to where he was. On the third pass, his attention was drawn in the direction of the cabin, and as I, too, glanced that way, I suddenly understood not only what he was searching for, what he was staring at, but also why.

Without preamble, he rushed to the chopping block and grabbed hold of the ax that was imbedded in a stump. I reached over, cautioning Neris to remain by my side. We continued to stand silent as he returned to the birch, raised the ax, and struck it a mighty blow. Initially, the thought occurred to me that this would be the end for his sibling, but I was hard-pressed to mention this due to the confused state that we all suffered.

Upon contact, the ax's blow was ineffective. Its handle shattered, sending the blade soaring through the air and landing yards away, leaving it imbedded in the grass. The other half remained in his hand. I could almost feel the vibrations that his strong arms experienced. He stared in disbelief, ran his hands over the limb, and then looked our way.

"Neris, dear. You stand behind me now, and don't move until I tell you that it's safe. Do you understand?" She nodded and did what she was told.

Warner approached. As he grew near, I was frightened by the fevered look in his eyes. His fist still clenched the remainder of the ax. In the few seconds that it took him to reach me, I thought that I just might be seeing Miriam much sooner than anticipated. Nevertheless, if I had to die this day, I would do so as Neris's protector, as I'd promised. Raising my right hand, I bade him to stop. He did, and I was impressed with his control. He was furious, perhaps even disappointed, along with a myriad of other emotions.

"You tell me what the hell kind of tricks that you're playing here, Tanner! You think that this is a joke, smoke and mirrors, or projections of some sort? You're messing with the wrong man." He pointed the handle toward the two birches. "If you lured them here so that she could have her way with them, you are both going to answer for this."

"I brought you here so that you would understand your brother's plight and that of his friend. You've yet to understand the full meaning of what transpired here when they chose to become a part of Neris's legacy and her mother's as well. I could have had you over to my home, shared this tale from beginning to end, and you never would have believed me. I, too, was a skeptic. I, too, disbelieved that there are things that happen that are beyond the scope of our imaginations. Now I suggest that you return to my place, and I vow that by the end of this day, you will give credence to Skip's temporary plight, or I will personally drive you to the closest police station." Throughout my dissertation, Neris peeked around me to assess his mood or acceptance, I do not know which. Perhaps she was hoping that Warner was warming up to my offer, or if her well-being was in danger. If I didn't know any better, I'd say that she was fascinated by this city dweller who appeared as large as some of the lumberjacks that she'd mended on occasion.

"I have to go that way to get my truck and camper, so I'll give you my undivided attention until we get there. You'd better be damned well convincing, or you and that pretty little lady of yours are going to be eating whatever it is that the sheriff serves up for dinner. Mark my words!"

Fortunately, he set off immediately, giving me the opportunity to send Neris home with the assurance that everything was going to be all right. She appeared to be none the worse for the wear. Did she know something that I didn't? I set that thought aside, gave her a reassuring hug, and bid her fare-thee-well.

Warner had made his way to my home, had the time to help himself to a beer, and sat on my porch.

"Did you go into my home?" I was angry.

"Cool your jets, pops! I got this out of the cooler in the back of my truck!"

"Then I beg your pardon. Not many people drink their Mic Lite out of a bottle these days, preferring cans."

"Well, I do. Now let's get down to business. I have no patience for this."

"Cool your jets!" I tossed his words right back at him. "I'm going to get one of my own before I settle in." I accepted his disrespectful tone, although rudeness normally rankled me. I'd always stood nose to nose, toe to toe, with the best of them, but his was rudeness set on by the disturbing sights that he'd just witnessed. So I held back. I inhaled deeply as I approached the door and into the house. "Here I go, Miriam. Wish me luck."

When I returned, bottle in hand, I sat. "I am going to tell you about how my Miriam, God rest her soul, Neris, and I came to be in this unique, albeit strange, situation."

"I'm listening. Proceed."

"All that I ask is that you keep an open mind. Now. From the beginning." We both sipped our beer, as I began from the time that I had met Miriam. He was very quiet, causing me to pause for a few minutes as he disposed of the empty beer bottle and returned lugging a red-and-white cooler. I took the opportunity to get myself another, then continued my dissertation. When I found myself speaking in a clinical manner. Admittedly, it was difficult to continue past my interactions with Miriam without breaking down. The realization that she could handle this situation much better than I made me fervently hope that this young man would understand how we all wanted a "happily ever after" ending. As I neared the conclusion, a thought came to me. "I am going to ask you to bear with me one more time."

"What now? Are the fairies going to do your bidding? Are the forest creatures going to join us, expounding on the details of their day?" He stood. "I need to use the facilities. Mine or yours?"

"You may use mine. All the way to the kitchen, then bear left. When you're done, it'll take me a minute to do the same, and then we'll take a walk to the Well of Dreams."

"Oh, great!"

"Whether you believe or not, that insolence is working on my last nerve. So can it!"

He never responded. He just did his business and was waiting for me outside.

"Let's move along. We have about another hour, an hour-and-a half, before it starts to get dark." I flipped a switch, and the spotlight came to life, bathing the entire area in front of my porch. "Just in case."

"Lead the way!"

While his tone was a bit more civil, there remained an undertone that seemed more angry than belligerent. I examined his footwear, concerned that he might be uncomfortable.

"Great hiking boots. They should do the trick." He raised one foot.

"They appear to be. Now, let's be off." As was my custom, I made certain that my footing was secure. It wouldn't do to fall on my keister now, for he'd probably just leave me where I fell. When I breached the area upon which the Well sat, that old, familiar, and pleasurable feeling overtook me. Quite frankly, I loved this place. We appeared to be the only sign of life within its surrounding area. Reverently, I spoke in a whisper. "Warner Trident, the Well of Dreams. I believe that you are south."

"What the he…"

He left the sentence unfinished as if he'd strolled into an empty church and heard the echo of his own voice.

"It's a well." He continued to speak in hushed tones.

"Yes. Please come with me." I led him to the portion of what I had come to know as the Table. I passed my hand along the top reverently. "Do you recognize any of these inscriptions?"

"Alex?" He leaned forward. "Alex?" The name was spoken on great exhalations. "I don't understand. My Aunt Mae and Uncle Harrold lived next door to us when I was a boy. Their only son, my cousin Alexander, he used to call himself Alexander the Great III. He was my best friend. We used to play Marine Special Forces. He made the game up as he went along." He appeared to be in awe. "He said that sometimes MSFs had to communicate in code so that the enemy didn't know what our maneuvers were at any given time." He wiped away an errant tear. "He joined the Marines when he was old enough and was true to his word; he was a decorated Marine Special Forces. He died in a desolate land and was awarded several medals posthumously." He turned to look at me. "Is this magic? I don't understand a couple of these."

"I am so sorry for your loss." My own voice cracked. "The others may have something to do with the part that you will play in this seemingly never-ending saga. I have, just now, become privy to the fact that you are Neris's champion."

"I don't know anything about that. You called this the Well of Dreams. What more can you tell me?"

"Hopefully, this will respond to you as mine did to me. Now place your left hand on your stone, and your right over your heart."

"This is crazy. I feel stupid."

"Just do as I say. I believe that you shall be rewarded by the effort." I stepped aside. "Oh, and I typically close my eyes. I am uncertain if you shall see better for it."

He followed my instructions. And within seconds, a smile surfaced, and soon he whispered, "Alexander the Great III! How they hanging?" He occasionally nodded, chuckled, or became quite serious. I imagined that they were on a mission of some sort, brave soldiers, children playing an adult game. Time passed quickly, and I was thankful for that because I felt as if I were intruding on some very private events in Warner's life. Some memories are better left experienced alone.

He returned to the here and now a bit wobbly. I placed a hand at his back, which startled him at first. Once he'd gained his equilibrium, I let go.

"Why'd I come back? I didn't finish! How am I supposed to finish if they push me back?"

"I've given that a great deal of thought myself. Perhaps we are only allowed to stay for a specific period of time in order to return to our present-day self, or too much time spent there is unhealthy."

"I think I need another beer." His eyes were still a tad glassy.

"Take it slow. By the time that we get back to my cabin, you should regain your center of gravity. Proceed straight ahead, and once we reach the path through the trees, you may follow that. I will be directly behind you. If you feel a little light-headed, stop for a minute. We still have about a half hour of sunlight remaining. You don't want to be in these woods after dark. You wouldn't even be able to see your hands in front of your face, let alone avoid new hazards along the route. Mother Nature likes to throw us a curve every once in a while. I also suggest that we have something to eat. We do expend a surprising amount of energy on our journeys."

"Whatever you say."

He followed my instructions and paused twice. The Well of Dreams had now found all four participants: Miriam, myself, Neris, and Warner.

"I'm going back come first light, and alone at that. I need to. Those symbols appeared timeworn, but it is possible to make them look that way. They do it in Hollywood theme parks all of the time. The kicker is, I don't know how you or that Italian could possibly have known about their existence. Alex swore that I was the only person that he shared them with. One day, when we were playing make-believe, he was captured by the enemy, and the only way that he could be saved was to send me a coded message about his whereabouts. His mom called us in for lunch. We sat there, eating, and when his mother joined us, I was about to mention a code translation. And he kicked me under the table. When we returned to the 'war zone' in his backyard, he made me promise to never talk about this method of communication with anyone, even our parents."

"It sounds to me like Alex was quite enthusiastic and that he possessed a vivid imagination. You cared very deeply for him, didn't you?"

"I did. His death did a number on me, and his mother was never the same. His passing sucked all the life out of her. I enjoyed whatever happened back there as I was re-living it, but the memories are bittersweet."

When we stepped out of the woods, I was relieved. One of my biggest fears was getting lost in the forest after dark. "I'm going to wash up and make some sandwiches. It's too late to prepare anything else. Do you like roast beef?"

"I do, but don't bother to make me one. My stomach feels like I just got off of a roller coaster. I'd appreciate a glass of ice water, though."

"In a glass receptacle?" Now where did that come from?

"What?"

"Uh, small, medium, or large?"

"Large, please. I'll go wash my hands."

As I prepared Warner's glass of water, I thought back to the times that Miriam had perched on my recliner and then left each of those glasses untouched. I placed the glass atop a coaster on my side table and returned to the kitchen.

"Sure you don't want something to eat? It's no bother, and I have plenty."

"Nothing. Thanks for the water." He sat in my chair.

"Not you too?"

"What?"

"Oh, nothing." I brought my meager meal into the living room and placed the plate atop the coffee table and my coke on a coaster. "This has been an eventful day for you. Perhaps you should take a day or two to think about everything."

"Not yet. I've decided that I'm going back to that well. I want to look it over thoroughly, and I want to do it alone." He sipped the water, unconsciously catching the drops caused by condensation.

"You may do that if you wish. However, I warn you. Enjoy a voyage into your past, but once a visit. The effects of these travels into the past are much too emotionally charged. We return a bit woozy. Why that is, I do not know."

"Maybe you don't recover as quickly as I would because of your age."

"That is a possibility. Nevertheless, if you do attempt more than one excursion, do it in the morning. At least if you lose consciousness, you won't wake up in the dark. Or let me know when you depart and give me some idea of the amount of time that you expect to be gone. That way, I can check on you if you don't return within the allotted time."

"What would happen if I tried to, say for example, use your stone or anyone else's for that matter?"

I swallowed a mouthful of delicious beef, and washed it down with a slug of coke. "Don't know. I've never tried that. Frankly, it never crossed my mind. I guess, now that you ask, I wouldn't."

"Why?"

"Because each is so very personal, their private property, I imagine, as if I would be violating a trust. There's a certain sanctity about each section of the Well." I paused. "I think that I would feel like I was walking in on an intimate moment."

"Maybe I just might give them a try."

"Let me ask you this. Would you have been willing to share with me that memory which you relived today?"

"Absolutely not!"

"And without a preface, would I have completely understood the dynamics of your relationship with Alexander the Great III?"

"No."

"I would have understood that you were two young boys at play, but your mission would have escaped me, yes?"

"Most likely."

"Then why would you want to walk in my shoes and relive moments in my life that I treasure? To better understand who I am, and how these events made me the man that I am today?"

"I don't particularly care about any of those things, Tanner."

"I see. And neither do you know or care about Miriam? Nor do you have a desire to peek into Neris's past?"

"Okay, okay. Point taken. My intention was to debunk the Well. Nothing more."

"Then proceed. However, please be respectful of this monument, our monument, that we cherish so deeply. Remember, it is yours as well now. You, too, will come to hold it dear, and we all will preserve our memories as long as we shall live."

"You've made your point. I don't intend to damage the thing. But you need to understand where I'm coming from. My brother is over at that woman's place, supposedly in some kind of limbo, maybe dead, maybe alive. You tell me a tale that's so bizarre that it's beyond belief, and then you throw that well in for good measure. This is 2020, and we aren't living in the dark ages." He stood. "I'm going to at least spend the night. If you don't mind, I'd like to keep the camper in your yard. I don't really think that I'd find another place at this time of the night. Then maybe, just maybe, I can make some sense of it all."

"You are welcome here. If I had an extra bed, I would offer you accommodations."

"Not necessary." He turned to leave and then paused at my doorstep. "After I'm done with that well, I think that we need to return to your friend's place. We have unfinished business, her and I."

"We shall see. That will depend on your state of mind. I won't have you tormenting or bullying her."

"Oh, and do you think that I'm not in torment? That's my brother over there, for God's sake!"

"We are all in a state of uncertainty and anguish. We are all on tenterhooks, and that can result in exasperation toward or with one another. It is my goal to see my life in order before I leave God's great earth, and I have a certain amount of responsibility in seeing that Neris's future is not left to chance, that she has someone to protect her. Remember this when you are quick to judge or think that we don't care about Skip and Clare. Our ultimate goal is to see them freed from captivity. Would if I could dash Jacob's curse to pieces!"

"Yeah, well, it's nice to know that you care." He exited, slamming the door.

"Lord, help us all!"

The next day dawned, and it was a pleasant one in Pittsburgh, New Hampshire.

Tanner showered, dressed, and walked over to Warner's home on wheels. It was a beauty. At approximately thirty-feet long, it shone as if new. Before settling on a place in the northernmost part of this state, he had given some thought to purchasing one himself, setting off for parts unknown across the vast hills and valleys of the United States. These rigs were complete with all the comforts of home, allowing the adventurous at heart to seek the places that piqued their interest. However, he couldn't trust his eyesight. His peripheral vision was poor.

He rapped on the side door. When there was no response, he knocked again. It appeared that Warner had set out quite early, so he returned to his own home and began to make a breakfast consisting of waffles and link sausages. As the coffee brewed, he popped the frozen blueberry pastry into the toaster, checked the pre-cooked meat for doneness, and set the table for one. He loved Vermont maple syrup and always kept two in the event that one ran low because he typically decided on his morning fare on the spur of the moment. After pouring his first cup of coffee, he sat down to eat.

Breakfast cleanup was not something that he looked forward to, but he was neat by nature. That done, he decided to enjoy his second cup of java on the front stoop. An unread book lay on the coffee table. He scooped it up on the way by, and wondered at the fact that he was a voracious reader, yet had been unable to concentrate long enough to get past the first chapter. It wasn't the tome itself, one of many written by his favorite author, but his inability to shift his mind from his worries.

He'd no sooner sat when Warner exited the forest straight ahead. He appeared to be talking to himself, perhaps preferring his own counsel than that of any other. He set that book aside, thinking it no more than a prop at this point.

"Tell me about Miriam." It was an order, not a request.

"Why is it that you are inquiring? I believe that I have only mentioned her name in passing."

"I want to know why she's so interested in your welfare."

"Wait one minute!" Tanner's heart tripped a beat. He inhaled deeply. "You'd better have a seat and explain yourself."

Warner complied, although he sat rigidly, then leaned forward, resting his elbows on his thighs. His general appearance was ruffled as if he'd jammed his clothing in a sack and had chosen to wear them as is. The cuffs of his jeans were wet with morning dew. His hair as yet uncombed was thick and jutting out here and there.

"Because I saw her this morning, she spoke to me." He looked straight ahead, staring at nothing in particular. Had he looked at the old man, he would have noticed a change in his pallor.

"Oh, saints preserve us!" He felt as if he was going to weep. "Why on earth would she come to you, and not me? I've attempted to summon her so many times that I've lost count. my Miriam spoke to *you*. How could this be?"

"Obviously, I went to the well this morning. I followed your instructions from yesterday, but was so anxious to see Alex again that I didn't realize that I was on the wrong stone. I waited a minute, thinking that you had duped me, had tricked me somehow, when all of a sudden, I saw this elderly woman who came walking toward me. She was very graceful and otherworldly. I didn't feel threatened at first. But then I thought of all those horror movies where a person approaches, and then they change at the last minute to scare the shit out of you."

"Please. Oh, please. Tell me, you say that she was lovely, and I don't doubt that. But what did she have to say?"

"When she got close-up, everything did change, but not as I had expected. I felt like she was directly in front of me, large as life. She said that she only had a few minutes before an appointment with Lady Libra."

"Really?"

"Please stop interrupting me, or I'll end this conversation right here and now!"

"Go on then." I couldn't bear to be left out.

"It felt like we were walking, she with her hand on my forearm. I felt really good. Like all of the weight of my responsibilities were lifted from my shoulders. I couldn't look at her without smiling. She was so warm and sincere. She said that she was in Atlantis, of all places! But that's what she said. She also said that she loved you and awaited her rebirth. Then she told me that I am Neris's champion. When I asked what she meant by that, she said that I was the one man who had the potential of releasing everyone from Jacob's curse. I said that I didn't want that responsibility. Furthermore, I told her that I didn't believe anything that you'd told me. I just wanted to get my brother and his friend out of whatever state that they were in and return to my life in the city." He was distracted by a low hum that the old man emitted, and saw that Tanner's eyes were closed, his arms wrapped about his mid-section, and tears coursed down his face, following lanes of wrinkles as if they sought an escape route.

"Hey? You going to be all right? I don't want you seizing up on me."

"I am. Continue, please? Please?" His posture remained the same. He wasn't able to sit still.

"If you say so. Then, she seemed to be distracted, said something to someone whom I couldn't see, and told me that she had to leave for some sort of meeting. Before she disintegrated into a flurry of particles, she suggested that I get to know Neris better and to tell you that she loves you." Warner realized that he was not immune to Trump's distress and reached over, patting him on the shoulder. "Hey, I'm sorry if all of this upsets you, but you wanted to know." He paused, giving Tanner the time to reach into his back pocket, retrieve a hankie, and dry his tears.

"So sorry. If the people back in the office could see me, they'd be shocked. I'm making a fool of myself."

"Yeah, I heard that you were a heavy hitter at one time. Had to get those scoops, didn't you?" His attempt at small talk was weak, at the most. He didn't really know how to comfort this senior.

"That's all in the past, and I'm thankful for it. You don't know what it was like. A person can fall from grace in the blink of an eye."

"Listen. All if this shit is getting us nowhere, and I'm losing my patience." He retracted his hand. "I took over my father's business when he passed away and turned it into a multi-million-dollar, Fortune 500 company, and was featured in their magazine three times. Our stocks soared, and I just implemented a project that will triple our worth within the year. I wear tailored suits, monogrammed shirts, and silk ties. Not because that's what I want but because appearances at the level that I do business are everything. No offense, but chasing down newspaper stories looks simple compared to my workday."

"You're so full of shit, Warner!"

"Oh, really! Please elaborate. I want to hear you expound on the life of a cub reporter!"

"Well, excuse the hell out of me, Mr. GQ! You are insolent, egotistical, rude, and self-absorbed! If you had pulled in the reigns like you should have, your brother wouldn't be in the mess that he's in!" He stood. "I can't bear standing in your shadow a moment longer!"

"Well, get used to it, pops! I'm here for the duration!"

"I'm going to check on Neris, and if you intend to join me, shelve that attitude!"

Tanner went inside, placed his coffee mug in the sink, and went back outside. He set out for her place without so much as a second glance. He inhaled deeply, hoping that he would be able to calm himself before reaching her home. As he approached the end of the path, the sound of several men gave him pause. Was there trouble ahead?

There were three men talking all at once, attempting to explain how the one in the middle, Steve, had come about injuring himself. Tanner knew Steve from previous visits when he sought Neris's ministrations after he had suffered wounds serious enough to cause concern. Two of his burly coworkers had escorted him here from a job site in the immediate vicinity.

"Here, here, gentlemen! You'll wake the dead!" He called out as he approached. "Steve? Have you gone and gotten yourself in hot water again? Your friends don't appear to be very pleased with you this morning."

"Oh, hi, Tanner!" Holding a saturated cloth to his damaged cheek, Steve welcomed the distraction. "Oh, this? It's nothing. They're making a big deal out of this." With that, he exposed the wound. It was a fierce, jagged rent in his right cheek.

"Hello, Barry, Ken. You can leave him with us. If Neris is unable to help him, I'll run him over the emergency clinic."

"Tanner! Thanks! We wanted to get Steve to the ER, but he insisted that Neris would be able to fix him up right as rain." Ken smiled, exposing a handsome set of dentures.

"You guys know that she can! I'm not going to pay an ER bill! Highway robbery is what it is!"

Neris stepped forward and took charge of her patient. She led him into her home.

"That's that, I guess!" Barry joined the conversation, shaking his head. "You know, he's going to get himself killed one of these days. That guy shouldn't work with sharp objects. He's so accident prone!"

"Carmen keeps badgering him about changing occupations. He loves the heavy equipment and flatbeds that come and go. With that in mind, she's told him many a time that he should get certified to drive something like a tractor-trailer." Ken shrugged.

"Come on, buddy. We have to get back to work." Barry shook Tanner's hand. "We know that he's in good hands. I'll call Carmen and forewarn her that Steve's had a bit of mishap."

"Okay, you go on. Get along. Don't give her cardiac arrest! We won't get pork pies this Christmas if she disowns us." He loved those meat pies. Serve them with some peas and cranberry sauce! His mouth watered just thinking about them.

"Later!" Barry and Ken chattered like two old hens as they returned to work.

He realized that Warner had been watching from afar and approached only when their discussion ended.

"Does this happen often?" He approached slowly.

"Only on occasion. Steve, the man that's with Neris, tends to be a bit accident prone. He's a great guy. His wife, Carmen, is a sweetheart. She has the patience of a saint, and she's an excellent cook."

"I imagine that talking with Neris about my brother's plight is out of the question."

"Absolutely. His cheek has suffered quite a blow, and the flesh is torn about an inch and a half. Numbing the area with natural herbs takes a little longer than procaine. Suturing outside and possibly inside, it's quite the procedure."

"Another day wasted!" His frustration mounted. "What the hell am I supposed to do with myself?"

"I know that your truck is still attached to that trailer, and I'm not familiar with how much work it is to disconnect everything. But if you want to use my SUV, you can. The keys are hanging on a peg in the kitchen. Bobby's place has pool tables."

"I don't know that I'll be welcome there, considering that he wanted to beat me to a pulp the last time that I was there."

"He doesn't usually hold a grudge. He's good like that. You have to be when even good men misbehave now and then." He paused. "Listen, you haven't been over to the pond yet. You can always take a swim, catch some Zs, get a tan, or read a book. You can read, can't you?" His gibe was meant to be good-natured and the proverbial olive branch.

"Comics. I like the *Avengers*, *Spidey*, *Superman*." He inhaled deeply and offered a tentative smile. "Truce?"

"A temporary stay." He shook Warner's hand. "If you go to the shed out back, I keep my swim stuff in there. Some large beach towels, sunscreen, a beach chair, and a comfortable little pillow for your head. Feel free to use anything that you want."

"No shovel and pail?"

Tanner was beginning to warm up to the young executive. Warner had a dry wit to equal his own. Verbal sparring challenged the mind, giving it the exercise necessary to stay sharp, keeping him on his "intellectual" toes.

"In the shop. Had a hole in it. I loved that thing. It was last year's mode, but hey!" He shrugged. "Now, the pond is, and I'm sorry, to the left of those fallen birches. You can't see it through the bushes, but it's just beyond that."

"Thanks. I believe that a swim and nap on the shore will help. I'm going into town later if you need anything. I have to check in with the office. If they don't hear from me, they'll start to worry. Unfortunately, there's no reception in this neck of the woods."

"You do what you have to do. By the way, there is a small igloo under the kitchen sink if you want to bring along a couple of cokes or some beer. If you pass by Molly's Sub Marines, I wouldn't mind a ham and cheese with the works, mayo not oil. You might want to try one. She bakes her own bread daily. I haven't had one in days, and I usually get one once a week. It's just down the road a piece. You can't miss it. I think that she used every color in the rainbow to paint her shop."

"How late is she open? I'm not sure what time I'll be getting back. Could be as late as six-thirty, seven o'clock."

"Until eight."

"Plan on it then. I'm going to head back to your place now. I need that swim."

"You do that. I'll check on Steve, see if Neris needs any help, then I'm going to the Well."

"Good luck with that!"

Warner gradually disappeared from sight. Tanner hoped that this young man was, in fact, Neris's salvation. As he entered her humble home, she was tending to her patient who lay atop a timeworn quilt. She was about to mend his wound with thread and needle.

"How is everything going in here? Can I be of assistance?" He prayed she was able to finish without his help. He felt queasy at the sight of that sharp object in her hand. It was Steve who responded.

"No, thanks. Everything is under control. Neris has done this before, and I trust her steady hand. She gave me something to ease my pain, and that mud that she uses miraculously numbed my face. She's about to do some stitching, so if you feel as green as you look, skedaddle."

He walked over to where she knelt, touched her gently on the shoulder, and smiled. "I'm going to leave now, going to the Well today."

She looked up, smiled, and bent her head in such a way that it touched his hand. Apparently, she preferred not to touch him with sterile hands.

"Give my best to Carmen, Steve. I've had company and probably will for a while. I'll stop by for a visit when I've got some free time."

"I will. Take care now." He winked. "She'd like that, Tanner."

I enjoyed my visit at the Well of Dreams; however, I was somewhat disappointed when I attempted to call forth my love, Miriam. Warner was fortunate to spend some time with her, but try as I may, it didn't work for me. When I backed away from my port, I felt calm, well rested, and pleased with today's outcome. I did not relive a time in my past, I was gifted with a pending dream, which I would enjoy this evening. You see, it was initially meant to do just that, as Miriam explained, but had somehow changed over the years to include jaunts into our past lives. I enjoyed both gifts, never knowing which to expect. Now if Warner returned with one of Molly's delights, it would bode well for me, my favorite sandwich, two Mich Lites on the porch, and a nice warm bed in which to dream away. The Well never served up bad dreams, only vivid, pleasant, heartwarming fantasies.

When I arrived home, I found my sandwich on the table along with a note from Warner. He'd made excellent time, contacted the office, stopped by Molly's, and was now at the pond.

The sub was delicious, and I ate the entire twelve inches. As I sat back, I decided that if I didn't work some of it off, I'd most certainly come down with a serious case of heartburn. Perhaps a walk to Neris' would do the trick. I hadn't had the opportunity to speak with her earlier because of all of the fuss over Steve's injury. After cleaning up my mess, I left my home, flicking on the outside spotlight in the event that I might lose track of time. The days are long in June, but I never took any chances.

I could feel the food that I'd consumed begin to settle, and I whistled a tune as I approached her cabin. When I'd rapped on the door and she hadn't responded, I went out back to see if she was working on her garden. There were implements lying here and there in random order. She never left them strewn about. Steve's unexpected visit must have interrupted her weeding. Then I remembered that she was a mess when she was bent over Steve, his blood transferred not only to her clothing but also to her body as well.

"I bet that she's at the pond." I often spoke aloud to myself, particularly if I'd spent most of the day alone. "She and Warner must be enjoying some time together. This is a good omen."

I decided that I would walk over there, and maybe even soak my feet. The walk there was quick, and when I reached the clearing, I almost called out a hearty greeting. But the words stuck in my throat. There before me lay Warner and Neris. He was covered from the waist down with my Charlie Brown beach towel, while my Betty Boop towel covered the better part of her body from underarm to ankle.

I suddenly had the urge to run, but I backed away slowly. Their eyes were closed, but I couldn't tell if they were sleeping. I caught a heel on a jutting root and fell on my arse, jarring my spine and scraping my right palm when I tried to catch myself by grabbing onto a nearby sapling. Cursing my clumsiness, I rose gradually and then returned home.

When I got there, I tended to my injury. My knee-length shorts were stained but undamaged, so I dumped them into the hamper and put on a clean pair. After seeing to my immediate needs, the initial anger surfaced. What the hell did he think he was doing? He was a worldly man, no doubt one who socialized often, with many women at his beck and call. He was handsome, fit, and a multi-millionaire. He didn't need to take advantage of Neris. A knock at my door interrupted this thought process, and I stomped my way over, turned the knob, and yanked the door open with a purpose. There before me stood the guilty party.

My reaction was two-fold. I called out, "You son of a bitch!" and put all my weight behind a right cross. Warner staggered backward. I cursed and supported my right hand with the left, certain that I'd broken every bone.

"Are you crazy!" He held a hand to his jaw, massaging the painful area. "Why the hell did you do that?"

"You took advantage of that poor girl!"

"She's not a girl! In case you haven't noticed, she is a woman! A very beautiful and healthy one at that!" He took me by the arm, led me to my recliner, and waited for me to sit. "You stay right there. I'm going to get some ice for both of us."

As I watched him, the rage gradually seeped from my body, and I felt very old and tired. "What...why?"

"Here, take this. If you can, spread your fingers out, lay your hand on your lap, and keep still."

He walked over to the couch, sat, and pressed the ice pack to his chin. "Not a bad punch for an old man with one foot in the grave. Now before you say another word, let me explain." He sat back. "When I drove into town, I thought about my brother and his buddy. I had to figure out a way to set them free, to help them in any way that I could. My brother is the only person that I have left, my only family. I also thought of my cousin Alex. What would he do in this situation? The answer was simple. If he had to, he'd lay his life on the line for those he loved and cherished. Then I remembered what you said. That if Neris were to bear a male child, they would be freed. But she had to get pregnant first, of course. That goes without saying. How's the hand? Do you need more ice?"

"Hurts like the dickens, but I'll live. It's numb right now."

"Good. That was a very stupid move on your part. You don't have to defend Neris's honor. Tanner, we are both adults, she and I. Furthermore, she is a very passionate woman. Combine that with dash of shyness, and you have the makings of an incredibly sensual woman. I can't say that I have ever been with another that can compare. Ah, I think that I'd better move on."

"Please do. I am not interested in the details of your coupling." It was obvious that Warner was remembering their tryst and that he found the memory of it arousing.

"That is between her and me. I never kiss and tell. Now, back to business. 'I' went to the pond for a swim, as you suggested, if I'm not mistaken. Neris was in the water, unclothed, and cooing a pleasant tune. She heard me step out of the woods, smiled, and waved me on. I told her that I didn't mean to interrupt. Again, she encouraged me to step forward, making several gestures that invited me in for a swim. I set the towels down, removed my clothing, and slowly walked to the shore. She obviously sensed my reluctance and came forward. She was the most magnificent sight. The sun shined off her skin, rivulets of water ran from her waist-long hair, and I thought, *She has no tan line.* I don't know why. It's a rather stupid thing to think of when such a beautiful creature holds her hand out to you."

"So you're telling me that she initiated this, this, whatever!" I was beyond words.

"No. I initiated it because I went to the pond. But I'll tell you, Tanner, when I let her take my hand and lead me to a spot where the water came to her waist, she smiled sweetly and pressed my hand to her breast."

"Don't…"

"Let me finish, please? I knew where this was going, and I knew the consequences of my actions. But I wouldn't have been able to stop if I had to. She's a bit timid yet curious at the same time. That she is innocent in the ways of making love with a man is quite apparent. I…" He passed the ice pack over his face. "Sorry. I had made the decision already, Tanner. When I was waiting for your sub at Molly's, I decided to make an attempt to impregnate Neris, knowing that if I didn't and if the curse is true, I'd end up beside Skip and Clare. As an aside here, do you know how long it will take before I know if…if…"

"If memory serves me, when the sun rises on the day after copulation."

"Well, at least I know that I have the rest of the night ahead of me. That said, if I have any time left after I take you to the emergency room, I may seek some comfort in her arms. There's nothing wrong with a man spending his last hours with a very special woman."

"You needn't take me there. I'd prefer to wait until morning."

"Want to witness my undoing?"

"No. I pray that you and I will then go to the emergency room first, then to Bobby's for a patty melt and maybe a game of pool." I was surprised at my attempt to ease his worries. I had, after all, almost decked him minutes ago.

"That sounds like a plan. Let me get us some more ice. I bet that my damn jaw is turning black and blue."

"Ha! It is. To think that I can still pack a punch!" I attempted to swing my hand but suffered too much pain to do so. "Ow!"

"Here. You have to keep it cold, or you'll be sorry. Do you have anything for the pain?"

"I'll get it in a few minutes. Thanks."

"Well, I tell you, Neris is a sweet and gentle lover. She is curious, adventurous, and blushes constantly when exploring my...shit, here I go again. Tanner, I don't want you to think that I'm being disrespectful when I speak of her this way, but if I don't talk to someone, I feel like I'm going to explode. Ah, that might not be the right word to, um, anyway! She didn't even really know how to kiss but learns fast."

"Look, Warner. I understand the risk that you've taken in an attempt to save your brother and his friend. I pray that all is well come morning, and at day's end, we will celebrate the fact that you will be a father in several months. Have you even given a thought about what you will do when that time comes? If she births a baby girl and passes, are you going to care for your daughter? Remember, Neris will perish, and you shall live."

"I hadn't gotten that far yet, and deliberately so. I can't imagine the worst-case scenario right now. I'm kind of worried about what will happen tomorrow, let alone nine months from now." He paced. "This...sucks!"

"It certainly does. Please sit. You're making me dizzy." He complied, leaned forward, placed his forearms on top of his thighs, and began to pick at the towel that he'd applied to his face. Here was this man—young, virile, handsome, and successful. He was the owner and CEO of a Fortune 500 company, a multimillionaire, who made split-second decisions that would affect hundreds of employees. He looked like a rakish boy with an errant lock of hair pasted to his forehead. I was at a loss for words, doubting that there was anything that I could say to ease his burden. I didn't doubt for one moment that should he survive and Neris perish, he would step up to the plate and be a responsible parent. I, too, felt a great sadness, because if we lose her and he brings the infant back to Boston with him, I'd be left here all alone. He raised his head, looked me in the eye, and spoke.

"Do you mind if I stay here tonight? I can sleep in the recliner. All I'll need is a pillow and that lap blanket over there."

I nodded, unable to speak. As I rose, so did he. I stepped forward, clasping the soggy ice pack in a bruised hand. Clearing my throat took great effort, but I was finally able to say the words. "You will always be welcome in my home as long as you do no emotional, mental, or physical harm to my girl. Now if you want me to sit up with you, I'll try damn hard to stay awake."

"Thanks, Tanner. You have my word. I haven't and would never do anything to hurt her, as God is my witness."

"That's good enough for me. Now how would you like to pass the time? Movies? Cards? Chess?"

"If you play cribbage, I'd like that although I can't guarantee that I won't skunk you." A sad smile creased his face. "Pops!"

"We'll just see about that!"

I moved my recliner, which was on casters, into the center of the room. The coffee table that I'd purchased served as both that and a higher eating surface by easily raising it with a tug. The exposed cubby held several items such as books, playing cards, and a cribbage board, to name a few. I prepared the board, a stylish handmade item, that I'd purchased at a local shop. Warner returned with a beer for each of us, placed them on coasters, and sat on the couch.

"This table's perfect for playing cards…where did you get it?"

"At a large furniture chain. I did think that it would come in handy sooner or later."

"How's the hand feel?"

"Surprisingly well. Perhaps I just bruised the stupid thing." I massaged it several times. "Nevertheless, you'll have to do all of the shuffling. I don't think that I can manage that right now."

"Got it. Red or blue?"

"I'll take the blue. They usually bring me pretty good luck." I waited as he placed a pair of pegs each at the starting point. "Please cut for deal." As he revealed my card, and then his, I noticed that his hands trembled a bit. With that in mind, I decided to keep the conversation flowing as much as possible in an attempt to keep his mind off of his worries. Then it came to me that no amount of good conversation or card games could possibly keep a condemned man from agonizing over his fate. This broke my heart. I was tempted to allow him to trounce me, but he was an intelligent man and would find me out in no time. "How do you like to play? Blood and guts or a more casual game?"

"Casual's fine. If I have to watch your every move just for the pleasure of calling muggins, I won't enjoy that."

Muggins, for those of you who are unfamiliar with this card game, comes about when a player miscalculates their points and the other player catches him making that mistake. Then the challenger is awarded the opponent's points. It is rather cutthroat.

"Shall we proceed then?"

"We're off!" I found it a bit clumsy latching onto the seven cards. However, when I discarded two, the remainder were more manageable. "I've got a hand like a foot!"

"Like a what?" He smiled.

"Like a foot. My father taught me how to play, and he'd use that term every time that I dealt him a lousy hand. Rather silly, isn't it?"

"I just couldn't quite figure out whether that was good or bad."

"Bad, exceedingly bad, at that. If you continue dealing me cards like these, you'll skunk me for sure."

"I'll do that all the same. Now let's get this game moving. I, for one, have one hell of a hand!"

We started playing at approximately eight in the evening, and were still at it come midnight. We drank and poked fun at each other's lousy cards, and in general, it was quite pleasant. I began to yawn at about twelve-thirty, and as is usually the case, it was contagious.

"Listen, Tanner. I appreciate the fact that you're trying to help me out here, but you look beat. Why don't you go to bed? I think that I'll be okay."

"I'll just sit back for a minute and put my feet up. They've swelled some because I've taken in too many fluids today. Just one of the wonderful benefits of growing old." I pushed my recliner away far enough to change from sitting to prone position. "There, that'll do me just fine."

"Can I get you anything? A pillow? A blanket?"

"No, thank you. This is fine. How about you? Do you want to stretch out? That couch is quite comfortable."

"Thanks. I think that I'll do just that."

He settled back, with a plush pillow behind his head and the knitted throw over his legs.

"You were a real heavy hitter back in your days as a reporter. How did you come by that career?"

I shared some of my background in reporting with him, and we each shared some of our adventures on the way to the top of our professions. I enjoyed his enthusiasm and found him to be quite an amazing man. His brother, on the other hand, at least in my opinion, lacked the drive that Warner possessed from an early age. Not that he imparted this in his dissertations, but it was simply evident to me. That he loved his brother, there was no doubt.

I cannot recall exactly what time it was, but I dozed off, slipping away without intention. Warner was nodding, last time I knew. My intention was to let him nap for a short time while I was deep in thought. I reached for that novel that I'd been attempting to read for such a long time. Soon, I slipped away, unable to remain awake any longer.

When I awoke, it was with a start. How could I have been so inconsiderate? A sudden and all-encompassing terror consumed me. There on the couch lay the pillow that still held the indentation, the shape of that poor man's head, and the throw, which had fallen to the floor. The morning sunbeams bathed my living room, dancing dust motes celebrating a new day. I laid my head back and released a mournful howl that sounded foreign to me. Had I not been its creator, I would have surmised that some poor animal was in the midst of deathful throes. Exhausting my breath, I repeated the sound again. Placing my hands atop my head and setting my right hand ablaze with pain, I welcomed it. I deserved that agony and more. I cried out for Miriam to soothe my emotional distress. Closing my eyes, I prayed that the grim reaper would gather my sorry soul, for no longer was I able to deal with Jacob's curse. That demon had torn a young man from us, a person undeserving of his fate.

"Tanner?"

Good Lord! I could hear Warner's voice through my emotional fog. Was there no end to my torment?

"Hey, buddy! Come on. Wake up! You're having one hell of a bad dream!"

I felt his hand. By all that was holy, I felt his strong hand comforting me! What is this? I opened my eyes, and there before me was Warner Trident, flesh and blood. I took his hand in mine and pressed it to my heart. "Thank you, dearest Lord! Thank you! Thank you!"

"Tanner? I survived the sunrise, Tanner! I'm still alive, and if I'm not mistaken, Neris is carrying my child! I'm going to be a father! And just maybe, just maybe, my brother will be saved!"

Warner invited me to join him when he went to share the wonderful news with Neris, but I decided to stay home. It was not my place. I felt that I would be infringing on moments that should be shared by the young couple. He bade me farewell, and I suggested that he bring along a couple of towels in the event that they decided to go for a swim.

After he left, I put my house in order. As I was doing so, it came to me that I had not dreamt while asleep. The Well had promised a flight-of-fancy yesterday. This was the first time that it had failed to deliver, and that troubled me. I set my concern aside for the moment, taking inventory of the food in my cabinets and fridge. It was time for me to refill the larder, so I dressed and went into town. I took a detour, opting for a midmorning breakfast at Bobby's, but went to a nearby clinic instead. Trying to drive proved difficult, convincing me that something was wrong.

I'd broken three bones in my hand and the little finger. By the time that I'd left the clinic, it was casted, and the doctor had written me a script for pain medication. I had it filled in town, netted four autographs, and made my way to my favorite spot for watching locals and strangers alike fly-fish. I didn't recognize anyone, but that was fine. After an hour or so, I decided to stop at Molly's. I didn't know what kind of sandwich Warner preferred, but I ordered mine and two for him, a ham and cheese and a roast beef. Molly humored me when I requested that she fill those little plastic cups with each fixing possible except mayo and oil. I had those back home. I assured her that I would pay extra for the custom order, but she waved me away. I felt that I'd shown my appreciation by buying some coleslaw and potato salad. A large bag of her homemade chips rounded out the fare.

Upon arriving home, I immediately put everything in the fridge. I had a dinner, thanks to Molly, fit for a king. That done, I checked the time and decided that I had more than enough time to visit the Well. It troubled me that I hadn't dreamt the night before. This had never occurred in the past.

The verdant carpet, which typically appeared as if it were mowed by an unknown lawn keeper, was a bit more-spongy as I walked along, and a few errant weeds jutted here and there. The afternoon sun shaded a bit, and I looked to the sky, searching to see if clouds had set in. It wouldn't do to be caught in a down-pour. There was not a one. Unusual as these were, what concerned me the most was the ever so slight smell of sulfur. I immediately feared fire. Turning 360 degrees, I couldn't see any smoke or flames, neither was I able to detect a direction from where it came.

Though good common sense told me to leave, I proceeded forward to the Well, vowing to make my visit short. It was short. As was the case yesterday, there were no pleasant travels to the past, but I hoped for a wonderful dream. Perhaps one of Warner and Neris' and a handsome son.

I was in deep thought as I returned to my home, a bit careless as I stepped on a few acorns. A pair of squirrels had placed them along the trail. Annoyed by the fact that I could have suffered a painful fall, I delivered a quick boot to their store. They dashed off, undoubtedly angry with me.

Warner sat outside my home, enjoying a tall glass of lemonade. "Tanner! Welcome back! Been to the well, I see." His voice matched his smile, cheery, but not overly so.

"I have. Not much to report today. I am anticipating a wonderful dream tonight. I see that you found the lemonade that I made. Is it too tart?"

"It's just right. Can I get one for you?"

"Not necessary. I'll go in, wash my hands, and join you in a minute. If you don't mind, I'd like to hear how your visit with Neris went today."

After taking care of business, I took the chair beside him and placed my beverage on the table between us.

"I see that you went to the clinic as I advised. Where's it broken?" He pointed to my right hand.

"Pinkie finger and a couple of small bones here and there. She said that it shouldn't take very long to heal, three weeks to a month." I proudly displayed the neon-green wrapping. "Like the color?"

"I think that it's great! Appealing to your inner child?"

"I just didn't want people to take this too seriously. Doc gives away free Sharpies per cast." I pointed to the signatures as I counted aloud. "Signed by five people already. Do you want to join my fan club?" I handed him the marker and watched as he jotted his initials atop the little finger. "How is your jaw, by the way? I can see that it's taken on a blackish-blue tint."

"Looks a lot worse than it feels. Just a slight twinge when I move it." He sobered. "Listen, I want to apologize for upsetting you yesterday. I didn't quite handle things the way I should have."

"You didn't, however, that's water over the bridge. I believe that you and I both have Neris's best interest in mind. I am also confident that whatever the gender of your child, you will be a good father."

"I'm sorry that I never met her, Miriam, that is."

He caught me off guard. "She was a wonderful woman. I am praying that we will reunite in another lifetime."

"How great would that be? You really believe that?"

"It pleases me to think it possible. That is enough for now."

"We can always dream. And speaking of dreams. We came to a large clearing. Apparently, the area had been harvested because there were tree stumps as far as the eye could see."

"I've been there as well. That is the place where Miriam walked into the sun."

"Exactly what does that mean?"

"Let's set that question aside for another day. Please continue with your tale. I am enjoying your slant on things." I decided to explain Miriam's departure, as well as what may be my own, at another time. This was his time, not mine.

"Well, I stood there for several moments, and suddenly, I envisioned a beautiful large log home in its center, a carpet of soft grass surrounding it. I then asked Neris to envision these and other highlights that came to mind. She smiled all the while and squeezed my hand as if she approved. Tanner, I think that I'm going to find out who owns that land. I'd like to buy it all, have the stumps blasted, and design the place myself. What do you think?"

"I've seen the spot, and frankly it's a blemish on this normally verdant area."

"I agree." He leaned back in his chair. "It'll take some time. That is if the owner will let it go."

"I don't see why not. They've taken what they wanted, and if you offer a fair price, it should be a done deal. What would your ultimate goal be? Electricity, running water, and all of the comforts of city life?"

"For the most part, I'd like a few woodburning fireplaces, but electric appliances are a must for me. I realize that Neris has the bare minimum of creature comforts as she knows them, but I think that she'd enjoy a place like that."

"Only she can tell you. I am not privy to her desires for a future with a family. If she lives beyond giving birth, I think that she just might live anywhere." Great job, Tanner! I chastised myself. It was a wonderful way to put a damper on things. "Listen, I'm hungry. Do you want to join me? I have some subs, and all of the fixings. Got enough for the two of us and then some." I prayed that he would let my comment of Neris and her potential doom pass.

"If it's from Molly's, I'm right behind you!"

So it was that. Warner and I enjoyed a peaceful meal at my table. We ate, each with his own thoughts and concerns. No matter what they were, they did not deter us from consuming all of the good eats, thanks to Molly. We remained at the table, speaking of this and that. The conversation was lighthearted. I truly enjoyed his company. As I said before, his dry wit was a match for my own. We laughed over the silliest of things, relaxing in the early evening. When I finally pushed away, in need of a stretch, he did as well. Unfortunately, those chairs made my legs numb.

"I think that I'll spend the night in that camper and give you some privacy. That hike through the woods was great exercise. I'll sleep well."

"I don't blame you. Neither my couch nor the recliner were meant for the purpose of catching a great night's sleep. I myself have every intention of getting past the first chapter of that book over there. And maybe, just maybe, my overdue dream will visit during the night." I wasn't totally convinced that it would, but only time would tell.

"Before I leave, I was wondering if you'd like a nice thick steak for dinner tomorrow. I have a small gas grill packed away in that thing out there. When I return from my visit with Neris tomorrow, I'll have the time to run into town to pick them up."

"I'd like that very much."

"Great. Good night then."

"Night."

There were several times that I caught myself dozing off as I, once again, attempted to read that novel, my apologies to the author. I secured the door, checked the windows, and retired to my room. My bed felt exceptionally comfortable. I sighed, content that sleep would not be elusive. As I slipped off to sleep, I hoped that the Well had gifted me with travels or exciting adventures.

Miriam called to me from a small chair in the corner of my room. It sat kitty-corner to the foot of my bed, and she was as radiant and as beautiful as ever.

"Tanner Trump. I apologize if I have startled you. I meant for you to awaken slowly."

"Miriam? Is that you?"

"It is."

"Let me turn the bedside light on so that I can see you clearly."

"That is unnecessary. That you are alert is sufficient. Please rest your head and hear the message that I am here to impart. It is very important."

"Is something wrong? Is Neris okay? And Warner? You have me wondering at the importance of your message, for I have not seen you since that day when you walked into the sun."

"I apologize. My nocturnal visits are very limited. Had the choice been mine, I would have come often. Now my time is limited. Please permit me to continue."

"Then go on. Permit me to ask one question. Are you still waiting for me, Miriam?"

"I am. That shall never change. I have been promised, and again reassured that it is so. Now for the reason that I am here this evening. You, no doubt, have been to the Well of Dreams these past two days and found it unresponsive."

"True."

"Do you recall the story of Jacob's curse? That it was a demon who initiated that most heinous pact?

"Yes, has he had something to do with the well's failure to perform?"

"He decided to take up temporary residency there. He is anticipating Neris's next visit. At which time, he will attempt to foil her relationship with Warner and hopes to either terminate her pregnancy or force her to pledge her child's life, her child's future, in exchange for sparing the life of her new love. Tanner, she is innocent enough to think that his life holds more promise, that she cannot live without him."

"How on earth are we to proceed? This is terrible. We can't let this happen, Miriam! Please help us! If you can. Because if you can't, then who will?"

"Mara."

"Neris's mother?"

"Yes, her mother. As we speak, she is doing battle with him. He who would cause such irreparable harm to her daughter. I tell you this because neither you, Neris nor Warner must ever seek out the Well again. Regardless if Mara is able to contain the demon within, it shall forever become a forbidden place."

"What will happen to Mara whether she succeeds or not? I don't understand."

"The bargain that Mara struck with All of the Good People dictates that she shall remain in the Well for eternity. In order to defeat the evil one, she must maintain a hold on him forever."

"How can that be done, and who are All of the Good People?"

"Sheer will and love for her daughter will give her the strength that she needs. All of the Good People is a group that watches over families who may be in danger of being torn asunder by evil. They attempt to intervene whenever they can."

"But that is excessive, isn't it?"

"Oh, it certainly is. However, it was her choice, not ours, not Neris's. She will not have her grandchild's life held in the balance. If there is the slightest chance that her daughter lives beyond birthing, Mara feels that this child deserves that right to know its mother."

"Please don't change anything about our rebirth."

"I will not. Now, allow me to finish. I am overdue."

"Go ahead."

"All of the Good People have resources available to them when it is apparent that a spirit surrendering their future does so selflessly. They pleaded with an Amazon Princess to avail them with the gift of a Golden Lasso. Their request was granted, and it was given to Mara so that she may secure this demon and render him helpless. As a rule, this lasso draws the truth from its captive. It may also be used to secure them temporarily or permanently. Once this is done, she must await approval to leave that pit."

"How can she endure such a fate?"

"Because her child, Neris, means more to her than life, than rebirth, than any demands, be they what they may."

"Are you beginning to fade, or is it my imagination?"

"I have overstayed the allotted time. Please be well, Tanner Trump. Until we meet again. I will always be with you in spirit."

That said, she disappeared.

As I lay there thinking of how wonderful Miriam looked, radiant and more lovely than I remembered, it came to me that, I was not privy to the young couple's plans for the morning, I reached over to reset my alarm. I had to intercept Warner before he set out for Neris's home. I laid back down, but my head had no sooner hit the pillow that the prospect of sleeping through was too worrisome.

I crept out of bed, dressed, and dashed to the kitchen, forming a plan as I went along. First of all, I reached under the sink for the insect repellant. I slipped it into my shirt pocket. Then I checked the flashlight to make certain that it shined brightly. Next, I tucked two cans of coke, one each into the front pockets of my cargo pants. As

I passed through the living room, I decided to bring that damned book with me. At least it would entertain me as I read by torchlight. Upon exiting my home, I sprayed a generous amount of repellant across arms, legs, and to be on the safe side, my clothing.

With flashlight in hand, I dragged a porch chair along. When I reached the steps at the door of Warner's camper, I established my post in such a way that he would be unable to leave without tumbling over me. The fear of missing his departure later this morning consumed me. I set the two sodas on the top step and then shined the light on my book. There I sat, prepared to man my post diligently. All good intentions aside, I slipped into a fitful sleep.

"Tanner! Tanner, buddy! Wake up!"

Warner gently shook my arm. I came awake so suddenly that I shot to my feet, prepared to do battle with the unknown.

"What are you doing out here? How long have you been sitting there?" He leaped off the top step. "Be careful now. I don't need you falling on your ass and breaking something else."

"Oh, Warner? That you?" My eyes struggled against the bright morning sun. "I need to talk to you. It's extremely important."

"Is Neris okay? Has something happened to her?" His concern was telling. Obviously, this man cared for her.

"She is as you left her yesterday, I suppose. I have not visited her since. However, I must speak with you immediately. Are you on your way over there now?"

"Yes, why? Come on, Tanner! Tell me what is so important that you camped out at my door, and why didn't you wake me?"

"I didn't want to disturb you. Now, I am going to walk to Neris's with you. I will share an abbreviated version of my visit with Miriam."

"Miriam? Your Miriam visited last night?"

"She did. Now come on. Let's get moving." I gave him a gentle push. "Miriam awakened me about an hour after I'd fallen asleep. The message that she imparted was complex and ominous. Bottom line, do not now, or ever again, visit the Well of Dreams. It has been violated by the very same demon that called on Jacob so many eons ago."

"Say what?"

"Yes. He now resides within. His intention was to lay in wait for Neris and do her and your child serious harm. He fears that she may be carrying a male child, which would put an end to this horrible curse."

"This whole curse thing is getting out of hand. If in fact, if what you say is true, I won't let it happen. I'll take her away…oh, damn it! You said that she can't leave this forest, didn't you?"

"I did. That is part of her penalty for being Mara's child." I stopped quickly, and grabbed his arm. "Don't you even think of attempting that, Warner. You can't possibly deny the truth of the events that have taken place here. You would be murdering Neris *and* your child!"

"What can I do then? What if she has a complication during her pregnancy? How am I supposed to handle that? Bring a doctor here? He'd think that I was out of my mind!"

"She cannot leave! Accept it and move on! No doctor. No man-made medication of any sort. None of it!" I became frustrated. How many times was I going to have to repeat myself?

"Okay, okay! I get it! Play by the rules. I just want her to be safe. I want her to be happy. I want her to give birth to a healthy baby boy!"

We were about to enter the clearing to Neris's home. I placed a hand lightly upon his arm. "Now, take a deep breath and simmer down. Listen, it will be easier if I tell her about the well. She'll heed my warnings."

"Okay then. Let's get this over with so that we can move on."

"I'll just say hello, tell her about the Well, and then leave you two to enjoy this beautiful day."

"Thanks, Tanner. I appreciate everything that you've done for her, for both of us."

After speaking with Neris, I decided to check out the Well of Dreams myself. Not to travel through my past, but to see if it still appeared as it had before.

I stopped at home to change my hiking boots then set off. As I navigated the path, most likely for the last time, I mourned the loss of that incredible time machine, for that was what it was, wasn't it? Fortunately, I was the one who'd missed it the most, and I could live with that.

My approach to the end of the path leading to the Well was tentative. As I peered through the thinning shrubs, I wasn't exactly sure what I expected. There were no flames bursting toward the heavens; however, I was able to hear a very low, mournful cry. If it were possible for the sound of despair to take physical form, I had no doubt that it would have been a deep, dark tower of smoke.

My initial step was tentative, for I was experiencing a fear beyond any that I've known in my lifetime. Before I could progress any farther, the smell of sulfur, which I had noticed on my previous visit, was so intense that my stomach roiled causing the soda that I'd drunk to rise in my gorge.

While the morning sky was as blue and beautiful as it had been when I departed, the light appeared to be filtered, dimming the surrounding area. I felt as if I was standing beneath a gray cloud that was about ready to shed a sudden summer shower.

I took a tentative step forward, sensing that I was about to sacrifice the safety of solid ground. I sank a wee bit but opted to proceed forward. I sank further with my next step and found that my boot submerged up to its thick sole. I felt very insecure. In addition to the sogginess of the turf, the sounds from the well intensified. I could have sworn that someone or something was calling out to me. So mournful were the pleas that my initial instinct was to rush forward and offer aid.

As I sank deeper into the ground, I felt my emotions shift as if somehow something reached into that secret place where I tucked away all of my meanest, most hateful feelings and stirred them up, encouraging them to rise to the surface. My body became rigid as hostility, bitterness, and revulsion drove me forward. Every affront, every injustice, and every selfish feeling that I had experienced in my lifetime swirled, fueling my progress forward. I did not heed the struggle that it took to progress as I sank deeper and deeper into the green murky sludge.

My breathing became labored, and had I had my full faculties, I would have feared cardiac arrest. When I attempted to take another step, my boot dislodged from my foot. In anger and, in frustration, I released a string of foul language that was meant to humiliate and debase whatever it was that impeded my progress. Then suddenly, I was unable to move.

As I reached into my back pocket for a cloth to wipe my dampened brow, I passed the folded handkerchief across my forehead. I screamed when it cut the skin. My initial reaction was to toss it as far as I was able, but then my curiosity got the better of me. Unfolding it carefully revealed that the culprit was the faux crystal bead that had fallen from Miriam's bracelet when she had walked into the sun.

I began to weep. I held it to my cheek, sobbing and moaning. My heartache was palpable. I was ashamed. I was lonely. I was inconsolable. I was stuck. I wanted to retreat, to run back to my home, the home that Miriam had visited, sitting in *my* chair, *not* drinking the water in a glass container. I wanted it all back, yet here I was, both legs submerged halfway up my calf. Was I to die here? I began to pray. I wept, pronouncing each word in a slurred and drunken manner. Woe was me, woe was me!

A sudden movement to the right caught my eye. Sniveling and attempting to wipe my eyes so that I might get a clearer view of who or what was about to overtake me. Friend or foe, I knew not. I heard a shushing sound that reminded me of my mother attempting to quiet me during Sunday mass. I twisted in such a way that I almost lost my balance. Suddenly he was upon me, a large, strong hand at my back.

My eyesight adjusted to the dimmer light caused by the shadow that he cast over me. And, there he was, as clear as day. This giant of a man stood well over six feet and had to weigh in at two-hundred-fifty pounds at least. His blond hair was thick and unruly. He was dressed in a pair of bib-coveralls and a pristine-white, short-sleeved T-shirt that fit his muscular body with little room to spare. A bright-red handkerchief peeked out of his back pocket.

"Who are you? Who sent you?" He was close enough for me to see the light stubble on his cheek and a sparkle in his beautiful blue eyes.

Now I don't know if I can explain what happened next in such a way that anyone can understand, but I shall try. He spoke to me but didn't actually talk. What I heard in the forefront was a lilting, harmonious chant. But woven into those harmonic sounds were words that he wished to impart. I made an effort to pay undivided attention for fear of missing his response.

"I...am...Guardian...Z."

"Why did you come? Oh, never mind that. Can you help me out here?"

He reached forward, slipped his strong hands under my arms, and lifted me. I swear that I heard a suction-like pop as my feet were freed. Without preamble, he then carried me thus all of the way to my property. With my back to the house, he set me down on shoeless feet, sodden socks revolting, for they were thus because of that terrible place. I sat immediately, removing them gingerly, attempting to avoid contact with that vile muck, and it came to me that his large feet had never touched that stuff. His footwear was pristine. I then regained my feet, and as I did, he handed me my boots. They looked as new as the day that I'd bought them.

"Yours...I...clean."

It was the same lilting sound. When he smiled, it wasn't overly done, but a soft curve that exposed even white teeth.

"Thank you, kind sir. Where are my manners? I am Tanner Trump, and you are who again?"

Placing his fist at his waist in a superhero pose, he responded... "I...Z."

"Z? Well, then, Mister Z, my sincerest thanks from the bottom of my heart. Had you not come to my aid, I surely would have perished for no one knew that I was there."

"I...did...you...not...listen...to...Miriam...do...not...do... ever...again...cause...you...die."

"Did she send you? Did Miriam send you?"

"No...she...pray."

"Then I will have to make certain that I thank her someday. Can I offer you something to drink? I'm very, very thirsty, and you are more than welcome to join me if you wish."

"No...thanks...have...to...go." He pointed a very large digit for emphasis. "Stay...away...from...that...bad...place... Got...it?"

"Oh, you needn't worry yourself about that. As it is, I will probably have nightmares for many days to come."

This time, when he leaned forward, he placed his right hand atop my head. I stood perfectly still, not knowing what to expect. His touch was warm, gentle, and weightless. I don't know why, but I closed my eyes.

"No...bad...dreams."

"If you say so."

"I...go...now."

"Can I offer you a ride to your destination? It would be my pleasure."

"No."

"Then I thank you once more and bid you fare-thee-well."

As I looked on, he slowly nodded three times and began to float atop the grass. With a quiet flutter, the most beautiful wings unfurled, large opaque feathers formed a frame behind this ethereal creature. I looked on silently, in awe of their majestic power, lifting him farther. A gentle breeze passed over my body, cleansing me both inside and out. It was as if I was renewed, reborn. When he was high enough to clear the tree line, he leveled off and then disappeared from view.

I don't know how long I stood there or if I anticipated his return, but I softly prayed until I finally gave up my vigil there in the middle of my front yard. A soft smile creased this old man's face. Never, ever, would anyone, other than Miriam, believe that I had been saved by an angel. My guardian angel.

I fasted the remainder of the day, with the exception of ice water. Warner hadn't had the opportunity to go into town and promised that we'd have steaks for dinner tomorrow. After he shared the events of his pleasant visit with Neris, I asked him to keep Mara in his prayers, and whether or not he did was his business. I only meant to emphasize that this poor woman's soul was not at rest and wouldn't be until this horrible curse had come to an end.

My experience at the Well affected me deeply. I wasn't, as a rule, a religious man. Nevertheless, it gave me pause to question my life choices and values. For whatever time I had left on earth, I vowed that I never would take it for granted, nor would I be so quick to judge. I was very happy that I'd chosen to retire here in this beautiful setting, with the few people that I had come to know. I can't think of a one that I didn't appreciate. Their values were beyond reproach, and I wasn't the one to judge.

Our days passed quickly. Warner stayed in touch with the office. Over dinner a few days ago, he shared his immediate plans for his father's company. It belonged solely to him, contingent upon the decree that he would take care of his brother, financially that is, for the rest of their lives. So, when it came time to sell Trident Enterprises, he sold it to one of his competitors. His choice was made based on the similarities in their beliefs and business practices. He made certain that loopholes were in place should they fall short of expectations. This deal made him one of the richest men in the country. The day after he signed on the dotted line, he remained in Boston in order to tie up some loose ends and returned bearing gifts. Each and every person that he knew, including Bobby, Molly, Steve, Carmen, and all of the others, were given something that he had chosen with forethought. I was impressed as he sorted through the boxes, garnering my opinion on all with the exception of mine and Neris's. She was to be given a variety of seeds. He had made certain that each would fit our climate and soil. As for myself, I received a beautiful set of binoculars, an assortment of cheeses, and a bottle of my favorite brandy. I had an affinity for cheese, and the occasional nip of fine spirits.

Clearing the parcel of land proved interesting, but the blasting unsettled Neris. With that in mind, Warner spent several nights by her side. He purchased a large tent and all of the necessities for a comfortable night. They washed everything that they could in the stream so that she would be assured the utmost comfort. She was showing, and what a pleasant sight she made, waddling here and there, about her chores.

One evening, Warner visited. We sat outside, enjoying a bottle of beer when he shared some very interesting news.

"I've hired on a former assistant from my days at Trident. Hurit was initially hired to work in our IT Department, but soon exhibited such a commitment to her job that, long story short, I took her on as one of the three people who reported directly to me. She's an American Indian. Just before I came looking for Skip, she went on maternity leave. Her husband was killed in a boating accident, so she went to live with her mother in Connecticut until she gave birth."

"Hired her in what capacity?" This was quite an unusual twist. Was he going to start another business from scratch?

"As an Interior Designer."

"Are you serious?"

"Yes, I am. It's a temporary position, and she will be able to work and be a mom at the same time."

"I have to ask a question here, and I don't want you to get all hotheaded on me."

"I'll try."

"Good. Was she then and now a romantic interest? Because if she was, is, I'm not going to like this at all. You can't do this to Neris."

"Neither you, nor Neris have anything to worry about. You have my word, and you must know by now that my word is gospel."

"Okay, an Interior Designer?"

"Her first priority is to outfit my tent. I want everything in there to be made of all-natural materials, from top to bottom, side to side. The weather is going to get cold, so I want Neris to be comfortable. I don't want her to stay in the small cabin. I realize that she's spent many a winter there, but things have changed. She's with child, and may find that the harsh weather is too much for her to handle. I figured that if Huerit could get some input from her mother and grandmother, it could be done."

"That's not a bad idea. It'll be my first winter here, but they have to get pretty bad this far up north."

"Yeah, well, time will tell. I've also asked her to consult with Neris regarding the new house. I want it to be warm and inviting yet practical. I also think that both of them will have some fun in the process."

"You may be right. Now, is this Hurit woman going to commute or live here?"

"She's looking for an apartment around here and will go home on weekends to visit her family."

"Sounds like you've been a busy man."

"Not as opposed to what it was like at Trident. Frankly, I don't miss it at all. I'm happier than I've been since I was a kid. I even think that I'll take up fly-fishing."

"Good luck with that. I'll tell you one thing: wrap a trout in foil with the right seasoning, and it is a real treat."

"There's something else."

"I'm all ears!" This was the most that he'd spoken since he'd arrived here in Pittsburgh. I enjoyed his enthusiasm.

"As I was about to say, when I went into town last week, I came upon a detour. They were doing something in the roadway. As I was driving on the back road, I saw a man outside of his home, and he was taking a chainsaw to a large section of tree. Behind him were the most amazing things that I'd ever seen. There were forest creatures, posed in various ways, looking larger than life. I turned around, pulled into his driveway, and then got out of the truck. I had to see these things close-up. He welcomed me, and as we walked through this menagerie, he explained that he'd been doing this for many years, and that although he preferred animal subjects, there wasn't much that he couldn't do."

"I've seen them myself, Warner. They are magnificent and so lifelike."

"I agree. As he was talking, I got this great idea. It was bothering me that Neris was troubled by the blasting. What if I commissioned this man to work on some of those stumps? What would it look like to have our own menagerie in our yard?"

"I think that would be very beautiful, perpetuating wildlife. What did he say?"

"He's coming over after dinner tomorrow night. I'll take him over there. If he can work with what we have, I'll hire him on. We can work out a price that both of us can live with, and since he's self-employed, he can start right away."

"I wonder if he will be able to do anything with the ones that are low to the ground."

"We'll find out tomorrow, but for now, I asked that the contractor to leave them as is. They can wait a day or two for me to make that decision."

"I'm pleased to hear all of this and look forward to meeting Hurit. What is she going to do with her child? Is she going to leave it with her family in Connecticut?"

"No, she is bringing him along. Lyon, named after his father, will tag along with his mom. He won't be a hindrance. Besides, if she finds that she needs the occasional sitter, Carmen will step up to the plate. I saw her at the grocers last week. She had a little one with her, and when I asked about him, she said that she occasionally babysits for the neighbors. I'll introduce Hurit to her, and then they can work something out."

"What did you tell this employee about Neris? She's bound to be asking questions, and you'll have to warn her about the ever-present dangers that Neris might be exposed to."

"Severe allergies. I made a list, and she'll be very careful not to cause Neris any harm, furthermore, I am her contact. If I have to keep her away, I will. If this doesn't work out, I'll give Huerit an excellent severance package. She'll be well compensated. After all, I can afford it."

"It sounds like you've covered all of the bases. You know, it might be beneficial for Huerit to bring her child along. If she needs to feed or change her son, Neris can watch and learn."

"My thoughts exactly. It can't hurt." He rose. "I'd better get back. I promised that we would go for a swim."

"You give my love to her and tell her that I'll be by some time tomorrow. I have to go into town myself. Hopefully, they'll be finished with that roadwork."

"Ha! Good luck with that! You know how it is with the DPW. Send six men out to do a two-man job, and then milk it for as long as they can. City, county, it doesn't matter. They're all the same."

"True, so true." I watched as he made his way to the tree line, and then went into the house. I made a list of the things that I needed to pick up. At my age, you can't even leave that to chance.

Warner's tent was replaced by an enormous teepee. Huerit's cousins saw to the task. Frankly, it was a beautiful sight, not far from Neris's small cabin, which it dwarfed. Warner's employee had explained that a wigwam was more practical, more comfortable, and easier to heat.

When everyone was busy working on one task or another, either Neris or I would care for baby Lyon. He was a precocious child, winning everyone's heart over in a trice. We both changed his diapers, which were made of a soft, white material. There was no store-bought disposables for our little prince. When he required more than his mother's milk, he was fed some sort of mush that was prepared by his grandmother, jarred, and then kept cool until we warmed it to room temperature.

After a period of time, Warner and I agreed that his dedicated assistant could be trusted with the details of Jacob's curse. She never so much as blinked an eye throughout the telling and promised to keep our secret. She arrived one day with, I believe that it was, sage, and cleansed all of our homes.

Zack performed wonders, transforming the remains of age-old trees into an array of forest dwellers. He worked on the smaller ones as well, turning them into natural birdbaths. He was in his element, enjoying the challenge.

Hurit also schooled Warner and me on midwifery. There were no guarantees that she would be here when Neris gave birth. I was reluctant at first; however, she convinced me that it was imperative that I, too, participated because Warner, being the father, might need my support. So it was that, I gained some knowledge about birthing. I feared that I might not be as reliable as they all hoped, but one never knows how well they will do under pressure.

Weeks and months passed like a blur. Before we knew it, Christmas was approaching. These roads were treacherous in the snow, at times restricting travel. Thanks again to Huerit. We were able to gift one another of handmade treasures that we would all cherish for a lifetime. Warner and I feasted on Carmen's pork pies with all of the fixings. She and Steve visited with me for a few hours, and I was regaled with Steve's fumbling antics. And we all laughed, Steve taking it in stride.

We asked Huerit if her mother and grandmother would be so kind as to fashion baby items, which we would gladly pay for. Our intention was to surprise Neris with a baby shower. Carmen also showed an interest in attending, and she, too, requested an item or two to give the mother-to-be.

When Huerit arrived with a bundle of treasures, she also brought along nappies and receiving blankets. She encouraged us to wrap the presents in the blankets, therefore, creating a gift within a gift. Everything had been handmade and then purified with water from a blessed stream. Frankly, I couldn't wait for the day of shower to arrive.

It was a complete surprise when Warner returned after a walk with her and found all of us nestled warmly in his teepee. It was a snug fit, but this cold winter's day in January found us welcoming the body heat. Neris wept on and off, passing her hand gently over each item, and then folding them before she went on to the next gift. We rounded out the affair with a glass of her favorite tea, which Warner himself had prepared. As I listened to all of the good wishes, I found myself wondering if Neris would ever dress her child in nappies and buntings. My sadness was so profound, that I found myself in tears. The other celebrants probably thought that I wept with joy. However, when I caught Warner's side-glance, I realized that he, too, was of the same mind for he dashed away a tear or two.

Their wedding was a simple affair on the fifteenth day of February. As it turns out, our artist friend Zack was a Justice of the Peace. After much consideration, Warner asked that I was the only attendant and witness to this humble event. I was honored. Because of the bitter cold, the ceremony was performed in the teepee, which it seemed had become the place to congregate. Neris was as beautiful as ever. She'd saved some of the dried flowers from her shower gifts, and placed a few in her hair. At the last minute, she crumbled a few of the remains into our hair, silently blessing us as she went along. It seemed that I was forever weeping for these special people. It both warmed and broke my heart. It was always one or the other. After the ceremony, Zack kissed the bride on the cheek, and shook hands with Warner and I before he left the warmth of the enclosure and waited for me outside. I believe that he, too, felt humbled. I embraced the newly-weds, reached a hand to their cheek, and said not a word. I simply was not able to speak. Zack escorted me along a narrow path that the workmen and Warner had shoveled. That was a constant task in these New Hampshire winters. I thanked him for everything, and went into my home, seeking comfort and solitude.

I did enjoy my first winter here. My wood-stove was a plea-sure, and didn't require as much work as a fireplace would have. I finally read my way through that book, and as I set it aside, I chuck-led. It wasn't worth a damn. Some people think that they are the next Koontz. I vowed that come spring, I would seek out the nearest library instead of buying books at the grocers. There was bound to be one or two that I would enjoy.

The Tridents' home was coming along nicely. He was constantly urging the contractor to hurry things along so that it would be com-pleted by the time that his wife gave birth. Because Neris was unable to shop for their furnishings, and ordering on-line, sight unseen, was out of the question, Hurit came to the rescue again. She ordered cata-logues. Although most manufacturers no longer offered these, claim-ing that they were obsolete, she was so convincing that they sent her any type of brochures and salesman catalogues that they could find. She left the young couple alone as Neris, in particular, was in awe of these colorful exhibits. Warner offered suggestions here and there and recommended that before their final selections and pur-chases were made, that they consulted with Hurit and myself. This, I surmised, was due to hodgepodge array of mismatched upholstery. However, all was not lost. Warner's assistant offered to speak directly to the company to see if they would consider a custom order, and due to the total sum of their purchases, the agreement was struck.

On and on it went. These were happy times for all of us, and I couldn't have been more content.

March first arrived with the promise of an end to the snowfall, which did not cease, but slowed. I don't know how these people lived year after year in this climate. Don't get me wrong. I like all of that white stuff, and it was beautiful; but enough is enough. I purchased a Farmer's Almanac at the grocers, and it did not bode well. There was more snow to come this year and more than normal. I was told that this annual publication was rarely wrong. Although I vowed to set it aside, it became daily reading in the water closet.

Neris was due in two weeks. She was such a trooper, waddling about and constantly reassuring Warner that she was able to do some minor chores without harming herself. I will say one thing, she was quite large, and it looked like she'd swallowed a basketball.

We hoped that Hurit would be here when Neris went into labor. However, she insisted that we be prepared for the eventuality that she was not. She prepared a large woven basket with everything that she could think of and explained each item to Warner and me. It frightened me to listen as she listed the use of each item, and I had nightmares several nights in a row.

On the fifth of March, Warner received several educational CDs about birthing. That evening, we sat in the center of the teepee, he, Neris, and yours truly. Fortunately, they were intent on the film, for I closed my eyes as often as I could. The sounds were bad enough to send me packing. When we were alone the next day, I asked him how the hell was he able to watch that stuff; and he said that while his eyes were open, his brain allowed him to escape to his "happy place." Now where the hell was that, and why didn't I know about it? Before I bid them good day, he showed me the biggest horn that I'd ever seen. He explained that the bullhorn would come in handy if his wife went into labor and I wasn't there. After warning her that there was about to be some very loud noise outside, he led me into their front yard, and then, without preamble, pushed its button. Well, I tell you, it felt as if my eardrums had exploded. Neris waddled over to him, grabbed it out of his hands, and brought it inside. Neither he nor I were able to hear for the better part of the evening.

The next day, we all attended to our chores; and when I returned home, I was exhausted. I was awoken just after midnight. Warner's bullhorn sounded several times. It took me a few moments to realize that he was sounding the alarm. Neris was in labor.

I dressed quickly, buttoned my shirt incorrectly two times, and then tossed it aside in frustration. I then selected a pullover and a pair of wooly socks. Once that was done, I went into the front room, put my boots on, grabbed my coat and hat, and hurried along my way, flashlight in hand. It seemed to take an inordinate amount of time to reach their teepee, but I cautioned myself not to run. It wouldn't do to slip and fall, for to do that could have been fatal. I would have frozen to death as Warner assisted his wife in delivery. When I approached, he was outside, fussing.

"What are you doing out here in your shirtsleeves, Warner! You'll catch your death!"

"I don't know what to do, Tanner! She keeps leaving this damned teepee and going into her old cabin! Every time that I bring her back, she just ups and returns to that place!"

"Let's keep our wits about us. I will see what I can do." Neris was pacing back and forth, and each time that she went by the wood-pile, she brought one piece with her and then placed it in the hearth. "Honey? How about we go back to your nice warm home? You don't want to catch a cold. It's freezing in here."

She stood before me with timber in hand and shook her head. She pointed to the cubby where her four-foot bed lay, so much as informing me that she wanted to give birth in her former home. Perhaps it gave her comfort. I was not certain, but at that moment, I decided to comply with whatever she wanted. I took her arm, walked her over to the palate, and asked her to sit, and told her that I would see to the fire after I spoke to Warner. When I exited the cabin, he stood there barefooted, partially unclothed, and holding the basket of necessities that Hurit had prepared.

"Okay, my friend, let's get you back inside so that you can get dressed." He offered me the tote, but didn't move so much as an inch.

"Yes, we will need those things, but you have to get back inside. I can't be worrying about both of you at the same time. Now, get your act together. Your wife wants to birth your child in the home that she grew up in and loves dearly. She is most comfortable there. Now I don't want to hear any arguments. I'll take that stuff and get back to her. There's a fire to start. It's freezing in there! If you want, you can get dressed and then heat up some water."

"The video said to…"

"To hell with the video. I believe that Neris is going to do this her way. She knows best what's happening, and she will not jeopardize her child's well-being. Move it!"

When I returned to the cabin, she was still pacing. The fireplace was ready to light, but for some reason, she had not taken the initiative to do so. It took me three attempts, but I saw it done.

Tanner entered appearing more alert, and went to his wife. "Honey? Is there anything that I can do for you?" His concern was apparent as he spoke. "Why don't we go back to where it's nice and warm and you can lay back in bed?"

As she refused, she reached into the basket and began removing items one by one.

"Neris? Honey? This place looks super clean. Have you been keeping it up?"

If I hadn't been scared half to death, I would have laughed. The look that she gave him was priceless. With a hand on her hip and, her head tilted, she looked at him as if he hadn't a clue. I absolutely love women. I vow that they possess a plethora of expressions, one for every occasion. This one spoke volumes like, "Where in hell have you been lately?"

"Warner, don't waste your time. She wants to have her baby here. Then let her have it here. She's kept this place neat and clean. Now I realize that we're in cramped quarters, but let's make the best of it, okay? Now why don't you go get the bassinet? We'll need it once the baby's born and we're cleaning up."

"Fine, okay, you win!" He brought the woven bed over and set it aside so that we wouldn't trip over it. Then he attempted to prepare some of the bedside necessities, and Neris arranged the bed. "Oh, man! Look! She just wet herself, Tanner!"

"She did not! Her water broke! Is there a clean nightgown in that basket? If not, you're going to have to get one. She can't stay wet like that. She'll catch her death!" I cursed my choice of words, but nonetheless, it appeared to jolt him out of his funk, because he gave me a look like he wanted to severely hurt me. When he returned with not one but three garments, he gently set them aside.

"Can you turn your back for a minute, Tanner? I want to get this gown off of her."

"Not a problem. Listen, it's too small in here for the three of us to move about without bumping into one another. I'm going across the way. If you need me for anything, just call out, and I'll come running."

"Don't you leave us, Tanner. I...we...she...we can't do this without you!"

"I'm just going to be across that way. I can spell you if you need a break or be here to help when it's time for the infant to arrive."

"Okay. Okay then." He turned to his wife. "Honey, you let me know when you're ready, because I want Tanner to be here to help. Okay?"

She smiled at me and then dismissed me with a wave. As I crossed that short path, I could hear that man speaking without pause. Lord, help us. It was going to be a long night.

I fell into a fitful sleep then awoke a couple of hours later. I was confused by my surroundings. My body was aching because I'd dozed off sitting up. When my head cleared, I arose too quickly, and the room spun. I sat again until I was awake enough to stand without hurting myself. All was quiet across the way, so I thought that I'd go put my ear to the door. They say that "timing is everything." I had no sooner rested my ear against the door when Warner opened it with a jerk. I fell into his arms, and if he hadn't steadied me, we both would have toppled over.

"It's almost time, Tanner. I need you to spell me for a couple of minutes. Mother nature's calling, and I want to go over to talk to Skip."

This poor man was terrified. His fear was a contagious thing, for I suddenly couldn't breathe. He guided me just outside the door and gave me the opportunity to take a few gulps of the fresh air.

"Are you going to be all right, Tanner? I really need you right now. Like I've never needed anyone in my life. Please, please, help us?"

"I..." I had inhaled a couple of deep breaths, and I found my voice. "I will...I am...just...I just needed some fresh air. You go and do what you have to do, and I'll stay with Neris."

"Thanks. I won't be long. Just give me a minute."

With that, he walked away. A heavy burden sat atop this young man's shoulders. Was he about to lose his brother and his wife all at once and at the same time? Was Jacob's curse to continue on with his daughter, who could, as well, perish in childbirth? "Miriam, if you're listening, please, please help. It's not about me. It's about Neris, the child that you raised as your own. If you've got any pull at all, please call in the markers." I left it at that and joined Neris who, at this moment, clutched the ledge over the fireplace.

"How are you doing, sweetheart? It's a little hot in here. Let me take this coat off, and then I'll help you sit down. You're covered in sweat."

I guided her to the bed, retrieved a cool cloth from a nearby bowl, and gently touched it to her face. She smiled weakly and nodded in thanks. I chatted continuously, and truth be told, I couldn't tell you what I said if asked to repeat it. Then, in tandem, Warner returned and Neris lay flat out on the bed. Her mouth opened as if to scream, but no sound followed.

Warner removed his jacket, and we swapped places. I immediately began to arrange several items in preparation for the arrival of their child. I intoned the requisite "push, breathe" when it was my turn to coach. But it was he who was by her side when the babe finally arrived. It was such a sorry sight, all wrinkled and covered in gunk. He passed the child into my awaiting arms as I held a clean blanket. We shared a knowing glance. He held his exhausted wife while I held their daughter.

He and I wept. My vision was clouded by so many tears as I washed this precious baby girl. My heart was rent by the knowledge that she would be raised by a widowed father.

It came to my attention that Warner was holding Neris as if against her will. She pushed him away and began to struggle.

"I don't understand. Neris?" He turned to me. "She hates me! I did this to her! I've killed the only woman that I've ever loved!"

I rushed over immediately and handed him his daughter. "Tanner! Stop this! Take your daughter now!" He had no choice but to listen. "Move. I have to get closer!" Again, he complied, not taking his eyes off Neris who was once again in the throws of excruciating pain. How does one help a person who was dying and in such agony? As I reached to gather her into my arms, my hand briefly touched her tummy. Quickly I understood her plight. There beneath my shaking hand, I felt a contraction.

"Oh my God, Warner! She is…she is having another baby, Tanner! She's not finished!"

"What? That can't be!"

"Well, it is! And, here it comes! Push, Neris. Push, honey. It's almost over. One more. Good one!" When that wee bit of a thing slid into my hands, I felt like the heavenly hosts were singing hallelujah! "It's a boy, Warner! It's a…" I was unable to finish. I passed him to his mother so that they could share a few moments together before we got him all squeaky clean. I walked past Warner and into the fresh air. This little family deserved some privacy.

As I stood outside, using a fresh pile of snow to wash my hands and arms, two very confused young men, dressed in summer hiking garb, called out to me.

"Hey, mister? Where the hell are we? Where the hell are we?" Skip and Clare were confused but none the worse for the wear. I invited them over, got them settled in the tepee, each with a warm cup of tea, and then excused myself.

"How are the babes doing? Do you think that they are ready to meet their uncle?"

Warner, who was kneeling over Neris and the twins, stood so quickly that he startled the babes, and they began to wail.

"No! Really? Skip?" He could do no more than choke out his brother's name.

"In the teepee."

He rushed past me, leaving me to babysit for the first time. I sat on the stool beside her. Neris wasn't at all embarrassed as she fed the duo.

"As my dad would say, 'you done great'!"

"I had a lot of help. Thank you, Tanner Trump!" The sound was but a whisper, but its impact was monumental.

"Did you just thank me, Neris Trident?"

"I did." When she was able, she took my hand. "Warner's brother?"

"Right as rain, although he'll have to borrow some clothing from Warner. Other than that, all's right with the world, my sweet Neris!"

Warner returned and made certain that his wife was covered before he invited Skip into the cabin. I left as the young family as they enjoyed their time together. When he introduced his brother, Neris's "nice to meet you" response sent him reeling. He sat on the floor, at the foot of her bed, and grinned like the proud father that he was.

I walked back home feeling twenty years younger and as if I didn't have a care in the world. And, frankly, I didn't!

The Trident residence was completed one month after the twins were born. It was completely furnished a month later, and the joyous family moved in. They were pleased to leave the confines of the teepee. Skip had moved into Neris's cabin, while Clare returned home into the loving arms of his parents.

The Tridents had invited Skip to move in temporarily, at least until he enrolled in Harvard Medical School. He preferred the now-vacant teepee, but joined the family for meals and a few other activities.

I, too, was extended an invitation, but I was happy to live on my own, with an occasional visit from Mara and Joshua—Mara, after Neris's mother, and Joshua, after her father. We had heard very little of the man, but they liked the name.

Time passed quickly as we all settled into our own routines. Warner and Neris doted on Mara and Joshua. There were gatherings at their home, which included myself, Skip, and several others. Neris was gradually introduced to the foods that we all consumed, and that in itself was very entertaining. She was tentative at first, sniffing, examining, and then taking a tentative bite. Warner was trying to encourage her at every turn and then chastised the poor woman when she spat out something that she found unpalatable.

Skip adored the new additions to his family and spoiled his niece and nephew constantly. He enrolled in the fall program at Harvard Medical School, still not certain if he wanted to specialize or work in the field of research. I believed that whichever he chose, he would excel at, for he was as brilliant as his older brother.

I became very concerned that Mara and Joshua would eventually be playing in the yard. These wooded areas, while tempting to an adventurous child, was no place to wander. Yes, I agreed that their parents would not allow them any unsupervised time, but it still troubled me. When all of a sudden, I thought of the Well of Dreams.

Without preamble, or concern for my own safety, I set off down that well-worn path, determined to investigate its condition. My step was lively, bringing me to the curve in the path that would take me to that meadow. I paused there for a moment, thinking about the promise that I'd made to my angel that I would never return here again. I prayed to be forgiven because my intentions were good. I needed to know about whatever exposures Mara and Joshua might be subject to. Taking those last several steps, I did so with my eyes fixed on the ground. When I felt brave enough, I raised my head and saw a wonder of all wonders.

A lush green blanket carpeted the scene before me, wildflowers peeking out here and there. Two rabbits scampered about, playing a game known only to their species. The sun shined from above and, in rays, split by the tall trees framing its circumference. There, in the center, stood our Well. But alas, it was no longer the Well of Dreams, for I immediately knew in my heart that it was different. An arch had been added to the rim. At its zenith hung a thick rope that supported a brown wooden bucket full of water. Whether the crank had been used to fill it or rain had collected within, I did not know, but several orioles flitted and dipped, bathing and flying, bathing and flying. This was a wondrous sight to behold. I stood at the end of that path, watching nature's miracle at play, then turned to leave.

There before me, blocking my path, was a lovely woman. With hands clasped at her waist and, dressed in a white stole, she was a vision. It occurred to me that she resembled Neris a bit. I did not fear her, for she did not come across as a threat. It was I who broke the silence.

"To what do I owe this pleasure, my lady? I am Tanner Trump." I did not offer a hand in greeting; it simply did not seem appropriate.

"I am mother to Neris, Mara. I wonder that you have come here today. You promised never to return, did you not?"

She wasn't angry but simply stating a fact. "I did make that promise. However, I was concerned that this place might be a threat to little Mara and Joshua, your grandchildren. However, it does not appear to be."

"Your intentions are honorable, good sir. I see that now."

"And the demon, then?"

"Banished upon the dissolution of Jacob's curse. There is no longer a place here for him. My daughter has seen to that. She and her champion, that is."

"I am so pleased to hear this, and thank you for your intervention."

"A mother's protective instincts, nothing more. Are you satisfied then?"

"I am."

"Then I shall thank you for keeping a watchful eye on my daughter throughout these times, past and present, and bid you fare-thee-well, good sir."

"There is no need to..." Before I was able to complete my reply, Mara vanished. I was starting to be accustomed to these disap-pearances. "Okay, then. It's off to home for me!" The trip back was uneventful. That night, I treated myself to some of that brandy that Warner had gifted me and limited it to two-fingers, no more. I told no one of my encounter with Neris's mother. I simply saw no need to since she gave me no message to impart.

I awoke early on the fifteenth of July, had breakfast, and tackled the housework. I did not care much for the domestic chores, but they needed to be done. Afterwards, I drove into town to do my laundry. I did a quick stop at the grocers for supplies and then an early dinner at Bobby's. I enjoyed a quiet evening and dozed off a couple of times, so I decided to go to bed before I ended up sleeping there the entire night. I reached into my shirt pocket, and came away with the hankie that held Miriam's bauble. I'd found it in my cargo pants just as I was about to toss them into the washing machine. For some reason, I tucked it under my pillow, changed, did my hygiene thing, and called it a night. And I dreamed of Miriam, my love.

She was smiling, dressed again in all white, and as she reached for my hand, I noticed that she was still wearing the necklace and bracelet that I'd given her. I held on for dear life because I needed her. I didn't want to go through the anguish that I would suffer upon wakening. We left my home and began to walk. Neither she nor I spoke a word. We were that content in each other's company. As we continued on, I recognized the tree stumps, where Warner and Neris's new home stood. Now how could this be? This place where Miriam had "walked into the sun" was no longer strewn with stumps. Ah, but of course, I reasoned, this was, after all, a dream. Wasn't it? As I looked ahead, I realized that the sun was setting in the west. "I am west," I told myself.

I was at peace. I, who lived by the word, am unable to explain this feeling of nothingness and completeness all at once and at the same time. To be sure, this was a dream that I would regret relinquishing. I also clung to the hope of rebirth, for everything else was unimportant.

"Hey, Warner! Wait up a minute!" Skip ran to his brother's side, the puppy at his heels. "You got a key to Tanner's place? He asked me to take a bag of clothes to Good Will when I went to Concord to get my driver's license straightened out. For some reason, I forgot to renew it, and now I have to go all the way down there to straighten it out."

"He keeps one hidden under that tacky frog by the shed."

"Yeah, well, it's not there anymore. Maybe he moved it or something."

"Okay, give me a minute, and I'll be right out. I think that I'll walk with you. You know how you are about returning things." He chided.

"Yeah, I know. I just get so busy that it doesn't cross my mind."

"Be right out." He returned, key in hand. They enjoyed some friendly ribbing on the way back to Tanner's. It was still quiet when the two arrived at his door.

"Let me go in first. He might be in the shower and didn't hear you knock."

"That'd have to be one hell of a long shower, bro. But hey, it's none of my business."

"No, it's not." Warner turned the knob, gaining access immediately. "Tanner? Let me check in the bedroom. Maybe he left the bag in there, 'cause I don't see it out here."

When his brother didn't return immediately, Skip went to find out what the guy was up to.

Kneeling at the bedside, Warner held a cold hand to his cheek. Tears flowed freely.

"Is he?" Skip whispered.

"Gone."

‹‹ꟻꟻꟻ››

ꟻhe ꟻringe

T HE FRINGE IS A FAR and away place. A setting where a
person's essential being, their non-physical self awaits rebirth.
It serves as an initiation for first-timers who have never before
been offered a second chance at life. It is a magical place. Here is
where the novitiate is given the physical form and attributes that will
carry them through their next life.

Understanding rebirth and its complexities is not easy. When
they arrive, they "were." When they depart from the Fringe, they
"are" to "be" is determined by teachers, and they may be at any age.
So, you see, while we use the term *rebirth*, it is for the ease of understanding because most humans will not grasp the concept of "being."
That said, an initiate shall return to be at any age because they do
not require a mother's womb or the birthing process. They are given
a structured life history that both they and their fellow humans will
accept as fact. They may share a memory with someone, when in fact,
that memory is fictional. They believe that their material possessions
were earned through dedication and hard labor, because we make
certain that they "have." After that, whether or not they improve on
their assets or lose everything is up to them. Their "were," "are," "be,"
and "have" combine to make them a person with the gift of second
chance to walk the earth.

The Fringe Overseer is Aegis. His assistants are Picket and Flanker. They, too, possess a physical form as do all of the characters who reside therein. These three are capable of mutation: Aegis, the eight-foot giant; Picket, the centaur; and Flanker, the cyclops. They may transmute at will, primarily when they or their charge is threatened. Standing at approximately three feet, they are often mistaken for dwarves, which they are not. They are simply short men.

You will find many unusual places or characters here, and you shall choose to believe or deny their existence. That is your prerogative, for it will not alter our world in any way. However, if you chose to believe, and keep an open mind, then anything is possible. When anything is possible, and the blinders are tossed aside, our eyes see differently, our ears hear all, and our heart soars.

As Aegis, Picket, and Flanker, along with their charge Aiden Wolf (the former Tanner Trump), go about their affairs, enjoy the journey, for someday you yourself may "be."

"Please be still, Circadian!" Tanner adjusted the leather hood. "I don't believe that you are not in a cooperative mood this morning. Let's set you on your perch, and I'll come by later." He smiled. "Perhaps I was a falconer in a previous life."

The squirrel, who took this all in while gnawing at a sweet acorn, paused for a moment and shared its thoughts. Tiny bits of saliva peppered with fruity bits escaped as it chattered. He enjoyed behaving poorly in the presence of the hare, whose manners were impeccable. As a matter of fact, his favorite taunt was farting in his presence. The noxious fumes rivaled those of a human. Why? The answer was beyond anyone's reasoning. Things were unusual on the Fringe.

"What have I told you about talking with your mouth full, Rata? That is so disgusting! You were not a falcon in a former life, you twit! You have had no former life." Slacker chastised. "You know nothing about this mortal's history because you failed to attend the briefing."

Rata took exception. His beady eyes focused on the enormous six-foot hare as he tossed the succulent treat over his right shoulder, raised his paws, and challenged the egotistical boor.

"You must be joking?" Slacker's ears stood to attention while his snout wrinkled, exposing two enormous teeth. "How ludicrous!" He began to laugh, snorting, taking in great gulps of air, and clutching his midsection. "Silly twit!"

Rata's rage suffused every pore. He lunged forward and bit a section of tender skin between the hare's first and second toes.

"Why you little…"

The cagey rodent evaded a swift kick that would have propelled him into the firmament. The three creatures usually got along, amazing as it would seem, considering the fact that Circadian could capture Rata without much effort.

"Stop that caterwauling, Slacker. You're frightening the bird." Tanner began to lose patience with all three.

"But, sir! He bit me!" The white hare attempted to display its injury. However, the human brushed him aside. "Now look what you've gone and done, squirrel! Both Circadian and Mister Tanner are perturbed. This is all your fault!"

"May the gods have mercy!" Nanna entered the small structure. "Do not think of bolting, Rata. I would have a word with you three." She removed Circadian's hood. The falcon spread its wings, and nodded in appreciation. "You are welcome."

Rata, the squirrel, remained silent. It would not do to upset this powerful woman. Slacker, the white rabbit, stood a full foot taller than their master's wife. He outweighed her by fifty pounds, yet felt small whenever she presented herself. She had chosen him for his ability to interpret the language of all animals, to transform their gibberish into human sounds.

"If you'll excuse me, I'm going to check in with Aegis and see what he has planned for today." Tanner was about to leave.

"Not quite yet, sir."

"I apologize, Circadian. Our daily exercise shall have to wait. I intended to serve omelets for lunch. However, that crotchety old rooster simply would not allow me entrance into the chicken coop. I suffered several violent pecks."

There was nothing unusual about that nasty pecker. Sometimes things are just what they are on the Fringe. "I'm sorry, ma'am. Would you like me to intervene?"

"No, thank you. I have chicken thawing on the counter. Perhaps tomorrow we will find that his disposition has improved."

"Good luck with that! You might want to bring along a baseball bat!" It struck him funny to picture Nana swinging away.

"I would never! All of God's creatures must be treated kindly!"

"That was a joke, Nana. You know, something to lighten the mood?" He hoped that not everyone was in a foul mood, especially his three little friends back in the compound.

"I am aware of that, sir. I was simply offended by your choice of... Now what is that word? Ah yes, material."

"Got it. Okay, then." He suddenly realized that he was alone with the woman. There was no squirrel or rabbit in sight. Smart little guys. "Well, I have to go. I hope that you enjoy your time with Circadian this afternoon. I'm sure that the exercise will do him good."

"I shall. Good day to you, sir."

"And you as well."

Tanner's arrival on the Fringe took place right after he'd had the dream of Miriam joining him as he walked into the sun.

He had been reluctant to begin another because he took such pleasure dreaming about his love. Unfortunately, his bladder began to scream, demanding that he relieve himself. Opening his eyes as he turned onto his side, he suddenly realized that he was not in his bedroom, in his cabin.

This place was a stark, clinical white. His first thought was that he might have been in a hospital room; however, there were no gadgets and gewgaws typical of such a place. The door directly to his right was partially open, and he was able to discern that it was the water closet. He arose, went inside, and was about to do his business when he peered down at the hands that held his, um, private part. They were not his; furthermore, his private part was impressive. His paunch had somehow been replaced with a firm, flat stomach. This had to be a continuance of the Miriam dream.

Upon completion of the task at hand, excuse the pun, he went over to the sink to wash his hands. Much to his surprise, he'd grown a full head of auburn hair. Chiseled, handsome features brought a smile to his face, revealing a set of even white teeth. A day's worth of stubble peppered a strong jaw. Unrattled, he moved on to the task of brushing his teeth. Or, did he really have to? This was a dream after all. His mouth did feel tacky, so he brushed in order to rid his dream self of the foul taste.

When he returned to the room proper, he was startled. There, at the other side of the bed, stood three short men who stood approximately three feet. Their features were perfectly proportioned to their size, and each wore any expression of…well, to be honest, they were expressionless. Their attire was a combination of business, military, and casual garb. Nothing that he had ever seen before.

"Tanner Trump, welcome to the Fringe." The one on the far right spoke for the three. "I am Aegis, Overseer. To my left are Picket and Flanker. They are my assistants."

"My pleasure, I think. Now where am I? Who am I? And what the hell is going on?"

"Please change from your bedtime garb to daytime clothing. You will find what you need in that closet. They have been selected with your comfort in mind." He pointed to the doors to the right. "We shall give you some privacy and will wait outside in the hall. Once you are appropriately dressed, we will go to my office." At that, they left him standing there, more confused than ever.

The jeans and shirt fit quite comfortably. Underwear, socks, and sneakers were gray, and they, too, appeared to be just his size. He returned to the bathroom, splashed some cool water on his face, and then brushed his hair. As he looked at his reflection, he spoke aloud, "Well, Tanner Trump, or whoever you are, let's get this done and over with."

He stepped out of the room, entering a hallway that was painted a pristine white. The three men immediately formed a straight column, with the one who had spoken at the lead.

"This campus is well organized, and you will find plates or signs that will guide you during your stay. As you can see, your billet has your name on the door, the compound is to the right, the mess is to your left, my office is directly ahead, etc. Nothing is left to chance. We, I, am very organized. This leaves less to chance."

"Am I in a military installation? An informal penal institution? Boot camp? Maybe a Boy Scout Camp?" He was becoming impatient and annoyed.

"Not quite, sir. My office." Opening the door, he let Tanner in, and then asked his assistants to remain out in the hall.

Tanner sat in the chair directly across from the standard-sized desk, and the odd little man assumed his place. Once settled, he folded his hands, leaned on his elbows, and began.

"You, sir, are on the Fringe. This is the place where you will prepare to 'be,' to once again, live among mankind. You will return to earth prepared to resume the life of a thirty-year-old, single man who earns his living as a contractor. You will reside in a place that is close to the woman that you love and wish to wed. However, the latter will not come about until you help her vanquish a very evil being who represents himself as a pious man, a spiritual leader. She is the key to his banishment. You will not remember any of the events that take place here, other than those that will be subliminally embedded in your mind. I will not know if you require anything over and above that until I have had the opportunity to evaluate you and understand who you are as a person. I will determine exactly when you are sufficiently prepared to 'be.' Now, this is an abbreviated explanation. Do you understand?"

"Hell! I should have brought along my tablet so that I could have taken notes! Don't you think that this is, like, information overload? Now how about you repeat that very slowly so that I can understand?"

Aegis was very patient. They discussed each edict until Tanner felt confident that he understood each one to a certain degree. He vowed to try his best to adhere to whatever plan, whatever schedule, and whatever it took to see him rejoined with Miriam. He wanted to "be." That was the bottom line.

Atlantis

THIS VENUE IS MORE COMPLEX than the Fringe. It hosts the council. It is a simple name for a complex group, addressing rebirth and specific assignments or conditions set forth for a few remarkable humans. The council consists of The First Seat along with, in this case, seven others. The First Seat must assign a specific task and conditions therein, to an individual who has had multiple lives. The belief is that these souls have matured. They recognize the gift that they are about to receive and understand that they must show appreciation and willingness to accept a quest that must be fulfilled. Failure to complete their assignment results in immediate death and forfeiture of any future reincarnations.

The other council members attend and witness the First Seat's decree as its plot develops and may offer suggestions to improve or expand on its merits; however, the First Seat's decision is final. Upon completion, a scribe will put ink to scroll, and then the subject will finally become privy to their assignment and ultimately return to earth. To "be." Should they disagree, a higher council will hear their reasoning. However, history has proven that to do so is ultimately for naught, concluding in immediate termination of any and all rights to exist.

Miriam's committee consisted of the following:

Poseidon—First Seat
Hercules—The Protector
Andromida—The Governess, Bearer of Grace and Dignity

Gifford—The Righteous Warlock
Angel Gabriel—Spiritual Sentry
Dame Puissant—The Pure Witch, Temptation's Dispatch
Freud—The Arbitrator
Jules Verne—Time's Transporter

A footnote. Committee members, including First Seat, may reseat multiple times, adjudicating the same subject over and over again. Poseidon had been First Seat twice before in Miriam's case. Unfortunately, ill feelings and hostilities between she and Poseidon existed, causing her great concern.

MIRIAM PAUSED AT THE CHAMBER door, awaiting her dear friend's arrival. She and Lady Justice, or Lady Libra were kindred spirits, had been for the span of six life cycles. Miriam possessed sufficient mortal genetics to walk the earth, to experience firsthand, while her friend remained but a symbol of man's clumsy attempts at justice prudence. They cherished these interludes; these respites were intended to rejuvenate the soul.

She welcomed Libra's arrival, and suspected that the other woman had wept away the morning. "Be done with those unsightly blinders, won't you?"

"Not today, Miriam. I have only just returned from the Hall of Sorrow and Shame."

Libra slipped a hand onto Miriam's forearm, allowing her to lead her through a narrow hall that led to an enormous garden. "Shall we sit by the roses?"

"Yes, please." Libra enjoyed the fragrant topiary.

"In all my travels, I have never seen such creative beauty. Have you had the opportunity to walk about freely without that blinder over your eyes? To see the multitude of colors and shapes?"

"On occasion. I do give all of my senses a treat now and again. However, having visited those miserable souls today, I find that I have overtaxed my eyes. Do not weep for me, Miriam. I am content in my lot. It can be quite interesting, to say the least."

"Perhaps it is better that you are unable to see. This place is unsettling all the same."

"How so?"

"There are fish circling overhead, to either side, and I imagine beneath."

"Of course, there are, Miriam. Atlantis has settled to the ocean floor."

"We are encased in a mystical bubble, a cocoon that is both enchanting and eerie at one and the same time."

"Those who sit First on the Council select its venue. Fear not. We are well protected."

"If you say so." Miriam rose. "I should have sought your company earlier. I do wish that you would not weep so often."

"I must visit the Hall of Sorrow and Shame periodically."

"What do you seek there? It is an unpleasant place, and I would keep you from it if it were within my power."

"Humility."

"You are humble, Libra."

"Pride's shadow bumps along at my feet. However, it is banished when I walk the length of the Passage. What troubles me most is that the cursed thing has elongated. I am no longer able to complete the morbid journey in two earth hours."

"Is it so horrible then?"

"Yes. And bound to get worse. We are witnessing evildoers exiting earth's Halls of Justice, liberated because deep pockets and notoriety attract barristers, legal eagles who are themselves self-serving. They run in packs, jackals to the last. I fear that televised trial broadcasts complicate matters. There are so many who believe that they are above the law. However, they shall suffer eternal punishment unlike any on earth. They shall spend eternity encaged and displayed along that hall." She shook her head. "Murderers, thieves, and perverted souls become celebrities, for goodness' sake!"

"I am not permitted access. What is their punishment once they die? I agree that they are deserving of the ultimate punishment, but exactly what is their plight?"

"The passage consists of two rows, one to either side of a walkway lined with horizontal bars. Cells are arranged alongside and atop each other, with three vertical rows. The cell itself is hollow, molded from Venus's vapors. Each is a four-by-four cube and transparent. While solid to the touch, they are designed to allow sound to escape and enter. When a deviant's soul departs from its corporal host, several sentries transport it to the Bench. As you know, former magistrates of exceptional character share that duty. After a review of their misdeeds, the sentry in charge is given a stencil listing these, and it is off to the Hall for eternity. When I am informed of a new arrival, I enter and, stand at the portal of their assigned cube, witnessing their entry. I, and only I, then seal the cube and watch as their crimes are indelibly stenciled on the portal. There is no maintenance needed. Once deposited there, they remain forever and a day as decreed by the Bench Judge."

"That sounds horrible, Li! I am not pleading their case or disagreeing with their final punishment. I am concerned for your well-being. Just the sounds alone would drive me mad. How can you stand the noise?"

"I must. I am, after all, Lady Justice. If the legal system is to remain accountable, I must oversee the just and final outcome."

"I do not envy you. Is this necessary then?"

"It is. However, there are times such as these that I am able to enjoy the company of a good friend. Now, let us move on. The committee has reached a midway point. I shall join the gathering as they review Poseidon's directive. Unfortunately, the time before last, when he sat First Seat, you angered him by questioning and disagreeing with his dictates. He is unaccustomed to his subjects casting him in a poor light. He was embarrassed, and humiliated. That does not bode well for you. I fear that your quest shall be a difficult one."

"I understand that he was displeased. However, I am hoping that the other committee members will plead my case to a certain degree. What will be, will be. I miss Tanner and am anxious to move on."

"Poseidon is an enigma to us all, I am afraid. However, we must deal with him. As to your companion, I am pleased that you have come to care for him. I pray that upon completion of your directive, you and he will find peace and happiness."

The Fringe

T
ANNER HELD THE GUARD ALOFT. "What the hell are you doing? Can't a man have a little privacy here?"

"Now what?" Aegis huffed. "Unhand him, Tanner Trump."

"You want a part of this action? I'm in rare form. Get in line!" He continued to hold the squirming guard aloft.

"I find no humor in this, sir. Release Picket or pay the penalty." There was no menace in his tone.

"What are you going to do, Aegis? Pummel my knees?" He shook the frightened little man several more times for good measure.

"Stop behaving like a petulant child. I have no patience for this."

"Bite me!"

"Very well. Consider it done." Aegis took the man literally, went to its knees, and sunk both rows of tiny teeth into his charge's calf.

Trump howled, dropped his captive, and clutched the offended area. The tender flesh suffered no visible damage. However, the pain was intense.

"Cease that cussing, sir. I will not have it." Aegis dismissed his associate and stood before the mortal. "Picket has been exceedingly patient with you. However, I am not cut from the same cloth. You deserved that and more."

"Why the hell did you bite me?" He continued to massage the tender area.

"Because you told me to. Is your attention span as short as your fuse? As short as your penis?"

"You little son of a…"

"I said, no cussing!" Aegis transmuted, soaring to a height of eight feet, his body mass plumped like a parched 'sponge' greedily absorbing fluid. He grasped the visitor by the throat, mirroring the treatment that poor Picket had endured. A deep, sonorous voice imparted several dictates. "You shall not threaten Flanker or Picket again." He looked into Tanner's bulging eyes. "You shall not cuss, misbehave, or permit that temper free reign. You shall treat us all with respect, courtesy, and kindness." He bellowed, releasing air from powerful lungs. "Have I made myself clear?"

"Sssssss!" Trump crumbled to the floor, gasping for breath.

"Very well." Aegis returned to his former state and began to pace. "When you are capable of gaining your feet, I will be in my chambers. Join me there."

Tanner sat, dumfounded, and humiliated. Were these strange creatures to be feared? He stood, adjusted his clothing, and sought the entity that had so easily brought him to his knees.

"Enter."

"Look, I want to apologize for what happened back there. This is all new to me. I know that you gave me a preliminary overview, but it's not enough." He settled onto a chair.

"It is Flanker who is entitled to an apology. You've frightened and offended my assistant. In the present state, he is the gentlest of all. Nevertheless, had he chosen to change, the raging cyclops could have trounced you soundly." Aegis, quill in hand, scribed several notes. "I will not tolerate it."

"Oh. I suppose that Picket mutates into a centaur." Tanner envisioned the fair one who sported thick eyeglasses.

"Yes."

"Damn! The lollipop kids gone psycho!" Tanner fumed. "You know, it's impossible to have a healthy difference of opinion with someone who is so passive."

"An argument?"

"Yes."

"Men who yammer incessantly, attempting to prove a point, are by and large buffoons. They tend to enjoy the sound of their own voice. It is a sin to waste valuable airtime. It is far better to listen, to learn."

"Ah, an analogy. My time here has not been completely for naught."

"Humph. On to the business at hand."

"Subject closed just like that?"

"Like it or not, we have work to do. As I explained previously, your progeny shall be the first woman to serve as commander in chief. It is imperative that you, as her parent, at least attempt to prepare her for this honorable seat." Aegis placed the quill aside and leafed through several sheaves of parchment. "We here have the ability to offer a great service. You have been given the opportunity to meet with some of her predecessors in order to garner valuable advice one-on-one."

"I fully understand my role as her father and appreciate the opportunity that you are giving me. However, I am, I will admit, a bit stunned by this revelation and can't believe that my child, that our child, will succeed in such a way. It is awe-inspiring."

"Then all I ask is that you behave with dignity."

"I have."

"Really? Then why has President Washington reported that you pinched his teeth, stole them while he enjoyed a late-afternoon respite in the arms Morpheus, or as you humans prefer, taking a nap?"

"I politely asked the man to remove them. I wanted to see for myself if they were truly made of wood. However, he refused. I slipped into his bedchamber and would have examined them then and there. But, the light was poor." Tanner shifted. "I took them to the balcony."

"And dropped that poor man's mouthpiece into the goldfish pond."

"True, but I returned them."

"You sarcastically quoted that exceptional man verbatim, did you not?"

"I'm not sure where you're going with that one."

"It is reported here." He pointed to a brief paragraph. "You repeatedly said, 'I cannot tell a lie'."

"I sure did." Tanner grinned foolishly.

"You quoted verse and verbiage in a disrespectful tone, at an inappropriate time, making a mockery of his admission when asked if he chopped down the cherry tree. You insulted the first president of the United States. That icon existed on your planet from 1732 to 1799. Do you honestly believe that he understands your foolish gibberish or tongue-in-cheek humor?"

"I'm sorry. I didn't think he was that thin-skinned. I'll apologize to him tomorrow. And by the way, he didn't."

"Didn't what?"

"Chop down the damned cherry tree! Pay attention!"

"Enough! You are guilty as charged, rude, and disrespectful! You are not permitted to behave in this manner with those who are devoting their time to assist you!"

"Fine. I said that I'll apologize to him. Are you happy?"

"He has departed."

"So soon? Hell, I was going to challenge him to a coin toss across the lake!" He raised his hands in supplication. "Just kidding. Just kidding! Frankly, I think that you need some R & R. You are wound tighter than my aunt Gussy's corset!"

"I shall take that under advisement. Now may we get to the business at hand?"

"By all means."

"Tomorrow you sit with Mr. Lincoln."

"Why have we skipped from one to sixteen, from a federalist to a republican?"

"The council has selected those they deemed appropriate for the task. While all have their merits, you shall not be required to interact with each. There simply is not enough time. Your choices will be taken into consideration later."

"That sounds reasonable. However, why am I asked to chat with them? I was under the impression that I wouldn't remember any of this, nor will I recall my previous life or who I was for that matter."

"This is true. All of the pertinent data that you learn while on the Fringe shall be saved deep in the recess of your mind. When applicable, recall will prompt it to come forward. It shall be such a seamless thing that you will not question your resources. You will simply know. Now, may I continue?"

"Who the hell thinks up this crazy stuff, anyway? And how much am I supposed to believe if I can't remember it? And I have no reassurances other than taking your word!"

"It is not for me to question. It is and shall be. Now, you are responsible for selecting the final five, those who will personally tutor your daughter early in life, and eventually act as advisers when it comes time for her to serve her country as chief executive."

"What am I supposed to tell people when they see a former, and dead president come waltzing into my home?"

"They shall appear just to her at a very young age. Children often claim that they enjoy the company of imaginary friends. The presidents shall act as her imaginary playmates while imparting useful information. Your daughter is very fortunate, indeed."

"I wish that you had told me all of this before." Tanner was suddenly humbled.

"You would have behaved with a modicum of dignity?"

"Yes. Just remember that it's in my nature, the very fiber of my being, to question that which with I am unfamiliar. I guess it's because my faith in mankind was sorely tested. I do have trust issues."

"Understood. However, it is never too late to reform, Tanner Trump. I believe that you shall redeem yourself."

"Thanks for the vote of confidence, Aegis." His stomach grumbled. "I believe that hefty slice of humble pie didn't appease my hunger." He rose. "I'm off in search of dinner."

"You shall fast until tomorrow."

"But!" Trump witnessed a brief wavering, a telltale glimpse of his keeper's alter ego. "Sounds like a great idea. I've got to keep in shape." He exited the chamber and sought the Well of Dreams. "Just a quick peek before I call it a day." Tanner had been thrilled when he'd seen a sign leading him to the Well. He'd sorely missed the one on earth.

Atlantis

P OSEIDON GRASPED A PARCHMENT SCROLL that listed those on his committee. Rarely did such an assortment of entities joined to pursue one common goal.

Before him, an intricately carved teakwood table spanned a raised marble platform surrounded by an assortment of salt-water pools, which teemed with sea creatures of varying size and color. In deference to the attendees, Poseidon exiled those with a penchant for human flesh. Council members donned in colorful garments posed before mounds of parchment, their neighbor beyond arm's reach. He brought the session to order.

"I believe Mr. Verne has the floor. Please proceed."

"Thank you, kind sir." He remained seated. "I am concerned about the logistics and have given this matter a great deal of thought. A cosmopolitan setting such as Boston, Massachusetts, will make it difficult to park the time machine without notice."

"Understandable." Poseidon agreed. "What do you propose?"

"A place farther north." Jules consulted a mammoth road atlas. "Litchfield, New Hampshire. There are several working farms located on Route 3A. In addition, this town is within reasonable driving distance to cosmopolitan cities such as Boston and New York. A large barn could accommodate the time machine, and keep it well hidden from the public at large."

"Point taken, Mr. Verne. However, it appears that Andromida is not in agreement. Would you care to voice your concerns?"

"Socially speaking, country humans, born and raised, do not possess the social graces or sophistication of the upper crust. Mr. Verne must seek an alternate solution." Her posture remained rigid.

"Dame Puissant?" Poseidon addressed the pure witch.

"Thank you, kind sir." She smiled, and spoke directly to the lovely woman. "Lady Andromida, I believe that you are capable of instructing your charge no matter what the venue."

"Thank you." Andromida nodded and attempted to keep an open mind, for the directive at hand required multiple entities, not solely hers.

"You are most welcome. Perhaps I may, in some way, put your mind at ease. I have had the pleasure of visiting a dear friend who resides not far from the area that Mr. Verne has chosen. These New Englanders are not at all country bumpkins. They are a proud people, well educated, and committed to family. A hearty lot, these men and women nurture family values, pass on age-old traditions, and teach their offspring to love the environment. These humble surroundings would be conducive to serving our purpose." Angel Gabriel nodded in agreement.

Poseidon nodded. "Then so be it. It is time to apprise Libra of our strategy to date."

The Fringe

TANNER PACED, AND COUNTED TO ten five times over. Aegis insisted on reviewing a summary of the topics that he intended to discuss with President Lincoln. Picket stood sentry, arms crossed, eyeglasses perched on the tip of a minute pug nose. He was about as intimidating as Casper, the friendly ghost, and as colorless.

"You may enter, Tanner." The overseer stood in the doorway.

"I'm accustomed to editorial posturing, but this is ridiculous! If you're doing this to get a rise out of me, it's working." He landed in the chair with a resounding thud. "I take it that you're not pleased with the list."

"I am not."

"Why?"

"Where shall I begin?" Aegis assumed a regal bearing. "Ah yes." He passed Tanner a parchment penned in a perfectly symmetrical hand. "This is the revised list."

"How neat and orderly." Tanner tensed. "Wait just one minute here! Who do you think you're fooling, little man? This thing was compiled way before I had the opportunity to document my list of questions. You dated it. I'm not a simpleton."

"I have neither stated nor implied that you are simpleminded, Tanner Trump. I am accustomed to intervening when necessary. My experience and knowledge surpass any that you could possibly attain in either one or several lives. I am your intellectual superior. I say this because it is a fact, not a reflection of the vast information that you have learned over one life span."

"Well, I'll be damned! Haven't you just made me feel insignificant as all get-out!"

"That was not my intention, sir. I tend to be direct at times, which may be unsettling to my charges."

"If that's an apology, then I accept. Now how about you tell me what it is you don't like about my list of questions and I'll tell you what to do with yours?"

"Ah, mirth! I assume that there are no ill feelings."

"Not when my daughter's future is at stake."

"Very well. We shall compare your inquiries and mine. Your question number 1. Why do bedbugs bite?"

"And mine. What prompted you to select a career in politics?"

Tanner nodded patiently.

"Question number 2. Do big feet stink worse than little feet?"

"My second. What is your stand on slavery?"

Both groaned.

"Question number 3. How come some birds can fly, and some can't?"

"Question number 3. What did you wish to accomplish during your term as president?"

"Ugh!" Tanner groaned.

"Let us not make this personal, Tanner Trump. Question number 4. Why do bears poop in the woods? Oh, for heaven's sake! What a ludicrous query!" Aegis tossed the parchment. "I simply cannot continue. What were you thinking?"

"I might ask you the same! My questions make perfect sense!" Tanner huffed.

"They do not!"

"They do so!"

"Fine. I am certain that I shall regret this. However, I shall proceed. Why do those silly inquiries make sense to you?" He sighed, making his way to the opposite side of the desk.

"I'm not going to tell you. It's obvious that you're taking a negative stance, and I refuse to humor a closed-minded troll!" He rose and made for the door. He had intended this session to be enjoyable regardless of what it took to please the little man. He huffed. It was an impossible venture.

"You cannot come here, into my chambers, and insult me endlessly. Do not think of leaving now. We have resolved nothing."

"Oh, is that so?" Tanner spoke through gritted teeth. "You pompous, short stack! You egotistical, tyrant! Come on, Aegis. Pull that quick-change act on me, and do it quick. I may not be able to beat you, but at least I'll have the satisfaction of getting a few licks in before you pummel me, before you transform me into an insignificant pile of shit!" He squared off, intent on releasing the rage, which he'd banked from the onset of his stay on the Fringe.

"I shall not resort to fist-a-cuffs. I am above that, sir. Cease and desist."

"Your mother serviced Barnum, Bailey, and half the sideshow freaks!" He pressed forward, hell-bent on cornering the self-righteous sentinel. "Your father was an abbreviated, ass-licking fool who didn't have the good sense to use birth control!" This felt damned good. "You pea brained, witless peckerhead!" He chortled, dancing on the balls of his feet. "Come out, come out, wherever you are!"

Within a matter of seconds, Aegis transmuted, dealt the disrespectful cur a sound thrashing, and then regressed.

"I guess...I deserved that." Tanner struggled to his feet. "You've got one hell of a right cross, Aegis old man."

"Tanner Trump?" The guard was quite shaken by the encounter, for it was out of character. "I...I..."

"Don't apologize. It'll ruin the effect." He rose gradually, uncertain of which part of his person hurt the worst. "I'm going to my room."

"Tanner?" Aegis was remorseful.

"Look." Tanner grasped the doorframe and turned before exiting. "Those questions, in my opinion, were better suited to a precocious preschooler, an innocent babe. I wanted be certain that the presidents were patient men, willing to appease the curiosity of a small child, willing to earn her trust. The second scroll deals with matters of the state."

"What second? I have only one, Tanner Trump."

"Yeah, well. While I was squirming on the floor, in agony, I saw it under the desk. I'd retrieve it for you, but I have a feeling that if I get down on my knees, I won't be capable of getting up again." He winked. "You get it, short stack. You're closer to the ground." That said, he groaned, found his bed, and remained cloistered for the next three days.

Atlantis

"**T**HE COUNCIL SHALL RESUME THEIR deliberations after a short respite; Miriam and I have no news to report as yet. With that in mind, I thought to help you occupy your time. Come. There is someone that I would like you to meet."

"You have enough on your mind, Lady Li. Do not concern yourself with me."

"It is no bother. Ah, here she is." Libra sensed the other woman's presence.

"Lady Libra! My, my what a beautiful place this is. I absolutely adore these colorful sea creatures!" She embraced Libra, turned to Miriam, and pressed a gentle, speckled hand on her forearm. "Now, please introduce me to this lovely woman."

"May-May, this is my dear friend, Miriam. Miriam, please meet May-May. She, too, is a person near and dear to my heart."

"Pleased to make your acquaintance, Lady Miriam. My given name is Loretta. However, Ms. Libra has called me May-May for eons. You may call me by either name. I answer to both."

"Ah, Loretta, May-May. The pleasure is all mine." She wondered what Li was up to.

"May-May is a babysitter, Miriam. I invited her to Atlantis. She has offered to bring you along with her as she performs her wonderful duties. I am afraid that I must return to the meeting, and do not have sufficient time to explain further. However, I am certain that she shall manage quite well on her own." She turned to Miriam. "I sincerely hope that you enjoy this diversion. She shall help fill the time until I return."

"I appreciate the gesture, Li."

With that, Libra left the two to get acquainted.

"Do you mind if we sit, Lady Miriam? This is such a beautiful place to lounge."

Without preamble, May-May selected an overstuffed chaise. "Ah! This is heavenly! My dear, please join me, and I will tell you about our organization, the Babysitters Elite." She closed her eyes momentarily. The previous evening had been quite demanding.

"I am very curious, ma'am." She sat across from the woman. "Please proceed."

"Members of Babysitters Elite are committed to aiding, assisting both mothers and infants in achieving pleasant, peaceful nap and bedtime experiences. Our founders, Wilhelm and Jacob Grimm, assigned Beatrix Potter as our directress. She personally selects each candidate, and we all undergo a rigorous training. Not all who apply are deemed fit to be called babysitters. There are those who are better adept at dream weaving. Should you like, after we see to tonight's assignment, I can bring you to meet a dear friend who exemplifies Dream Weavery's work to perfection."

"You will permit me to observe the act of babysitting first-hand?" She was intrigued.

"Oh, yes. Lady Libra has requested that I do so, and I must say, I am honored. She is a gem, that one."

"You will hear no argument otherwise from me. Please continue."

"Our tasks are quite simple but valuable to the mothers of infants who refuse to nod off at nap or bedtime. Our charges are typically newborn to three months old. Occasionally, there are babes that require more time. However, it is rare." May-May stretched. "I apologize. Last night was a challenge. Now, shortly after our children are tucked in, we quietly enter the room and observe them from afar. Typically, before they get vocal, they will toss about, which is our cue to step in. Some babes simply need to know that there is a presence in the nursery, and we approach their bed. We are not permitted at any time to touch the child. That is taboo."

"And why is that?"

"We cannot risk personal attachment or alienation from their birth parents. We do not want them to prefer us over their mother and father."

"That makes sense. Has this occurred in the past, and what is the penalty, if any?"

"Yes, it has and results in immediate termination."

"That is severe."

"It is absolutely forbidden and emphasized repeatedly in the classroom."

"A proper safeguard, I imagine."

"It is necessary. Now where was I? Ah yes! Once a child can see us, we mime various actions. Such as thorough examination of each and every digit, a suckling motion, first with one finger, then two, and my favorite, attempting to place the entire fist into the mouth." She chortled. "What fun! We will then proceed to grab the toes. Once captured, it is possible to nibble a bit. Should there be a colorful mobile, blowing gently will attract the babe's attention nicely."

"And if they soil their diapers, then what?" Li was right. She was enjoying this visit with May-May tremendously.

"Oh dear! We allow the child to become very vocal. There is no pleasure in lying abed unclean. You can hardly blame the wee tyke. Yes, we permit the cries. The more vocal, the better. Now, once they are nice and dry, they will typically nod off, and their parents are able to enjoy a peaceful night's sleep."

"I imagine that there are exceptions to the rule."

"Of course. Those challenges are few and far between. Some do it well; others disappoint. I myself have experienced a few difficult assignments. I shall admit to possessing a stubborn streak and have been known to dig my heels in. I have been told that I am steadfast. If so, then so be it. When a child is cantankerous, I attempt all amusements, and then I softly sing. You must understand that we are not perfect and there are exceptions to the rule."

"What is to be done in those cases?"

"We continue for an additional month. I will admit that it is difficult to give up on a child. Nevertheless, we accept the fact that we must terminate our visits and move on. Personally, it breaks my heart."

"I can only imagine. Your purpose, the group's missions, are to be applauded. How wondrous!"

"It is a rewarding endeavor for the most part." She stood. "Shall we?"

"By all means." Miriam stood as well.

"Now may I take your hands?"

"Of course."

"I shall forewarn you. Upon arrival, you may feel a bit unsteady. That is expected, for you are unaccustomed to travel in this fashion. All you need to do is keep your eyes closed until it passes. I shall hold your hands all the while and then release you when your eyes finally open. Now, let us depart."

Miriam experienced a slight tug as May-May held her hand securely. All of a sudden, she felt her feet touch a firm surface and wondered at the fact that she hadn't felt herself leave the path. Once she acclimated to her new surroundings, she opened her eyes.

May-May released her hands and immediately pressed a finger to her lips. "Shhh."

A brief nod confirmed that silence was understood.

The babysitter guided her to a lovely pink cradle within which a beautiful baby lay. The tyke possessed thick raven locks, wondrous brown eyes, and rosy cheeks. She was alert, as if expecting their visit. For a moment, she had to resist the urge to coo and reach out. In order to avoid temptation, Miriam grasped her hands behind her back and looked on as May-May mimicked suckling her index and middle finger then silently clapped.

May-May turned to Miriam and winked. It was apparent that this exceptional woman loved her work and that this cunning child was smitten with her.

Time passed quickly, and when the sitter grasped Miriam's hands in order to depart, she paused a moment to gaze at the wee mite who had fallen asleep with two fingers firmly planted in her mouth. They shared a smile, and closed their eyes. What a beautiful memory she took with her.

Miriam opened her eyes prematurely and swayed. A gentle hand steadied her.

"Damned IT department! How do they expect me to do my job if this blasted system is down! Jack! Jack? Where are you? Don't go trying to hide your sorry ass from me! First, I'll find you. Then I'll beat the… Well, okay then…never mind. System's back up. I'd better not have lost the file that I was working on! It's due tomorrow, and you know how hard it is to get overtime approval around here? Let's just give it a once-over? Oh, oh! I think that we're not alone! Shit!" Terry spun in her chair. "Oops! Sorry about that, May-May! You kinda snuck up on me! And let me guess, it's show-and-tell time?" A large grin replaced an unpleasant frown, transforming her completely. She rose and approached the two women, offering a hand. "Terry here. Sorry for all of the commotion. While May-May is always welcome, it would be nice if she made an appointment. I am running late with this one, wicked awesome, if I say so myself, dream catcher. I've outdone myself!" She inhaled noisily, then offered each woman a seat. "Okay, May-May! Who do we have here? A babysitter in training?"

"No, she is a guest of Lady Libra's. They are presently visiting Atlantis. My Lady requested that I treat her to a visit with my current charge and with you as well. Lady Miriam, this is Terry. She is a Dream Maker."

"I am pleased to make your acquaintance, Terry." Her hand was met with a rigorous pump.

"My pleasure! Listen, I don't want to be rude, but I'm in a time crunch right now. So I'll give you the nickel tour. *If* that's okay with you, May-May."

"That is better than nothing. Go on."

"Okay. I imagine that you, Miriam, know what a dream catcher represents."

"I do."

"Great. We can, for the most part, dismiss what the dream catchers, as you know them, represent. Now my catchers are the complete reverse of the Native Americans. Theirs 'catch' dreams; mine 'dispense' dreams. I spend my days, and sometimes nights, developing and creating those dreams." She turned to an enormous screen and, typed a few commands, and a beautiful image of the Grand Canyon appeared. "Now, a few flicks of the wrist, and I can super-impose a parasailer." Her fingers touched the left side of the screen. She placed the aerialist above the Canyon, and he immediately took flight. "Add an eagle." Again, as if by magic, the beautiful bird took flight. "Whatever your pleasure, I can make it happen. But I refuse to plot nightmares. That's Judy two doors down, but I don't suggest that you disturb her. She left her door wide open after lunch, and if the sound effects are any indication of what she has in store, it's a huge, emphatic no for me. Anyway, I apologize, I tend to ramble and digress. So, once my dream-catcher is programmed, with the requi-site requests if there are any, I download it over there." She pointed to an industrial-sized printer. "Let's go over to that stupid contraption that's always giving me fits. Depending on the order, if it's a pickup, I'll print out a beautiful dream-catcher of my own design. The size depends on the, yeah, you guessed it, the order. I can also e-mail the finished product as long as the recipient owns one of our printers, and stocks supplies." She checked her watch. "Sorry, but I have to get back to the computer, and I don't like it when people look over my shoulder. I know it sounds like I'm rudely dismissing you, but it is what it is." She addressed Miriam. "So, do you understand that abbreviated lesson?"

"I believe that I do. What a wonderful creation." She chuckled. "The flip side of an American Indian dream-catcher!"

Terry laughed boisterously. "Yeah. But by all that's holy! You've made it sound so simple!" She sobered. "But don't you think for one-minute that it is!"

"Oh, I do not! One final question before we leave you to your work?"

"Okay, but then I have to ask you to excuse me. The boss is on vacation with the Candy Man. What a life! A two-week cruise to the Bahamas while I'm here slaving away!"

"I am sorry to hear that. I was hoping that Miriam could meet the boss himself." May-May was disappointed.

"No dice! Now, Miriam, your question?" Terry was becoming impatient.

"Who is your boss? Who submits the requests for your amazing dreams?"

"Why, the Sandman, my dear lady. The Sandman!"

With that, May-May grasped her hands and transported them back to Atlantis.

"What a marvelous adventure! And the Dream Weaver? What can I say? Terry is a creative genius. A bit high-strung, nonetheless an amazing individual."

"She certainly is, my dear."

"And you, May-May! Your way with infants is heartwarming. Your calling is one more than likely goes unnoticed or unappreciated by the parents. However, let it be known that the entities that you interact with, no doubt, find your labor impeccable."

"Thank you, my dear. No need for the kudos. I am fortunate to be doing what I love. That's enough reward for me."

"By the by, who is this Candy Man? Are you able to share that with me?" Her curiosity had been left unsatisfied.

"He, ah, let me see, how can I put this without offending your sensibilities? He, his workers, that is."

"Do not fret so! If my inquiry causes you discomfort or embarrassment, you may leave it unanswered."

"No, it's okay. He designs and manufactures edible underwear."

Miriam chortled. "Everyone has a calling, my dear. You needn't blush! Is there any one particular flavor that you prefer?"

The question was so unexpected that the portly woman responded without thought. "Strawberry."

They were enjoying a bout of hilarity when Lady Libra approached.

"I see that you have become fast friends. You enjoyed yourself, Miriam?"

"Oh, yes, my Lady! This woman is a gem!"

"I don't know about that. At least my charge didn't vomit 'through' me tonight."

"There are some pitfalls in most assignments. Do you agree?"

"I do. Now quick hugs, and then I have to leave." May-May embraced both women and quietly departed.

"Li? You appear frazzled. Was it all that unpleasant?"

"While you were away, the council concluded their task. Each of them has sought a brief respite." She raised one corner of the satin mask, exposing a fatigued blue eye. "Your fate has been sealed."

The two women strolled along the verdant subterranean gardens, each in her own thoughts. This would be the last time that they would share each other's company until the next time that Miriam concluded a life on earth. Should she complete the mission set forth by Poseidon, that is.

A page interrupted their walk, requesting that they join the council in chambers. They shared a brief look and then followed.

The opulent chamber was a bit ostentatious, the massive table in its center. Poseidon stood at one end, while the council members remained seated. The silence was ominous. No one spoke a word as Miriam took her seat at the opposite end, while Lady Libra stood behind her, resting her hands atop her friend's shoulders in a possessive manner. When Poseidon nodded to his scribe, a bespectacled aged man who unveiled a large scroll and began to read.

"As set forth by Poseidon, First Chair of this Council, with all present consisting of He, respected Council Members in toto, Miriam, and Lady Libra. The following mandate has been determined to be a just requisite in return for Miriam's next life on earth, in order for her to "be.""

Poseidon raised his right hand and, opened it palm up, and as all looked on, ten orbs appeared, forming a circle, and began to rotate. They were iridescent, quite beautiful, and a bit smaller than the size of a dime.

When the page deemed it appropriate, he cleared his throat and resumed.

"You shall be returned to earth upon the conclusion of this reading."

"You shall seek ten subjects who carry within themselves a terminal malediction. The order and time span between each are to be at your discretion."

"You shall, with the consumption of one orb per subject, have the power, the ability to draw forth their malediction, seamlessly transferring said into your person with the touch of two hands."

"You shall then carry within yourself said malady for the period of one to ten days as determined by the contents of each orb, which in itself is a living, mythical thing. The orb's purpose is to transform that malediction into liquid form as it resides within you."

"You shall, at the end of that period, spew forth the vile substance into a placket provided for your use. Said vomitus will be toxic and must remain in the placket [pouch] until disposed of in such a manner that it shall not be a present and ominous threat to others. Upon completion of your final and tenth purge, you are to be charged with the destruction of that storage reservoir. Heed this well for what once would cause certain death does not change. It is a vile stuff lethal to humans."

"You shall, as set forth, complete all ten purges and the destruction of the reservoir within one earth year with no exception or relief."

"You shall, after the satisfactory fulfillment, be entitled to completion of this life cycle, for then you shall 'be', and then many more at the discretion of subsequent councils."

"You shall not fail, for to do so will terminate your current life cycle. It shall also forbid you further rebirth. You shall cease to 'be' forever. Forfeiture of that privilege shall be of your own doing."

"So it is declared to be, so it is said, and so it is set forth. This declaration has been witnessed by Poseidon, First Chair, and committee Members Hercules, Andromida, Gifford, Gabriel, Dame Puissant, Freud, and Jules Verne. Further witness and subject to this Declaration, Miriam. Finally, we acknowledge the presence of Lady Justice, Libra."

"If the First Chair would please present the orbs and placket to Miss Miriam, then I may complete this document with my signature and seal, confirming its authenticity and delivery."

Poseidon produced a small vial, watched on as each orb committed itself to the container, and then secured an intricately carved golden lid. He made a great production of shaking hands with each committee member, who stood as he passed and bestowed a quick kiss on the hand of each women, of course.

He all but tossed these items before Miriam, causing them to come close to slipping over the edge of the table. She stood and nodded to each committee member, displaying her respect for each and every one. She was certain that they had tempered the First Chair's edict as best as they could. With head held high, chin jutting, she took possession of the orbs and placket, refusing to acknowledge Poseidon who stood to her right. She walked to the door without so much as a glance at her tormentor. The tension was palpable as she opened the door, stepped aside to let Libra pass, and then closed it behind them.

No sooner had the ornate door met its frame, Miriam faded away.

The Fringe

"**AEGIS! THANKS FOR SEEING ME!**" Tanner had vowed to be on his best behavior. Deep furrows ran a course across Aegis's brow. "Are you okay?"

"I have much on my mind, sir. Shall we proceed?"

"Okay, then!" This was bound to test his resolve. "I just wanted to fill you in about my visit with Abe."

"Abe? Abe?"

Well, hell and damnation! He was already second-guessing the direction of this conversation. "Calm down, buddy!"

"I am not your buddy, and President Lincoln deserves, at the very least, a modicum of respect! You assume too much, addressing him by his given name!"

"I didn't. That is, I didn't at the onset! Give me some credit! I'm not stupid!"

"I never accused you of being stupid, Tanner Trump. However, your manners are nonexistent at times. Now, let us not bicker. Time is of the essence."

"Your posture belies your temperament, Aegis. Your shoulders have crept up so high that your neck has completely vanished. Not to mention that road map on your forehead!"

His mentor sighed and attempted to adjust his physical demeanor, for his charge was very observant and offered his comments freely. "I shall attempt to listen to your report without interruption. Please continue."

"Thank you. Now, Mister Lincoln, President Lincoln, was a pleasure to meet. He was very forthcoming in his responses to all questions, both yours and mine. I learned a great deal, and just when I thought the session complete, he asked me to address him as Abe. I, in kind, asked him to call me Tanner. We set the political patois aside and talked about our personal lives and pleasant memories." Tanner paused for effect, and a fond smile surfaced of its own accord. "Did you know that when Ab…Mister Lincoln was a young man, he wrestled? He fought three hundred some odd bouts and only lost one. He does admit to being boisterous and downright cocky, often challenging anyone in the crowd to test him. It was apparent that these bouts were fond memories of a man whose later life imposed such demands. Anyway, we talked about other things. But you look busy, so I'll save them for another time."

"He was a very impressive man. I am pleased that you enjoyed passing some time with him. Would that I could have made his acquaintance. I was occupied elsewhere."

"I wanted to report to you right away and give you my list of the remaining five presidents."

"I shall make note." With quill in hand, he nodded. "And they are?"

"John Quincy Adams, Franklin D. Roosevelt, Dwight D. Eisenhower, Ulysses S. Grant, and John F. Kennedy."

"Interesting. None later than President Kennedy?"

"I have many profound feelings and opinions regarding political persona. Please don't let's have a discussion of that nature, for we would more than likely kill each other."

"Agreed. Now if you are finished, there are matters that we need to discuss. An extremely important mission has called myself, Picket, and Flanker to duty." He raised a hand, interrupting Tanner's apparent query. "Please do not interrupt. Circadian has accepted the task of programming the Think Tank for the purpose of you and your choice of five presidents to Skype. I believe that is the present-day jargon. I realize that this manner of interviewing each lacks the 'one-on-one,' 'let's shake hands', personal approach. However, we have no say in the matter."

"Circadian? Circadian is going to program the Think Tank?" He was taken unawares and didn't like that. "You mean to tell me that this falcon is a computer programmer?"

"Of the first ilk. We have found his work to be impeccable and error free. You have yet to accept the fact that the unexpected should be expected on the Fringe?"

"Fine. Then tell me about this Think Tank. I don't know what that is."

"It is a large glass cube. There is a chair, what you call a recliner, therein. One enters, and once seated in the chair, reclines. When ready, push the play button on the remote. The introductions will ensue, and then your conversation may begin. You are permitted to pause only between presidents, and may resume after a brief respite. Upon completion, select the off button. Is this clear?"

"As a bell. Thanks!" He was about to continue. However, it abruptly came to mind that his time on the Fringe may be coming to a conclusion. "Wait a minute! What happens after I'm finished with the presidents? Who's going to be my keeper after you've gone? What..." Aegis' raised a hand, putting an end to his queries.

"Cease, please! Permit me to continue." He collected himself and proceeded. "Nana will monitor your progress, and she shall forward daily reports directly to me. I do suggest that you refrain from testing her resolve. She is quite adept at wielding that wooden spoon, and it can be extremely painful."

"Yeah, I've experienced that firsthand." He unconsciously rubbed his upper left arm where she had dealt a seriously effective blow just the day before. "Don't even try to sneak a warm cookie when she's baking."

"Heed me well. Do not rush your interviews with each president, for to do so will displease her. Be prepared for several question-and-answer quizzes. She also taught American history in a previous life."

"Okay. Okay, you've made your point. Now what comes after these history lessons?"

"You shall be returned to earth."

"Now the million-dollar question: How am I supposed to get from here to there, and will Miriam be waiting for me?"

"Why, Jules Verne, of course! As to Lady Miriam, she has already returned to earth. Mr. Verne has been told where she resides, and you will be brought to within a few earth miles of that place."

"And I'm supposed to just 'be.' I already exist, per se."

"This is your first rebirth. You are unfamiliar with our ways. You must trust us to have seen to all of the details."

"I don't know that I can do that. Isn't there someone here who gives shit about sending me back, holding nothing but my dic..."

Before he could continue further, Aegis disappeared in a puff of smoke. Poof. Gone.

"Well, I'll be..."

Reincarnation

"**C**OME ON, SWEET CHEEKS, COOPERATE. I'm going to strangle that man for allowing you to escape. Don't even think of biting me. I'm not in the mood." Eevee, formerly known as Miriam, reached farther into the drainage pipe. "Let's go, baby."

"Excuse me? Ms. Smith?" Aiden Wolf, formerly known as Tanner Trump, remained at a distance, uncertain what the woman was about.

"Not now, please. Can't you see that I'm busy? If you're responding to the ad, I'm still interviewing, so you haven't missed out. Don't you dare bite me!"

"I wouldn't think of it!" He grinned as the woman's posterior rose.

"Not you! Please get Bent?"

"I beg your pardon?" Her suggestion seemed inappropriate.

"Bentley. Do me a favor and get Bentley. He should be somewhere in the blasted house!"

"Sure." He entered the woman's home and wandered about the first floor, calling the man's name.

"All right! I heard you the first time! Jeez, Louise!" Hercules in the guise of Bentley Braun hesitated. "What now?"

"Don't know. She asked that I come in and get you."

"Oh, no! Don't tell me that she-devil has gotten loose again!" He took hold of a roughly hewn walking stick and brandished it for emphasis. "I'm going to throttle her. She's going to lay all the blame at my feet and not for the first time!" He headed for the back door.

"Don't you think that's a tad excessive? I mean, she'll clean up and be as good as new before you know it." Aiden opted to shadow the irate man in hopes of preventing disaster. He had no use for any man who beat his woman. "Just stay cool, ok?"

"Don't interfere!" Braun paused within three feet of the petite woman. "Eevee?"

"You didn't mend the screen, Bent. I've been asking you to do that for a week. Now look what's happened."

"I knew I'd take the blame for this. I say we drown then incinerate her."

"We'll do no such thing! Ah, ha! Gotcha!" She squirmed backward, sat, and began scraping mud from what appeared to be a scrawny kitten. "Oh, sweet cheeks! What am I going to do with you?"

"Give her a bath, that's what. For that matter, the two of you can share one."

"May I please have that?" She reached for the walking stick, turned onto her knees, and managed to make her feet without dropping the cat. "Stop screeching, kitty. I sense a migraine coming on."

"Can I help?" Aiden reached for the feline and withdrew his hand before the cat could inflict any serious damage. "Not very sociable, is she?"

"That she-devil will scratch your eyes out, man. I suggest that you keep your distance. Eevee's the only one who can handle her without getting mauled."

"She's a bit high-strung, is all." Eevee smiled at the stranger. "To what do we owe the pleasure, sir?"

"Aiden Wolf. We spoke on the phone yesterday. I'm here about the job. Building a chicken coop?" He slowed his pace as the woman lumbered toward the farmhouse. She relied on the makeshift cane to support some of her weight, and it was obvious that she was paying dearly for the effort it took to rescue the cat. "If this is a bad time, I can come back."

"If you don't mind waiting until I rid myself of this muck, then I'll join you. There's coffee brewing, cookies, and muffins on the counter. Make yourself at home."

"Join me in the kitchen." Bentley huffed. "I need a cup myself." The two men entered the warm, cozy kitchen. Bentley reached for two large mugs. "Here, help yourself or go without." The coffee smelled amazing. "Cream and sugar are on the table." Bentley tensed as he carried his own coffee. He'd broken several of the porcelain receptacles, forgetting his own strength. He made a mental note to pick up a metal travel mug the next time that he went to the store.

"Dame Puissant." Eevee whispered. "Whatever possessed you to crawl into that drainage pipe?"

"Do not address me by my surname. Someone could hear you!" This translated into a long meow. Only Eevee was able hear the words that were interspersed.

"Please answer my question."

"That wretched bird was tormenting me, and I lost my footing! You mark my words! When we are finished here on earth, Gifford shall suffer the consequences of his actions. He is a bully."

"He would never harm you intentionally, Dame. He's just being mischievous. Besides, he told me that he was leaving today. He's needed elsewhere." Eevee tested the water.

"That pleases me, although it is unfortunate that he was unable to transport the placket for you."

"That poor Oriole almost died trying. I hope that he hasn't suffered any permanent effects." Eevee tested the water. "Bubble bath?"

"Yes, please. I believe lilac scented today. And, a clean eye patch, for I fear this one is beyond repair. Oh, yes. Put that entire sponge in the sink, I do so love reclining on it in lieu of the porcelain." Dame loved to soak. "I will admit that he was brave. Perhaps I shall let this incident pass."

Her temples throbbed, and she had yet to shower, get dressed, and meet the stranger. "Is this the way that you want it?"

"Yes, please, and thank you, my dear. That powder I prepared yesterday will help rid you of that headache."

"I will. I thank my lucky stars that I have only two more children to help. Although I wish that I could do more. There are so many of them, Dame. Such little troopers!"

"Please do not dwell in this today. Make yourself presentable, my dear. You true love awaits in your kitchen."

"It is him, isn't it? I don't think that I made a very good first impression. Well, I can't do anything about that, now can I?" She set the kitten atop the large sponge. "Here you go. Now, how does that feel? It smells great!"

"Bless your heart! This water is so very soothing, I vow that I shall slip onto the arms of Morpheus."

"No, don't do that. You'll drown, and then who will Gifford tease?" A brief smile. "I'm getting in the shower. Enjoy!" Once the tiny feline had settled in, she removed the soiled clothing and tossed it into a nearby hamper.

"My dear! Look at you! You are far too thin!"

"You worry yourself too much, Dame. I stand at five-one and weigh one-hundred-ten pounds. Would you have me carrying a roll around my midsection?"

"No. However, you must take care of yourself. This last purge kept you abed for eight days, and I vow that you should have taken two more days to recover. It is not good to push yourself." Dame was concerned about the ramification of being subjected to such powerfully nasty stuff.

"Okay! I promise to be more patient the next time. But just think about it. There are now eight children out there that are no longer terminally ill. Freud has made the selection process so much easier, and Mr. Verne has been very gracious in freeing his personal schedule to transport them. Of course, they'll never remember any of it."

"I am anxious for this to end. Poseidon's edict left him looking as if he was a hero. Bah! You, my dear, are the hero, or better put, the heroine."

"I am no such thing. Now this discussion is over. I have to take a shower. Tanner has been kept too long."

"Mmm."

"Don't you fall asleep!"

"Mmm." She dozed.

Eevee felt refreshed, although she was tempted to let the water run until it cooled. She dried herself, and then reluctantly yet gently woke Dame.

"May I please lounge on the fainting couch? I would be oh so appreciative if you would set me atop my coverlet, my dear."

"I can do that. You enjoy the remainder of the morning in here. I'll leave the door ajar in case you want to make an appearance." She dressed in a clean pair of jeans and a T-shirt, opting for bare feet. "No shoes right now. My feet need to breathe." She pulled her thick black mane into a ponytail and dabbed a bit of lilac water behind each ear. "There, that'll have to do."

She was able to bank the pain in her head temporarily with a dose of Dame Puissant's magic elixir and hoped beyond all hope that it would disappear completely.

"I see that you two are getting along fine. Thank you for your patience. And if you can bear with me for a few more minutes, I'll make a quick cup of tea, and join you." Hercules had already set everything out for her. "You are a gem, Bentley!"

"You're welcome." He complained. "That feline is a mean, vengeful one. Do you know what she did?"

"Oh, oh! What now?" For some reason, Dame found it funny to torture this huge powerful man.

"She pooped in one of my slippers after chewing a hole in the toe. I just purchased those last week, replacing the previously damaged set. I am losing my patience with that feline menace!"

"I'll reimburse you, Bent."

"You needn't bother. It is not you who are to blame. Now if you have the time, Mr. Wolf is here to give a quotation for that chicken coop. Mr. Woolf, this is Eevee Smith, the owner of this estate. Eevee, Mr. Aiden Wolf." He remained standing for the introductions as did Aiden.

"It's a pleasure, Ms. Smith, or is it Mrs.?"

"Eevee is fine. I apologize for the drama. Dame, my kitten, can be a handful."

"I have never seen a cat wearing an eye patch."

"She is a bit vain." Oh lord, what was she thinking? "Theoretically speaking, that is." Eevee stopped before saying anything more about Dame. Her brain wasn't functioning properly, and she might appear like an empty-headed dolt. Never had she thought that reuniting with Tanner would affect her emotional balance so strongly. And oh, how handsome he was.

"I could stand here for the rest of the morning holding your hand, but I have a lunch appointment that can't be put off." Aiden grinned. He wondered if this beautiful woman was a bit off, or simply if the events of the morning had flustered her. "And I didn't mean anything derogatory about the cat. It was just an observation." She pulled back.

"I, um, frankly, I hadn't expected to be prone on the ground, rescuing my kitten, when you arrived. I do apologize, Mr. Wolf. Would you care for more coffee?"

"No, thanks. I had a couple of cups before I came over. And, please call me Aiden. I'm not much for formalities."

"Right then." She made a mental note to refrain from calling him Tanner. "Do you have a quote for me?"

"I do, and you'll have to excuse all of this scribbling. Your friend and I were discussing the project, and he offered to lend a hand with the construction, which will save you money. Would you like to take a peek at the design? I've added a couple of features that I think you'll like."

"Yes, thank you." Keep the conversation to a minimum, Eevee. It'll be safer that way. "And the final cost, of course."

"Sure enough."

Aiden was efficient, pointed out the benefits of his design, and offered to perform the work at a reasonable cost. "I can start next week if you'd like."

"I'm very sorry, Aiden. Next week is not a good time for us. Is that going to move us to the end of the line? Because I'd really like to have it completed by the end of the month. You see, I barter with the Andrew family, and they are going to be opening their farm stand soon. They sell the eggs, and I receive fresh vegetables and such in exchange."

"I'll make sure that it's done in time. How about I contact you week after next and make the arrangements? Is it okay if I bring the materials over next week, though? It'll save me a trip? I have another job nearby. If that's inconvenient, I'll understand."

"I'd prefer that you do it all at once. I have other business to deal with. One thing at a time."

"No problem." Well, that was rude, he thought. "Oh, I meant to ask you, have you met the new preacher up the road apiece?"

"No, we haven't. However, we keep to ourselves mostly. The Andrew family leases several acres of my farmland, so we know them well. But I've only moved here recently and haven't had the opportunity to socialize much. And I'm afraid that we aren't members of any congregation yet. Why do you ask?"

"I stopped by to introduce myself this morning. Several men were working on the old church. You know, the one with the cemetery in back?"

"I've seen it in passing. What denomination is it?"

"That's a good question. When I asked the guy in charge, he pointed toward another man in a wheelchair. This dude was covered from head to toe, with exception of his face. He also wore sunglasses, don't know why. It's been really overcast out there. Anyway, when I approached him, and I don't want you to think that I'm one short of a six-pack, he just didn't smell right, like food that's gone all funky. I offered my hand as I introduced myself, but he didn't shake. He said that he had a skin condition that prevented him from having contact with people. I think that smell must have gotten to me because I felt a bit off my feed. He must have thought that I was three sheets to the wind with the way that I wobbled. I'd no sooner introduced myself, when he dismissed me with the wave of a hand. Frankly, I couldn't wait to get out of there and sat in my truck for a few minutes in order to get my bearings. That was the weirdest encounter. And you know what? I got the feeling that he didn't like me because he backed away when I initially approached as if I'd violated his space. He did introduce himself as Afleet, or something like that. I did inquire as to the name of the church and denomination. The Sanctuary. That's all he said, 'The Sanctuary'."

"How odd." Eevee spared a quick glance at Bentley. "I imagine that we'll all have to wait until he shares that with neighbors or places a sign in front of the church."

"It definitely wasn't the highlight of my morning. I just can't see people warming up to that man."

"Bentley and I are not churchgoers, I'm afraid. We're not atheist, by any means, and do attend an occasional service, a baptism, wedding, and the like."

"Me too. I was just trying to be neighborly, but I doubt that he'll draw too many people unless he cleans up good."

"Thank you very much for sharing that with us." Eevee reached into an ornate basket. "I hope that you don't think that I was being rude regarding the delivery. Please accept these cookies as a peace offering. They're oatmeal-raisin and were baked just yesterday."

"My favorite. Thanks! And don't worry. I understand." Aiden turned to leave, and decided that one final question wouldn't hurt. "By the way, have we met before? I have the strangest feeling that we have."

"No, I'm certain that I would remember you as Aiden."

"As Aiden?"

Oh, for the love of Pete! This was going to be a challenge. "Aiden, I mean."

"Okay, then. I'll see you in two weeks, and thanks for the cookies!"

They watched as he drove away, both craning their necks to make certain that he had departed.

"Good grief, Eevee! I didn't think that Tanner would arrive this soon. You have yet to complete the tasks set forth by Poseidon. Do you think that he will interfere? I do believe that he has taken a liking to you, which is all well and good. However, how are we to explain anything to him if he does not remember his past as you do?" He paced from one end of the kitchen to the other and back. "This worries me."

"First and foremost, everything worries you, Bentley. I am going to stop calling you Hercules all together. That way, I will get accustomed to it and hopefully will avoid a slip of the tongue. You might want to do the same, my friend. I am no longer Miriam."

"I agree. Eevee it is. However, this is not our greatest concern."

"Of course, it's not. To be quite honest with you, that man that Aiden met today may be someone that we should keep an eye on. If he is the threat that we were warned about, he must be kept away from the Splenetic Tree at all cost. I still have two orbs left, and Freud scheduled one child for next week." Eevee fretted. "I cannot ask Gifford to fly over and keep sentinel. The last time that I made this request of that poor tiny oriole, he almost perished; and for some reason, when he attempted to transform, he was unable to do so immediately. I believe that was the result of his exposure to the Tree. It took so long for him to recover."

"We shall persevere, my dear. Do not despair. You are nearly at the end of your journey." He stopped and placed a hand on each of her shoulders, shoulders that were asked to bear so much due to the edict of a vengeful entity. "I shall not fail you, my lady. I have sworn an oath to Andromida, and I shall not be deterred."

"I thank all of you for your kindness. I don't know what I would do without you."

"Your circumstances are dire, but let us move forward. To dwell on it is contrary to our final goal."

"You're right. One thing at a time. Hopefully, Aiden's curiosity will continue to pique, and if we appear to be interested in the local gossip, we may garner all that we need to confirm our suspicions."

"That is a good point." Bentley, as he was known on earth, offered a dazzling smile. "But for now, I am off to Trader Joe's. One of the simple pleasures that I know. Do you have a list prepared?"

"I sure do! I hope that they have everything. There's a good movie on tonight, and I feel like rewarding myself with a few delicious treats!" She rummaged through the notes clipped to the refrigerator. "Aha! Here it is!"

"Very well. I shall be gone an hour or two. Try to keep a positive attitude." He turned to leave. "What movie?"

"I don't remember the exact title, but it's one of the ones on the Hallmark Channel."

"Not one of my favorite choices."

She began to gather cleaning supplies so that she could tackle the upstairs rooms. Suddenly there came a resounding crash followed by what seemed to be multiple voices coming from the upstairs bathroom. She reached into the nearby desk drawer and retrieved the Ruger thirty-eight revolver, praying that it would not be necessary to use it. She was actually afraid of guns, but had allowed Bentley to talk her into purchasing three, one for each floor of the farmhouse. She had dutifully taken not one, but two safety classes and was certified to carry a concealed weapon.

As she made her way to the second floor, the noise appeared hushed. Were the intruders laying in wait, or had they intended to catch her unaware in another part of the house? Oh, what did it matter? She silently made her way to the open door, leaning against the wall. "Count to three, Eevee," she whispered. After doing so, she pounced into the small room, pointed the gun, and was greeted with a high-pitched scream from the three-foot man who wisely raised both hands in surrender.

"Please, my lady! Do not engage your weapon! I am Aegis, Overseer of the Fringe. We, that is myself, Picket, and Flanker, have been sent by Lady Andromida. We are not a threat. My lady..."

Before he could continue, another peeked out of the shower curtain. "Have we arrived then? For a moment, I thought that I had returned to my mother's womb. Oh, dear! Is this Miriam, our charge? I have forgotten her new name."

"Flanker, do be silent. Do not move. I have yet to gain our lady's trust. Have you not taken note of the weapon that she wields?"

Eevee breathed a bit easier but didn't lower the Ruger. This visitor knew her name.

Aegis spoke once again. "My lady? We three are protectors. Your Tanner spent some time with us prior to his rebirth. We would not harm you. We have accepted the task to act as protectors, or sentries or whatever my lady decrees." His hands remained up and steady. "Mr. Verne, that is Jules Verne, transported us to earth. We had anticipated a more appropriate introduction. However, he received an emergency message, and unceremoniously dropped us into your lavatory."

The third sentry shed the shower curtain, irritated by the interruption. "What does a man need to do in order to enjoy some peace? I was about to nod off, but this incessant chatter is very distracting!" He tugged a few errant strands of red hair into the queue at the back of his head. "And, as for the weapon, my lady, please be rid of it!" Picket spoke boldly.

Eevee immediately responded to this demand by pointing the Ruger to the ceiling. "Well, I'll be a…"

"Please no cussing, my lady! Have you the same temperament as Tanner Trump?" Picket exited the tub, followed by Flanker. "It is very unbecoming for a lady to speak in a 'language' peppered with vulgarities."

"Enough!" Aegis's patience waned. What a debacle! How was he to convince his charge that they were quite serious about this mission and that they were not a troop of fools? He yelped when the woman's weapon discharged.

"Do I have your attention now?" Driven by the need to take control of the situation, and the return of that migraine, she'd opted for a dramatic pose.

The three stood side by side, shoulders back, chins high, proud as peacocks.

"You needn't have done that! Are you high-spirited? We were not informed of that! Nevertheless, we shall do our sworn duty to protect you." All three saluted.

She sighed audibly, lowering the gun and placing it securely in the waistband of her jeans. She was about to offer a handshake to Aegis first when another shriek rent the air. "Oh, oh! We are in trouble now. We disturbed Dame's beauty sleep." The minute feline dashed into the room, and swiped a paw across Aegis's shin, earning a yowl of pain for her effort.

"You come over here this minute, Dame! If you don't, you will go to bed without your supper." Eevee knew that the cat would be hungry after a long nap. "You've been asleep long enough, and these men are guests in my home. Now, apologize."

Dame wound her way through Eevee's legs and gave the decree a quick thought. Was it worth sacrificing the meal to strike out again? No, she was deterred by the sound of her own stomach betraying her need for victuals. Settling between her charge's feet, she purred. Better to have them think that she was complacent. She would have plenty of time to treat them to a good dose of vengeance for waking her.

"All right! Let's get out of these cramped quarters, and go downstairs to the kitchen."

The men queued behind Eevee who herself followed the kitten. Once in the large kitchen, she felt more comfortable. This was her domain. "Please have a seat." Flanker immediately dropped to the floor. "Oh, no. No, not on the floor!" It was obvious that she'd have to be specific when dealing with them, for he'd taken her literally. "On the chairs, at the kitchen table."

"Thank you, my lady." Aegis spoke for the three.

"Okay, then. Now, please refrain from calling me 'my lady,' I prefer Eevee, not Miriam. I do understand that you are being polite. However, in order for you to be less conspicuous, it will work out better that way. Now how about some refreshments? We can have a snack while you answer a few questions."

"Ah, we all three are quite fond of cookies, my l…Eevee."

Okay, that was a very direct, no-nonsense approach. He was a bit stodgy, but his intentions were pure. "Sure. Now, would you like milk, lemonade, coke, beer, or wine?"

Flanker was the first to respond with a resounding "yes!"

She found herself softening. He appeared to be a sweet-tempered sprite. "Yes, what?"

"Yes, please!"

Aegis interjected, "All but the wine, Eevee. We tend to nod off after our first glass."

"All?"

Flanker revised his request. "Yes, please. No thank you for the wine."

"Very well." As she removed nine glasses from the cupboard, she wondered how she was going to explain this to Bent. Oh, well. Another day, another entity! She set the beverages on the table three at a time, and decided that there was no better time than the present to explain some of the kitchen rules. The foremost being that she was not a servant and, that they would either help themselves or go without. "Let me get some treats." She found two opened packages of cookies and, arranged those along with her freshly baked oatmeal raisin confections. As she helped herself to a cold beer, she made her way to the table. "Now, I want to make one thing perfectly clear. I ask that you help yourself to whatever is in the fridge or cupboards. If you empty a container, or bottle, jot it down on the list that I have hanging on the front of that cabinet over there." She pointed in that direction. "We all share duties such as washing dishes, vacuuming, dusting, and pretty much all household chores. That goes for mowing the lawn, although that might be difficult for you to accomplish."

"Oh, you shall be surprised at what we are capable of, Eevee. We are very cleaver at adapting to our environment."

"I don't doubt that a bit, sir. These salient points are made in order to avoid any misunderstandings."

"We shall do our share. We do not wish to be a burden but a valued addition to your home until such a time as you no longer require our protection. Furthermore, we are a tidy lot. We will not destroy your property. I do apologize for the damage that we caused to the fabric that hung in your privy. Picket and Flanker struggled with the desire to remain wrapped therein. You see, the very fine texture of this cloth resembles the sensations that we experience in our mother's womb. When we are wrapped in the arms of Morpheus, sleeping, that is, there is no other place that we would rather be. That fabric is so comforting."

"You can recall being inside your mother's body while she carried you to term?" She was in awe of these little guys. "For nine months?"

"Yes, we remember this. However, we are cocooned therein for twice that long."

"Eighteen months?"

"Of course. Transmuters require the additional time."

"How much did you weigh at birth, and what are transmuters? I'm afraid I have never heard that term." There were more surprises! Eevee was intrigued.

"Five pounds. Transmuters are shape changers." He drank the remainder of his beer. Picket and Flanker finished devouring their treats and nodded every now and then as Aegis, who appeared to be their superior, continued. "There is no better time than the present to expound. Whenever appropriate, or on demand, I myself assume the persona of an eight-foot giant; Picket, a centaur; and Flanker, a cyclops."

"Are you able to change at will, or is this wonder controlled by emotion?" She no longer doubted the veracity of his disclaimers. She'd experienced many strange and wondrous things in her lifetimes.

"Either. However, you needn't concern yourself. We must be in a full rage for this to occur, and we are quite a patient lot, particularly with humans. However, to test our resolve could be very, very disturbing." He noticed that Picket was nodding off. "I believe that I must impose on your hospitality. It has been a busy day, and time travel does tend to make us drowsy. Is there a room where we may rest our heads? We require very little of our accommodations."

"Of course." As she arose, her cell phone chirped. "If you don't mind, I'll take this and then see to your comfort."

"Shall we give you some privacy?"

By the time that she retrieved the thing from her pocket, it stopped ringing. "I'll call them back in a few. Now let's go upstairs, and I'll get you settled." Along the way, she retrieved several items from the large linen closet. "This should do. I think that you'll be comfortable in the bunker."

"We are not at war! At least for the time being."

"No. That's what my nephews call it." She opened the door, switched on the light, and invited them in. "It may be a little dusty. As you can see, my cleaning bucket is on the floor in the corner. After you've taken a nap, I'll come up here and dust."

"You needn't bother, Eevee. We shall save you the trouble. We are not averse to household chores. After all, we are bachelors."

"Okay, if you insist. Now let's get these bed linens on." There were four built-in bunk beds, two on each side of the room. Pleasant quilted comforters adorned with cars, trucks, wildlife, and general boyish themes lay atop each mattress.

They made quick work of setting everything to rights, and then she reached for the three packages that she retrieved from the linen closet. Having opened each, she passed them out. "I bought a supply of these at the dollar store last week. It's the best place to find them. Now, I'm not sure where you prefer these, over or under you. Perhaps wound around yourself?"

Aegis was touched by her thoughtful gesture. "I thank you for your kindness. For the refreshments, and now this. Rest assured that we shall take care not to damage these." He bowed gracefully, reached for her hand, and made as if he kissed it; a true knight never let his lips touch a lady's skin.

Eevee curtsied, feeling a bit silly, yet she appreciated his sincerity. "Have a good nap. Shall I wake you for dinner?"

"Oh, that is not necessary. Flanker possesses quite the nose. He is able to smell a biscuit in the next county. Upon awaking, we shall freshen ourselves and then join you."

"All right, then. Would you like the door open or closed?" She remembered the sounds that were coming from her bathroom earlier and prayed for closed. Not that they were horrible, just loud.

"Closed, please."

As she descended into the kitchen, she could not help but wonder at their capacity to eat and drink so much. She'd better text Bentley a list of things that she would require in order to keep these little guys fed. She tore the short lists from the cabinet and fridge, sat, and began typing.

Dame made an appearance. She was not happy at all. "Am I to have to put up with these three? I vow that I shall require food and water upstairs in our bedroom, and you may as well move the litter box there as well. I refuse to relieve myself in front of those three!"

"Oh, Dame, please behave for just another few minutes. I have to get this list sent over to Bent, and then we can discuss your needs.

I just don't understand why you're so cranky. You're a good witch and so sweet to me."

"Beg pardon. This is not the preferred guise for me." She broke down into tears. "I found a flea on my underside today!"

Eevee pressed send, hoping that she hadn't forgot anything and then picked the cat up very gently. "A flea? Oh, Dame! I am so sorry! It pains me to see you so miserable all of the time. Was this Poseidon's doing? Sending you here in the form of a feline?" She examined the cooperative Dame's tummy. "I don't see anything. Maybe it was a sand flea."

"My disguise was Gifford's doing. We made a pact, a lasting pact that he would select my camouflage, and I, his. Within reason, of course. Nothing vulgar, or ugly. At the onset, I thought his selection cunning and enjoyed the eye patch, a nice touch. However, had I anticipated that we would reside in this climate and formidable environment, I would have allowed for more restrictions, further rules. We were acting silly, and now we pay the consequences of consuming too much champagne."

"We all have our crosses to bear, and hindsight will not change our destiny. Pride and egoism are faults that we should check at the door when dealing with the future." Her telephone chirped again. It was Bentley. She would have to answer this time. "Excuse me, Dame." Eevee gently placed her on the top shelf of the unit that she had configured for the kitten. It consisted of several shelves and was quite a luxury, as Bent had opined.

"Hi, Bentley! How are you making out with that list? I'm sorry for the last-minute additions. We have three new visitors, and I don't know how long they'll be with us. I promise to explain when you get back."

"Then Aegis, Picket, and Flanker have arrived?"

"You knew about them? Why didn't you tell me? Why am I always the last to know? Lord, help me. My head is pounding!" She sat at the table, and absently moved the cookie crumbs to form a circle.

"I was told that there was a slim possibility that they would be permitted to venture away from the Fringe. Although I specifically asked that I would be apprised of their arrival so that I might share this with you." He sighed wearily. "I am so very sorry. Do not think for one moment that I take your plight lightly. First, the church and its new leader, and now this!"

"It's not your fault, Bentley. I'm in need of a friendly hug. Anyway, was there a specific reason that you called? Any luck at Trader Joe's? I want to sit down tonight with a lapful of goodies, and watch Hallmark." She reminded him of Aiden's visit as well. "Seeing Aiden, Tanner, left me feeling kind of tilted, off-center. I was unprepared. I knew that this was coming, but never anticipated these emotions."

"I shall join you in the parlor this evening. You know how I dislike that channel. Different actors, sometimes, same plot. It is as they say 'corny.' However, I believe that you need the company."

"You would do that for me?" She chuckled.

"I would. Now, may we discuss this list? Do you think that I should purchase triple the treats? Perishables are another thing, but I have been told that these men have a voracious appetite for sweets and all other junk food for that matter."

"Please do. How about a barbecue for dinner?"

"That is a wonderful idea. Shall it be steaks or a pork roast?"

"No time to marinate the pork, so steaks it is. I'll get started on the potato salad and slice some cukes and tomatoes. I missed lunch, and am as hungry as a bear, or an Aegis, or a Picket, or a Flanker!" She laughed at the clever comment, and Bentley soon joined her. "Okay, that was a bad joke, but thanks for humoring me, hun. I'll see you in a few! Drive safely!"

"I am looking forward to your potato salad. Are you considering with onions or without?"

"Without chopped onions on the side. I don't know if our company likes onions. Or I'll make one bowl with and one without. How does that sound?"

"Delicious! Ciao!"

"*Au revoire, mon amie! Je t'aime!*" And she did love Hercules. He was the brother that she never had, and what a brother! He was always turning heads and had no clue how he affected women. He was humble, handsome, and strong, and was her bodyguard. Furthermore, he was capable of transporting the placket and disposing of its vile contents within the Splenetic Tree. She decided that they, as a group, would discuss this matter tomorrow. She'd had enough disruption for one day.

"Eevee, my dear, a favor, please." Dame had yet to settle down. "Would you please set me upon the windowsill? The sun appears to be shining there. It always soothes my disposition, and since you prefer that I refrain from walking on the countertop, it would be an impossible feat for me. My powers are useless in this current state, and I am not permitted to transform until you require my care."

"No need to explain, Dame. Would you like it if I place a dish towel on the sill first?" She sorted through several that were no longer useful and found one that was a bit plusher than the others. "Aha! This one should do nicely." After pleating it and setting it in place, she reached for the kitten.

"You are a sweet woman, Eevee, and have been exceedingly patient with me. I thank you." She purred. "Oh, yes, this is just the thing." With feline grace, Dame stretched and then settled. "The irony of all this is that I am my very own familiar!" She smiled broadly. Not a Cheshire smile but still a tad eerie.

"You never cease to amaze me, Dame!"

They settled in, Dame dozing on her perch and Eevee preparing the potatoes for the salad. There was, she had to admit, a certain domesticated pleasure at hand, and she vowed to enjoy it as long as she could. She heard the old truck enter the driveway. That darned thing sounded like it was on its last leg, but it simply refused to take that final journey to the junkyard. Her mechanic's impressive knack to doctor her sole means of transportation repeatedly was astounding.

Just as Bentley pulled into sight, a resounding crash from overhead startled her. "What now?"

Eevee climbed the stairs gingerly, cursing her inability to move faster. The last time that she ingested a malady, it had weakened the muscles and nerves in her right leg. She had yet to fully recover and was concerned about entering into another commitment in a weakened condition, fearful of another debilitating recovery. However, this was not the time to obsess over her plight.

"Is everyone all right up here?"

As she approached the closed door and paid full attention to the ruckus, she realized that Aegis and friends were, in fact, laughing. To be more succinct, giggling. She paused, smiled, and allowed it to continue for a few more minutes. They appeared to be having a great time, and she hated spoiling it. But when another louder crash resounded, she felt that she had no choice but to enter the room. She knocked on the door, which was an effort in futility because of the din, and gradually opened it.

"Is everything okay in here?" The scene inside was that of a classical pillow fight and your basic fun time, other than the cans of furniture polish that each combatant brandished. They dodged the spray, and then crashed to the floor in a fit of giggles. Giggles, mind you! Even the stodgy Aegis was enjoying himself and seemed to have the upper hand. "Um, excuse me? Gentlemen, may I ask what on earth are you three up to?" She planted both feet a shoulder-length apart, rested fists on her hips, and attempted to appear stern. That failed miserably when she was unceremoniously struck in the face with a throw pillow. "All right! Which one of you did that?"

The men finally acknowledged her presence. "I do believe that it was Picket." Flanker accused.

"I did no such thing! Aegis is to blame!"

"Okay, okay! No harm done, but would one of you care to explain what you are doing? This seems so out of character for you. And why in blazes are you spraying one another with furniture wax? I'm confused here!"

"Oh my." Aegis covered his mouth before another laugh escaped. "I do believe that our festivities must come to an end, gentlemen." He reluctantly collected the aerosol cans and returned them to the bucket from which they came. "Peekit and Cranker, heel! Oh no, that is not correct. Pillet, no, ah, Picket and Flanker, do sit for the moment."

Aegis appeared to sober a bit, and addressed their hostess. "I apologize profusely, my l…ah, Eevee. Upon awakening, we pro-

ceeded to set our pallets to rights and then decided to rid the furniture of dust particles. Those containers and sections of cloth were
right there. Rather than trouble you, we took up the task with verve.
Unfortunately, your End Dust must contain a substance that prompts
immediate inebriation in our race. We suddenly, and without con-
sent or effort on our part, got cock-eyed."

His bottom lip quivered ever so slightly as she attempted not to
laugh. Eevee had a feeling that they rarely got drunk, and that they
were contrite. "I don't have very much knowledge about your race.
As a matter of fact, I'll admit to none. You can't be held responsible,
you were just trying to help out, and your intentions were honorable." Lord, she was rambling. "I tell you what, why don't you take
a nap and sleep it off. And nobody else needs to know what happened." She suddenly remembered that dinner would be ready in
about two hours. "How long does it take for you to sleep it off, I
mean, get sober?"

"Two days, Eevee. We are not overly vinous. Yes, a brief two-day
period should do."

"Okay, well then, Bentley and I will try to be as quiet as we can
so that we don't disturb you."

"No need. We shall sleep without interruption regardless of our
surroundings. It is difficult to wake us."

"Sleep well then."

"Are those three up to something?" Bentley had already begun
to sort through several bags, and the cupboards appeared to fill nicely.

"No, but we won't be seeing them for a couple of days. They
have to regroup. Maybe it's that time travel, you know, like jet lag?"
She regretted not apprising him of the afternoon's events. However, a
promise is a promise. "I think that we should freeze those steaks and
keep it simple. How about hot dogs and potato salad? I'm already
halfway through fixing it, and now that I've begun, I'm craving a
healthy helping of it myself."

"Anything served with potato salad will be a pleasure for the
palate."

She stored the remaining items and then returned to the counter
where the potatoes were cooling.

"I will explain everything to them as soon as we all five are together. While they hail from the Fringe, and being who they are, I don't think that they will doubt me."

"I drove past the church today. There are several men seeing to its completion. They are in the final stages of painting, and a large sign has been erected. As told by Aiden, it simply states 'The Sanctuary'; its overseer goes by the name of Afleet. He shall welcome all who wish to attend services at his nondenominational sanctuary next Saturday at ten o'clock in the morning."

"Do you doubt, for one moment, that he is our nemesis? That he is looking to gain his evil power through the Splenetic Tree?" She trembled at the thought. It was bound to be very powerful at this point, and had yet to ingest two more doses.

"I am certain of it, my dear Eevee. We are approaching the final stages of our quest. I apologize if it is difficult for you to discuss, but discuss it we must. Evil powers are at play here, and their game may challenge the good in all of us, especially you. Know that you are not alone, that your champions are fierce, and the love and purity of your heart shall be our greatest weapon." He placed a hand atop her petite shoulder; it's such a small shoulder to carry this immense burden. "Now, let us set this aside for the next several hours. We shall dine and then watch however many installments of Hallmark that you wish to see." He refrained from telling her that the last time that he deposited the contents of the placket into the Splenetic Tree, he was able to feel its burl vibrating beneath his feet. Although slight, it was bound to intensify with the next two deposits. And he wondered how much of an effect Overseer Afleet's presence had on this recent change. "I cannot promise that I will not fall asleep, though."

She set aside her task long enough to embrace him. Without a word, each to their own thoughts and fears, they sought confirmation of their dedication to each other. "Thank you for everything that you have done for me, and for volunteering for this horrible assignment."

"You are welcome." He released his hold and smiled. "Now when would you like me to grille those hot dogs? I vow that if it is not soon, I may pass on those and devour that entire bowl of potato salad in one sitting."

They went about their household tasks, and spoke no more about the Sanctuary or the overseer. Eevee found great solace in performing mundane chores.

The days went by quickly as she prepared herself for the upcoming visit from Freud. The next child was an eight-year-old girl who was diagnosed with terminal brain cancer. She had been a patient at St. Jude's Hospital for the past two years. Her condition had deteriorated lately, and he suggested that they delay no longer. For this reason, she had left her bed a couple of days earlier than she should have, having just rid child number 7 of tumors as well. Thus, the pain and weakness, which she insisted, were minor. Hercules and Dame knew differently but were unable to convince her to wait longer. She prayed that she would improve over the next three days because when she began a 'heal' in a weakened state, the subsequent recovery was even more difficult.

Eevee finished cleaning her bedroom and then walked down the hall into the kitchen. There sat all four men, sharing a beer and lively conversation. "Good afternoon, gentlemen. It's good to see you up and about. Are you three all rested, refreshed, and ready for dinner?"

They politely stood and nodded in unison. Aegis was the first to acknowledge her.

"Miss Eevee! We have recovered from the effects of your polish. I beg your forgiveness for causing such a ruckus. The room has been set to rights. Thank you once again for the shower curtains. They bring us much pleasure."

"No need to apologize. I imagine that you were as surprised as I was that a cleaning product would get you drunk. As far as the curtains, I'm happy that you are enjoying them. Sometimes it's difficult to sleep in a strange bed." She noticed that Bentley had taken the steaks out of the freezer. "Will those rib eyes be ready tonight? I'm fairly drooling at the sight."

They enjoyed the steaks, a fresh garden salad, and rolls. Bentley cooked each rib eye to order, and was applauded at his ability to do so. Their guests rarely had the opportunity to sit down and eat with one another, enjoying the meal all the more.

"Oh, Lordy! Lordy! I vow that I am about to burst from the seams! Gentlemen! Kudos to all who contributed to this magnificent feast!" Flanker appeared to be on the verge of tears, frightened. She realized that he, of all, would take her literally. "Oh, no, Flanker! Please forgive me. I am not going to burst. It's just a saying, a play on words, another way of saying that my tummy is full." She was about to stand when Aegis calmed his friend, for all three were truly friends at heart.

"A lighthearted quip, Flanker. Do you comprehend?" There was a gentleness in his tone.

Flanker swallowed with some difficulty and then, completely out of character, blurted, "So what's for dessert?"

They laughed for a few minutes. These are humble beings that fate had brought together. She felt truly blessed.

"Let's see. Bentley bought an apple pie, brownies, and carrot cake from the farm stand, and I can attest that they are yummy. Should I put them all on the table, and let everyone help themselves?" She smiled. "A silly question, of course! Now if each of you will rinse your plates and put them in the dishwasher, I will prepare the sweets." She warned, "Bentley is very particular about the way the dishwasher is loaded, so I imagine that he will supervise."

He winked and joined in the fun. "There will be an inspection later."

Aegis calmed his partners down. Assuring them that this, too, was a joke, a witticism. As she spared them a brief nod, she wondered at Aegis's patience. It would probably be in short supply by the time that they returned to the Fringe.

She hated to disturb this domestic bliss, but there was business to tend to now that the three visitors were rested. The nineth child would arrive in three days, and she would be incapacitated for the better part of a week to ten. There was no putting this off.

"Thanks to all who contributed to this wonderful meal, and I am very pleased that you all enjoyed those desserts. I detest leftovers."

They applauded, only Bentley catching her meaning. He was astounded at the amount of food that the three were able to consume in one sitting. He made a mental note to check the freezer and perform a quick inventory. It just would not do to exhaust their coffers, depleting their supplies so quickly. Eevee would depend on him to take the reigns while she was incapacitated.

Eevee took a moment to cover Dame with a dry dishcloth. It could get drafty on the window ledge. Her kind gesture did not go unnoticed.

Flanker dropped a fork on the floor, interrupting the discussion. He apologized and crept under the table to retrieve the errant place setting.

"While you're down there, hun, don't you dare look at my legs. I am in dire need of a shave! They're so darned fuzzy. I vow that I'll need a lawnmower to do the job properly!"

Flanker, missing her meaning, called out from beneath. "I shall fetch that for you as soon as we are finished with our discussion!" No one laughed at the offer. It was too sincere.

Lord! She was going to have to be less creative in her speech in order to spare these men any embarrassment.

"Thank you. We'll talk about that later." She paused as he took his seat, brandishing the fork proudly. "I've given this some thought. If anyone asks who you are, I'm simply going to tell them that you three are cousins. If that's okay with you?"

"If you feel that is believable, then so be it."

"Aegis, I don't know what people will believe at this point, but for lack of anything better, we'll go with that."

"I guess the best place to start would be my layover in Atlantis and my misfortune at meeting Poseidon." She shared each detail with them in a clinical manner, her tone never once giving way to the emotional scarring that she endured. Each quietly listened hanging on her every word. "I'm going to take a break right here so that we can grab a soda, and then I'd appreciate it if Aegis would share some of the details of Tanner's stay on the Fringe. I am unfamiliar with that particular layover, and I think that I'd like to know how he spent his time while we were apart. Are you agreeable to that, sir?"

"I am." He selected two beers from the fridge. Aegis was beginning to experience warm feelings for their hostess. "Is everyone settled, then?"

Eevee listened intently, her beverage left untouched. She felt emotions attempting to rise to the surface, but tamped them down. Now was not the time to get misty-eyed. This day forth called for an inner strength that brooked no-nonsense, such as weeping or sadness. She needed to focus; literally and figuratively putting one foot in front of the other. When he concluded his narration, he bowed his head, and sat. Raising the beer bottle toward the center of the table, he toasted. "To the Fringe, to Atlantis, and to those who pass through our doors, may they possess the strength of conviction, the power to right the wrongs, and to make us proud." They all approved with a hearty "Here, here!" with the exception of Eevee, her plea silent, her vow singular in purpose; may we all survive our quest!

"Thank you, sir, for sharing that with us today and for taking editorial privilege. You, no doubt, spared my feelings during your 'soliloquy,' and I thank you. Tanner can be difficult at times."

"These are trying times, my dear. We have all been joined for a purpose, and personalities set aside, we share a common goal. Now, please tell me what we can do to be of assistance. That was not made clear to us."

"Then I will tell you. After I have ingested a malignancy, I must be rid of it. When the evil stuff is deposited in a placket, it is then emptied into the Splenetic Tree. To date, this has been done eight times. The nineth will be deposited next week. A child is scheduled to arrive in three days, and then I never know how long it will take for me to recover from the effects of that putrid stuff."

"Oh, dear!" Flanker fretted.

"Yes, my friend, oh dear, indeed."

"Hush, Flanker." Aegis chided. "Give Ms. Eevee time to finish without interruption."

She inhaled deeply. "The Splenetic Tree contains an evil that could potentially attract those who would consume it in order to do very bad things. To gain power. To do with it as they may. We believe that there is a threat that resides just down the road from us. He calls himself Overseer Afleet. He has refurbished an old church with the intention to attract people who do not worship, people who do not believe in anything but pleasures of the body, people who have been disappointed with whichever beliefs have let them down, and negative people who have lost faith. He gains power from that, but wishes more."

"He is not a very nice person," Hercules volunteered.

"The worse! That is why we ask that you three guard the Splenetic Tree night and day. Twenty-four hours, no more, no less. He is not yet powerful enough to take possession forcibly."

"Then, we shall assume that duty, Ms. Eevee. I shall plan a schedule that will allow for uninterrupted coverage. We are proud to be of service. And if he attempts to approach, our alter egos will give him pause. You have our word."

"Thank you, Aegis. Hercules and I would never have been able to do this alone."

Eevee convinced Dame to change into her human likeness so that they could take a walk together. While rare, she complied. As they walked along the peaceful country road, they came upon a black Dodge Ram with a decal of an American flag on the rear window.

"Dame, that truck looks familiar."

"Approach carefully, Eevee."

"No flat tires."

Suddenly, a terrible retching sound followed by a deep moan caught their attention. "Shoot me! Just shoot me! Someone put me out of my misery!" More retching.

"Aiden? Is that you?" Eevee ran around to the front of the vehicle. "It is! Oh, you poor guy! What can I do to help you?" She placed a hand gently on his back, unconsciously rubbing.

"Shoot him." Dame Puissant wrinkled her nose. "I cannot abide this smell!"

"We can't shoot him, Dame!"

"Yes, we can. I see a weapon on his hip."

Aiden stood quickly, a hand automatically touched the sidearm. He passed a sleeve over the corner of his mouth and turned to Eevee. "What? Is she crazy or something? You don't shoot a man just because he's hacking by the side of his truck!" He was embarrassed at the thought of these beautiful women catching him in a weak moment, especially Eevee. He'd have to make up some ground if he was to get her to go out to dinner with him.

"It's okay, Aiden. She just took you literally. She's from a country town in England and not quite accustomed to our quirks of speech."

"Is that what you call them? 'Quirks of speech'?"

"She does. Now, are you okay? You didn't sound very well a minute ago. Was it something that you ate?"

The three stood at the edge of a cornfield as Aiden explained that he had received some mail for Afleet, and that he, as a good neighbor, was bringing it to the overseer. He had walked to the back of the building in order to see if he could find anyone there. Nothing. There was no one to be seen. Just as he was about to set the mail on the stoop, Afleet appeared behind him as if by magic. "I'll admit, I was spooked. There he was, sitting in a wheelchair, all dressed in black, covered from head to toe, in this weather no less; and he didn't make a sound on that gravel. Maybe that's why he stinks, wearing all that clothes in the middle of summer. He invited me to join his congregation, and I begged off. Told him I'm Catholic, born and raised. I don't like him. Anyone who makes me feel grimy and unwashed like that can keep their distance. So I left. Told him I had things to do. Then when I got in my truck and left, I felt sick to my stomach and made it this far before I puked."

"Hmm. I'm sorry that you're not feeling well."

"Oh, I'm fine now that I sicked it out. But I would have preferred that you didn't catch me in the act. I get kind of cranky when I puke."

"Not a problem. It happens." She suddenly remembered that he hadn't met Dame yet. "Where are my manners? Aiden, this is my cousin from England. Dame, this is Aiden Wolf."

She had been resting on the kitchen windowsill when he had visited the first time, licking her behind. How disgusting was that? It was more disgusting than witnessing this man's stomach revolt. "My pleasure, Mr. Wolf. I might add that you are quite handsome when you are not bent over the side of the road, vomiting."

"Dame!" Eevee blushed. "That's not nice!" Speaking to Aiden. "She does have a habit of speaking her mind."

"Nothing wrong with that. At least you know where she stands." He refrained from offering his hand.

"Likewise. Now, Eevee, we have been gone far too long. Let us return to the homestead."

"I can give you a ride, if you'd like."

"We don't want to be a bother. And I don't think that Dame would be able to climb up that high to get in."

"Truck has a nice step that'll drop down so that it makes it easier to climb in."

"No, thank you." Dame took Eevee's arm. "Perhaps some other time!" And off she went, dragging Eevee along.

"Bye, Aiden! See you next week!" She grumbled. "Let go of me, please? How am I supposed to get him to like me if you don't give me the opportunity to spend some time with him?"

"In a ditch, on the side of a thoroughfare, with sputum at our feet, is not the proper social setting for pecking!"

"That's petting, Dame, and I haven't reached that base just yet."

"So now we must go to a ball field in order for him to kiss you?"

"Why me?" She gave up. It wasn't worth it.

"Because you, my dear, are Eevee Smith, formerly Miriam, and are in my care. Until such a time as that changes, you are stuck with me! Like it or not!"

"Love you, Dame." She never could stay angry with the woman.

"I do care very much for you, my dear. Would that, you act more the lady."

Eevee slipped her arm into Dame's, and the two enjoyed a mutual silence, each absorbed in their own thoughts.

And so, it came to pass that Aegis, Picket, and Flanker stood as sentinels, guarding the Splenetic Tree as Eevee saw to her latest, and nineth child.

Eevee showered, dried her hair, and slipped into a night shirt depicting Snow White and the Seven Dwarfs. She checked the time once more, curious as to the whereabouts of Dame Puissant. Just as she settled in the oversized recliner, slipping a round pillow behind her neck, the woman entered the room. She wore a set of scrubs, solid pick slacks with a lively tunic depicting kittens at play. Their attire was chosen specifically for the purpose of easing their charge's anxiety in the event that she woke while in Eevee's lap. It had happened only once, but fortunately, the small boy thought that she and Dame were nurses.

Freud carried an eight-year-old girl into the bedroom. She appeared to be asleep but was, in fact, under hypnosis. Most of the time, these chosen few would remain that way until he and Jules returned them to their hospital beds. Occasionally, when they did stir, he would be called upon to hypnotize them again.

Eevee reclined farther, feet up and spread sufficiently for him to lie the child on her back, with her head resting on Eevee's stomach. He placed a colorful blanket over the wee tyke then took a seat at the far corner of the room. She shifted a bit, getting in a comfortable position.

Dame stood to their right and placed a hand on her friend's shoulder. Their eyes met, and the pure witch schooled her face, offering silent encouragement. A single tear escaped and found its way down Eevee's cheek. This is the only telltale sign that she anticipated the oncoming pain and misery. "Shhh, my dear." Her throat clenched. It was difficult for her to remain unmoved. "Shhh."

Eevee placed a palm at either side of the girl's naked head and breathed deeply. As quickly as it began, it was over with. Her arms fell to her side, and her head lolled.

Freud took the child away. Mr. Verne, who anxiously awaited them in the kitchen, led them to his time machine and escorted them back to Shriner's Hospital. She was back in her room, sleeping comfortably. Her oncologist would soon discover that the tumors had vanished and, that his patient was cancer free, and able to return home, a healthy eight-year-old girl. Although he delayed her release for a few days in an attempt to understand this miracle.

The time elapsed, for the aforementioned event was no more than one-half hour. Thanks to the time machine and Eevee's preparedness. So little time for a child to receive the promise of a pain-free existence and a brave woman exiled to her sickbed. She had not recovered fully from their previous and eighth mission. Everyone knew that her recovery this time was surely going to be a difficult one.

Dame chose to let her patient sleep in the chair until she stirred. The longer that Eevee slept, the better. She placed the placket on a side table along with a basin of cool water and several facecloths, a tumbler of iced water, and some Tylenol. It was only a matter of time now. Soon the torment would exhibit itself, and the evil bile would fill the pouch.

The silence in the ranch house was oppressive, and was broken only by Eevee's cries of pain. Never had the five visitors encountered such sorrowful moans. Hercules chopped wood, cooked meals for those with little appetites, and performed miscellaneous chores with a lack of purpose. Flanker, when not on duty, wound his body snugly in his shower curtain, wept, and slept fitfully. Picket ran— first around the barn, then into the barren field behind the house, and then farther into the woods. He ran, not for exercise but to exhaust himself, hoping to keep the bad dreams at bay. Aegis scribed. Journalizing his experiences had begun several decades ago when his charge had been a young girl who had been abused. Her body was battered and violated, yet her sweet temperament was a testament to the reason that she had been selected for reincarnation. Her spirit remained unbroken, and she had become a child psychiatrist. How apropos. Eevee (Miriam), was an exceptional woman. She refused to permit adversity to damage both character and spirit. And, so he documented these recent events, adding them to his archives. Aiden Wolf labored beside Bentley for seven days, and while they had come to be friends, and respected each other in many ways, he could not get the man to open up about Eevee. It was frustrating. She never once came outside to inspect the progress of the chicken coop, which he had taken the pains to incorporate various functional and quaint designs in order to please her and make her job of collecting eggs easier. Initially, he thought that perhaps Bentley had a romantic interest in her. However, after a time, he appeared to be more like a big brother. He would recount lighthearted, comical events that involved her attempt at farming. He never once used so much as one single derogatory remark, exhibiting only a deep fondness of her antics. Well, he was determined to win her favor and would not give up.

Eevee awoke with a start, tearing the section of cloth from her brow. With labored breathing, she sat, drew her knees to her chest, and gently rocked.

"Slowly now, my dear. You must not rush. You've been abed for seven days." Dame rubbed the woman's back. Cooing and reassuring her to the best of her ability. Magic was forbidden. That was the hell of it!

"That can't be right. I just sat in the recliner a minute ago." She turned to the woman who had remained by her side, thinking out loud. "Dame, I don't care if people think that I've lost it, fussing over a cranky, one-eyed kitten. You're so kind." A weak chuckle escaped. "You must be more than ready for a bubble bath in the bathroom sink!"

"Oh, never mind! I say that we two should share a magnum of the best champagne that money can buy, sweetling!" She paused. "Only after you have recovered though."

"Oh no! Not me! The last time that we did that, I got snookered and put the moves on Hercules!"

"I shall never forget that man's mortification when you offered to neck on the back porch! It was priceless! Thank you for that memory!" Dame relaxed.

"What number was this? Do you remember? My mind is as foggy as the air in a Pookah Lounge."

"Nine. You've but one remaining."

"That's awesome." Eevee knew that there would be no tenth child. She had a better use for the tenth and final orb.

"Come now. It is time for you to enjoy your treat, and then rest for the remainder of the evening. In the morning, you may shower and join us for one of Bentley's famous blueberry pancakes; but after that, you will spend the remainder of the day resting on the couch. Now what color shall it be?"

"Red!" She stated with great emphasis.

"That bad, was it?" Eevee had lightheartedly created a chart one evening, listing the various colors of ice pops as they related to the severity of her discomfort.

"A real corker!"

Dame entered the kitchen just as Aegis was about to narrate his report.

"Dame. Shall I delay my dissertation while you select your refreshment, or may I continue?"

"If you could wait a minute, I am getting Eevee a frozen pop and shall return forthwith."

"And how is she faring?"

"Fairly well, considering… Let us be thankful that she is…oh, never mind." She feared that her emotions were about to cause her great embarrassment. Leaving the kitchen quickly, she tamped errant feelings.

"Here you are, my dear. A crimson treat!" Eevee jumped with a start. She'd been just about to doze. "Oh, I am so sorry, dear. Would you prefer to sleep?"

"I'll have that popsicle and then try to sleep a little longer. Unless, you need me for something?"

"No, no. Enjoy. I have an errand to see to, and will check on you when I return."

"Thank you. This pop is delicious. Fare-thee-well, Dame, and thank you for everything. You have no idea of how much of a blessing it has been to have you here by my side. I would have lost my mind if you hadn't been here nagging left and right." She winked, assuring the good witch that the latter was a tease.

"Enough said. Thank you. This has been an eye-opening experience. We shall all see it through to fruition. I promise. Adieu."

"Adieu, Dame." Eevee had no trouble whatsoever drifting off. If she hadn't known any better, she would have sworn that Dame had put a spell on that pop.

Dame went to the ice box, looking for her favorite beverage. "Please begin." She enjoyed a cool Coca-Cola now and then. However, there were none to be found.

"I am going to the market after Aegis completes his oral report. I beg pardon, my lady. These have been difficult times. We have been fretting over Eevee's obvious torments, the sounds filling our hearts with fear for her. The Splenetic Tree's animation, earth tremors, and Aiden's constant harping on the fact that we have kept Eevee at a distance. I vow that he fears we have murdered her and hidden her remains somewhere on the property."

"If she is up to it, he may visit with her in the parlor for a very brief period of time on the morrow. I believe that this may be beneficial for both parties."

"I am off to relieve Flanker in a few minutes. I regret to report that the tree and its surrounding area appear to get worse by the day. If Ms. Eevee has one more child to heal, the addition of more putrid malediction may animate it further. Who is to say what happens next?"

"I see. Please continue your vigilance. Afleet is gaining in strength. I can sense it."

"As do we all, Dame." Aegis rose from the chair. "We shall not fail you. Now I must set off. Safeguarding that area is exhausting. We have decreased each shift to five hours, for any time longer than that is not possible. It drains our strength."

"I know of a sleep potion that is temporary and may help you to recoup your reserves quicker. It has no ill effect, and you will rise refreshed."

"Thank you so much. Any assistance is welcome." He turned to leave. "Oh, if you would, please add a pleasant flavor? Flanker will not ingest fluids that resemble a medicinal quality or taste."

"As you wish." She addressed Hercules. "I must also go. I have important business to see to, and when I return, I shall prepare the potion for Aegis and his friends. Please watch over Eevee. She was weakened by this last challenge but still may attempt to overdue."

The remainder of the day was uneventful. Dame had yet to return. Eevee had risen and quietly suffered Bentley's fussing. He insisted that she recline on the sofa and do nothing more than watch television and eat. Her appetite had not returned, so he offered several kinds of soup, served with crackers and tea with honey. It all tasted wonderful. She dozed off and on and greeted Picket and Flanker with a wave, and immediately returned to sleep. When evening arrived, she was allowed to have a bit of peanut butter on wheat crackers, more tea, and soup. When her hunger was replete, she decided to return to her room and call it a night. She was awakened by a ruckus in the kitchen and drowsily made her way down the hall. It was Aegis. He had fallen just after entering the house and was making unusual sounds that brought fear to her heart. She ran to where he lay, fell to her knees, and then sat abruptly. She gently reached for his head and placed it in her lap.

"Aegis, oh, Aegis! What is it?" His wails grew mournful. They pulled on her heart, and she, too, began to weep. "Aegis, what is it?"

"My lady! Do not weep for me, your humble servant, for I am unworthy. I have failed you." He rose and attempted to assist Eevee to her feet, but she had exhausted all of her strength and was firmly rooted to the floor. Hercules came to his aid and carried her to the couch. Aegis placed a pillow beneath her head, and a coverlet to help subdue the tremors that shook her body.

"What has happened? Aegis, please tell me now!" Bentley was adamant. "Tell us immediately!"

"With deepest regrets and my wholehearted apology, I failed. The Splenetic Tree is no longer. Its contents depleted." A sob escaped.

"How can this be? Eevee has yet to finish with the children. There is one more!"

"What is this all about?" Dame Puissant strode into the room in a fury. "Why is Eevee out of bed? And pray tell, has it come to pass that Afleet has feasted at the burl, drunk of the putrid, festering liquid? Is it so then?"

"Yes, my lady." Telling of it sounded more and more disgraceful. "I was patrolling the area when a young woman approached me. She said that she and her friends were playing a game, but she had become disoriented and was now lost. As she approached me further, she sneezed into her hand, and I felt a light spray hit my face. I now believe that she had discharged a powder, a sedative, for all of a sudden, I collapsed onto the soil and lost consciousness. When I awoke, the surface encircling the tree lay dormant, and the tree itself, a shriveled mass, transformed into an ugly perpetual grimace." He sighed deeply. "I am the strongest of us three, but still I was unable to do my duty."

Picket and Flanker joined their leader along with the others, sensing that not all was well. They refrained from inquiring what was amiss and understood that Aegis would explain in good time.

There came a knocking at the kitchen door, summoning Hercules. He reluctantly excused himself, and came face-to-face with Aiden.

"It took you long enough. Please let me in. I need to speak with all of you, and I won't leave without some answers. I also have news regarding the Sanctuary, and I know that you all are concerned with its activities. I want to know why!"

Hercules allowed him to enter, however, detained him in the kitchen. "You cannot go into that room until you promise to calm down. All is not well here. For Eevee's sake, be silent until you are asked to speak. Is that clear? Otherwise, I shall remove you from the premises."

"Okay, okay! But never forget that I, too, am here to help her. Do you understand?" Aiden stood firm. Hell! He had hardly spent more than a few hours in her company, but he recognized love when he felt it. "Now, lead the way."

Dame Puissant was speaking to the group as Hercules and Aiden entered the room.

"I regret to inform you today that I must leave. I'm needed elsewhere. I shall not linger, for parting is difficult for me. I ask that all present support Eevee and help her achieve her final goal, which is to see this Afleet and his minions dispatched. This mission has been replete with hazards, some of them potentially mortal." She turned to address the one person present who had touched her heart so dearly. "Eevee, I shall remember our times together and pray that you are awarded a lifetime of peace and happiness."

Eevee took Dame's proffered hand and gazed into her beautiful azure eyes. "Lady Andromida, Hercules, Aegis, Picket, and Flanker have all taken up my cause. You, Dame, have stood staunchly at my side. You, Dame, have performed tasks that even a mother would find difficult. You, Dame, are grace, beauty, courage, and love. You, Dame, are a friend whose absence I will grieve." Eevee gently kissed the good witch's hand. "A parting embrace, please?"

The hug was brief but priceless because Dame was rarely demonstrative. She rose gracefully and then departed.

Eevee's voice trembled when she finally spoke. "So what is this? Am I holding court? If so, then I ask Sir Aegis to join me here." She pointed to the chair that Dame had just vacated and, for the first time, noticed that Aiden had joined the group. "Welcome. Do you have specific business with me? Can it wait?"

Aiden responded sheepishly, "No, ma'am. I've had enough of standing out in left field. I sense that there is some serious business at hand, and I will help as much as I can. Count me in."

She smiled. "Very well. Now what is it that you want?" She turned to Aegis.

He sat ramrod straight on the chair and spoke clearly. "I am prepared for whatever punishment you deem fit for the failure to perform my duty."

"Relax, my friend. There is no need for forgiveness. We are all at the mercy of our pre-destined fate. Now, let me hear from Aiden, if you please."

"Last Saturday, I decided to attend one of Afleet's meetings, for lack of a better word because it was dislocated and frenetic. I stayed toward the back of the room, trying not to be conspicuous. He talked briefly, welcoming the congregants and offering them the pulpit. Men and women alike spoke fervently about the world's injustices and those that affected them personally. It was hateful! From accusations of adultery to racial slurs. Anything that they were pissed off about. Excuse the language."

"No offense taken." She feared that the demon had grown more powerful as he fed on the anger, rage, and displeasure of his congregants. "This can't be allowed, gentlemen." She turned to Aiden. "Is that all?"

"He's called for a special gathering. Late tomorrow afternoon. The sign says that they will all be offered communion or something like that. I can't quote it verbatim. I don't know about anyone else, but I think that it's going to be a big thing, a turning point. They never got bread and wine, at least according to the rumor. That's one thing that people have been talking about. How can a church validate their existence, if not through communion? This whole thing scares the hell out of me. You have good, law-abiding citizens acting strange and losing their tempers. Furthermore, what I'm really concerned about is you, your cousins, and Bentley cleaning up Afleet's mess. I get the feeling that each and every one of you, except Eevee, are not who you appear to be. Now I'd appreciate it if you would come clean, because I'm here for the duration. Nobody, but nobody, is going to touch you, Eevee, not without going through me first!"

"Well, Mr. Wolf. Would you care to meet my three protectors? Those that you have vowed to stand with?"

"I would. I do."

She nodded to Aegis; he, in turn, to Picket and Flanker. And they, as a unit, transmuted. *Baptism by fire*, she thought.

Bentley picked Aiden up off the floor and gently slapped his face several times. Aiden awoke with a start. Hercules offered a hand. "And I am Hercules. No joke." He steadied the man until he was able to stand on his own. "All right, then?"

"Aiden, please sit down before you topple over."

"Sure. Any more surprises? You going to tell me that your kitten belongs to a witch?"

"She is a witch, well, was a witch; Dame Puissant, the good witch; and a very good friend. I regret that she was called away."

"You're a woman, right? Nothing kinky about you?"

"I am what you see before you. A simple woman who has a challenge to complete before I can go on with my life. A peaceful existence on my farm, raising chickens, and making quilts for the county fair."

"As long as she does not bake an apple pie!" Hercules teased, lightening things up for a moment. "The last time she tried, it took two days for the smoke to clear!"

"All right, Bent! I promise that I'll stick to oatmeal cookies." She rose to the objection of everyone in the parlor. "Stop fussing right now! I have a lot to do before attending services at the Sanctuary tomorrow."

Aegis released her arm. "So this is it? The culmination of our visit here on earth?"

"It is. Hercules, I'll need a ride after I shower and change. I have to pay Father Bell a visit. Aegis, Picket, and Flanker, I ask that you accompany me and prepare to reveal yourselves one more time if necessary. I'd really like to get his blessing before we confront Afleet."

"I'm with you, come hell or high water!" Aiden stood.

"So, it comes to be." Aegis replied. "Our finest hour! Picket, Flanker! We have received the call to duty."

Eevee showered, allowing the hot water to soak away some of the residual aches and pains. Her headache was so bad that she could feel it pulsate. Her stomach roiled, giving her pause to question her physical ability to defeat Afleet. She had faith in Hercules, Aegis, Picket, Flanker, and yes, even in Aiden. If she could convince Father Bell to accompany them, all the better. "Now, father, don't make me have to reveal the true nature of my friends. I'd prefer that you take me at my word."

She dressed quickly, pulled her wet hair into a ponytail, and joined the men. "We need to swing by the store. I have to purchase four gallons of water."

Aiden helped her into the truck. He could tell that she was weak. "You sure that you can take this guy on? Wouldn't it be better if you rested for another week?"

"I'll have to rely on the strength of my friends and my faith. This can't wait. If Afleet has kept some of the contents of the Splenetic Tree and intends to share it with his congregants, there is no telling what will happen. These people may be unhappy now, but jeez!" She shivered. "I had that stuff inside of me, Aiden. I know how it feels and how it affected my mental state. Thank God that Dame was there, encouraging me to sick it up! After I'd filled the placket, I was relieved." She turned to him with conviction in her heart and a courage that she found somehow. "I'm going through with this even if it kills me! To hell with Poseidon!"

"Another of your 'special' friends? This Poseidon?"

"He is no friend of mine!"

"Okay. So what if his flock decides to revolt, to riot? We could be in real trouble. It's not that I'm a coward. I just want us to cover all of our bases, and be prepared."

"At the first sight of a physical confrontation, Aegis, Picket, and Flanker will step in. The mere sight of the three should give them second thoughts. Of course, there's always Bentley and you."

"Thanks for the vote of confidence, but I can only handle so many. Of course, I could always bring my Smith & Wesson along. The sight of that might change a few minds."

"Lord, no! No firearms!"

"Have you ever stopped to think that maybe some of them might be packing heat? Have you?"

Eevee had, in fact, discussed it with her four friends, and they had, in total, pushed it aside. Was that a good thing, or bad? She just didn't know. Should she allow him to carry a hidden sidearm for his own protection?

"Then, carry one if you will, but only use it as a last resort and to protect your life, not mine. Please."

"I tell you what. I have an ankle holster. No one will be able to see it, and I'll feel a little better, a little safer. I just don't want to go in there without a means to defend you or me. Yes, I said 'you.' Give me some leeway here."

"Aiden, let's move on. I don't want to argue with you." Would she be okay? Even if everything went well, would she be able to recover? Was the residual power that she carried within her be sufficient to serve her cause? There was no way of telling. Her resolve wavered a bit, and she set it aside. Don't be coward, Eevee. God hates a coward.

Hercules and Aiden volunteered to go into the market and purchased the water. Once that was done, they drove to the rectory.

"Okay, we're here!" She turned to speak with the three guardians in the back seat. "You come inside with me. Aiden, and Bentley will have to stay outside. Father Bell may feel overwhelmed. I don't like revealing our ace in the hold, but you guys may have to convince the good priest that we have some muscle on our side. Is that okay with all of you?" Aegis, Picket, and Flanker understood her reasoning and nodded. They were, after all, here to protect her, even if it meant exposure. Worst-case scenario, they had the option of returning to the Fringe.

Father Bell was outside, pruning a row of beautiful rose bushes. He wore a set of head-phones and hummed as a seasoned hand snipped away. Eevee approached the good father from the front, concerned that she might frighten the man of the cloth.

"Father?" She mimed a gesture, pleading with him to remove the headgear.

"Well!" He hung the buds around his burly neck. "If it isn't Eevee Smith! It's been far too long, my dear!"

"Hello, Father Bell. I know that I haven't been to mass. I'm sorry, but circumstances beyond my control, well, you know?" She truly felt repentant.

"You've been ill. I can see it in your eyes. Your face is gaunt, and you've lost some weight." He was most gracious. "Come, let's go inside. I just made some fresh lemonade."

"Thank you, Father. That would be wonderful." She opted for as honest an approach as possible. "I have had a few bouts with tummy upsets. I believe that the worst has passed."

"Glad to hear that." He held the door. "To the left, two doors down. Have a seat. I'll be with you in a moment."

"Got it!" She propped the door open so that she could hear him coming, and offer a hand with the refreshments. "You'll like him, guys. He's a good man." She sighed wearily. When the cleric came to the door, she offered a hand.

"I've got it, Eevee. Now tell me. Something's wrong, isn't it?" He set the tray down and handed each of them a glass of the bittersweet drink. "Talk to me. I'll try to help if I can." He assumed his place behind a beautiful enormous desk that befitted a man of his size.

"I'll get right to the point, Father. I need you to join us as we confront Overseer Afleet. He is about to agitate his followers in a way that you could never imagine. If they partake in their first communion, the unholy kind." She shifted uneasily in her chair.

"Please, if you can be any more specific, I might understand exactly what is going on here."

"From the beginning?"

"Please, from the beginning."

Eevee offered an abridged explanation of her ability to heal nine children, leaving out Atlantis, and her tenth reincarnation. She reluctantly fabricated some of her history for fear of sounding too far-fetched. Although, her friends in attendance might reveal far more than she wanted. She admired and respected this man of the cloth. Before she could finish, Father Bell came to his feet. He was angered that she could think him gullible enough to believe her.

"To say that I am disappointed in you, Eevee, is an understatement. How dare you come to my rectory, wasting my valuable time, with such nonsense! You know the way out." While spoken softly, his words held a great impact. "Now, if you will."

Eevee stood as if to leave, and turned to Aegis. With a nod, he and his men transmuted. It still didn't make her feel better.

Bell made a sign of the cross and sat heavily. His office was fair to bursting with a giant, a centaur, and a one-eyed cyclops. "This is the devil's work!"

Aegis returned to his former self, annoyed. He motioned to the others to remain as is while he spoke for the first time. "This is most certainly not the devil's work. Miss Eevee has pointed out who the demon is here, and it is Afleet. We have been sent here to protect her. There is naught but good in her heart. Once we see this finished, we shall depart, but then and only then. I have come to know her well, witnessed her unselfishness firsthand, and my heart weeps for her each time that she sets her best interest aside in order to help others. Believe what you see. What your eyes tell you is true." He turned gracefully and nodded to his compatriots. "Picket, Flanker, at ease. We have made our point. If Pastor Bell refuses to find it in his heart to believe and keep an open mind, then so be it. We are done here."

Eevee sat tall throughout Aegis's dissertation. She thanked her lucky stars that she had brought them along, for her tale was so far-fetched, even she would be hard-pressed to believe it.

"Please resume your seats. I don't believe half of what you've told me, Eevee. I will admit that your friends are unusual. I've never witnessed such a thing and am still not sure that the devil is or is not at play here. I don't like what is happening at the Sanctuary. But this is a free country, and people are permitted to practice whatever doctrines they chose. It's called freedom of religion. Until they cause harm to others, rather than just to themselves, I cannot step in without permission of my superiors. It is not for me to decide."

"I appreciate that this is all way over the top and wouldn't believe it if it weren't happening to me. We are moving forward tomorrow as planned. I regret that you will not be there to perform last rites, because, there are no guarantees that my life will be spared." Having spoken the words frightened her even more.

"I'm sorry, dear. There is nothing that I can do."

"Aegis? Could you please go out to the truck and bring in the four gallons of water?" As the men departed, she faced Bell. "I know that I can bless water myself if I want to. However, I don't put a lot of faith in that. I would prefer it if you could bless it yourself." She reached in the pocket of her shirt and held out a lovely rosary. "This was my grandmother's. She passed it on to my mother. Each had it blessed by their parish priest, and I have yet to see it done. Please do this for me?"

He offered his hand, palm up and as she reverently placed this beautiful treasure on it. He took her hand, placed it over the rosary, and said a blessing. "God be with you, Eevee."

Father Bell blessed the water and then stood on the stoop of the parsonage, watching them drive out of the parking lot. There was both good and evil in the world; he'd seen it first-hand. There were many things that went unexplained, and who was he to doubt any of it? No answer. He decided that he would return to pruning the roses. And while he was doing that, he would pray for Eevee.

She accepted the good priest's decision with grace. She could not fault him, for her tale was, although true, far-fetched. With the courage born of several difficult quests over her past nine lives, she spent the evening planning her strategy.

At first light, she made her way into the kitchen and began to brew the first of three pots of coffee. Hercules, always the early riser, greeted her with a warm smile.

"Would you care for some blueberry pancakes?"

"Yes. That sounds great, but can that wait for now? I'd like to go over my strategy for our confrontation with Afleet."

"If you wish. I hear our three friends shuffling about upstairs. As soon as they join us, you may begin."

And so, the five of them sat at Eevee's kitchen table as she revealed a crude diagram of the Sanctuary.

"Here is the stage. Afleet invites all new members to come up and introduce themselves and share some of the reasons why they chose to attend his services. Aegis, Picket, and Flanker, you let me speak first, but make sure that you are up on the stage with me, acting as if you're waiting in line. Hercules, you sit in the back, close to the two doors. You'll leave…"

"Hey, everyone! What's this? What have I missed?" Aiden placed two boxes of doughnuts on the table. "Why'd you start without me?"

"Thank you for the treats, Aiden. I was going to fill you in later, but come and sit. I've barely begun."

Once he was brought up to snuff, she continued. "Aiden, you sit here by the side door. On our way in, you set two of the gallons of holy water just outside. Hercules will set the other two outside of the building as well. It's a simple strategy."

"It is, Ms. Eevee," Aegis commented.

"Afleet will not suspect that anything is amiss. Wear light clothing, nothing that could hide weapons. We want him to feel like he's in control. He'll be more vulnerable."

"This holy water is our weapon?" Flanker inquired.

"No, Flanker, *I* am our weapon."

"Oh, no, you're not, Eevee! You can't challenge him and think that you'll come out of this unharmed! I'm not even sure if he's human. He may appear frail, but I doubt if that's the case. No! I won't let you do this! You're frail as it is! You haven't fully recovered yet! No!"

"While I appreciate your concern for my safety, I have to ask you to sit back down and shut up! I'll say this now, and only once: if anyone here wants to back out, now's your chance. I am going to do this with or without you! It's my way, or the highway! The end!" Her fist struck the table soundly. "Shall I continue?" As she gazed at each one, they nodded. "Good. Now after I step up to the podium, I'll speak briefly; and when I make my move, Aegis, Picket, and Flanker, I want you to change into your alter-egos. Aegis, you will jump off the stage and take your place immediately in front of it in order to discourage members from coming to Afleet's aid. Picket and Flanker, you, too, will transmute but remain on the stage with me. This should discourage any intervention."

"Then, what do Hercules and I do? Stand there and twiddle our thumbs?" He was being difficult. This was brought on by fear, not belligerence.

"Aiden, I am about to ask you to leave! Your sarcasm is making me angry and nervous all at once and at the same time. Now, either reign in that temper, or I'll be done with you!" She regretted having to speak with him that way, but unless they each played their parts, this plan would go south at the drop of a hat.

"That came out the wrong way. I didn't mean it to come across as sarcasm. But I'm not leaving, Eevee. It would kill me if you left me out of this. I think that you know that."

"Apology accepted." She nodded. "Okay, Aiden, Hercules, please make sure that the doors are open to allow people to exit. I believe that once they see our three friends transmute, they'll have nothing to do with the Sanctuary or Afleet. We will need all of the that holy water on stage. Picket, I want you to watch Afleet and keep an eye on 'us' right away. Flanker, you, Hercules, and Aiden are on the clean-up committee. You're to be ready with that water when I call for it, because if I succeed, that stage is going to be in need of an immediate cleansing."

"Why are we going to clean the stage?" Hercules inquired.

"Because, if all goes as planned, it's going to be one heck of a mess and nothing that you're going to want to step in. Which is why I suggest that you wear boots!" She stood, exhausted. "Now, if you'll excuse me, gentlemen. Hercules will make you some of his delicious blueberry pancakes, while I get some sleep. It's going to be a busy afternoon, and I need some rest."

And, she did sleep. It was fitful, but at least it was better than nothing. When Eevee rose, she showered, dried her hair, and pulled it back into a bun. Placing a small basin in the sink, she reached for one of the plastic bottles of holy water and poured a small amount.

"Please, Lord, I beg your forgiveness. It is not my intention to disrespect this blessed water but to seek Your protection by anointing my body. I face the demon that is Afleet this day and ask for your blessing. Please give me the courage to see this through to fruition, and protect the men that walk with me. Amen."

She prayed as the cool water passed over her arms and legs, then before she continued dressing, she reached for the ornate container that held the last orb. Without hesitation, she swallowed it, washing it down with more of the sacred water. After a moment of meditation, she rose from the bed, grabbed the container of holy water, and then strode into the kitchen with a purpose. Thanks to Poseidon, she was now armed!

"Gentlemen, any time that you're ready, I'm off to seek my destiny and destroy Afleet!"

And so Eevee Smith, followed by her champions, set out with a purpose.

She stood at the podium, all poise and grace. Her introduction to Afleet's followers was brief yet succinct. Aegis and the others remained in line behind her as if they, too, would share their story. When she turned as if to leave the rostrum, she lunged at the being in the wheelchair, knocking it over, and landing with an audible thud.

Chaos reigned.

Aegis intercepted three brave men who thought to come to their overseer's aid, while Hercules shouldered his way to the stage, assisting those who had fallen in the aisle. Aiden's fear and frustration grew, as he had no choice but to allow the few who opted for escape from the side door to pass. He was eager to get to Eevee.

"Flanker! Flanker! Please help me hold him down. I can't get a sound grip on him!" She twisted in an attempt to wrap her legs around Afleet's hips. The cyclops grabbed the demon's legs and lifted him a foot off the floor, while Eevee wrapped both arms and legs around the overseer as he struggled to get away. His exposed skin bubbled wherever Eevee's anointed limbs touched. "Okay, now. Okay, Flanker, you can let go now!"

The five men stood witness in the empty hall as this slip of a woman, this valiant woman, placed one hand on the demon's torso, the other on his stomach. They covered their ears as piercing cries of fear and torment escaped the writhing creature.

He, it, began to deflate before their eyes, to collapse within himself. Its cries weakened as Eevee consumed the evil that possessed his writhing form.

She never wavered, never relinquished her hold, until there was naught but a collection of damp clothing left. As she rolled to the side, a great pain suffused her body. She writhed, crying out, "No!" as her companions attempted to come to her aid. She suffered this torment for the better part of several minutes. It felt like an eternity. When she rose to her hands and knees, the retching began. Between 'deep intakes' of air, the stomach spasms were almost beyond her capacity to endure. "Holy…" She pointed to one of the containers on the stage. "Water…"

Their attention temporarily distracted, all but Flanker saw the mound of clothing begin to move toward Eevee. He immediately stomped on the mess, took hold of it, and began to wring whatever evil remained onto the floor. When he was satisfied that it was no longer a threat, he tossed it to the floor and kept it underfoot for good measure.

As they poured holy water over Eevee and the vile mess that spread across the stage, she finally sagged, too weak to do naught but rest her cheek and close tear-filled eyes.

Aiden rushed to her aid, cradling her gently in his arms. "Shh, now, love. It's all over. You did it. You did it." He rocked her, cooing and whispering words of endearment as the others made certain that there were not so much as a drop of evil fluid left to be seen. "Come on now, love. Let me carry you out of this damned place."

Eevee gently pushed Aiden aside. While she enjoyed the intimacy of his touch, she meant to walk out of the former church with her head held high. She allowed Aiden to help her to her feet and, guide her down the stairs, and she did not oppose the steadying hand that rested on her arm. Aegis, Picket, and Flanker had returned to their normal state, as Hercules approached, taking Eevee's left arm.

They exited the structure together, pausing a moment as Aegis went back inside. Who would know that it was he, and not a fleeing member, who had knocked a large candle to the floor, setting the age-old timber aflame? He had no fear that any neighboring home or the distant forest would be endangered. That done, he rejoined his compatriots as they descended the stairs.

As these champions walked off of the last step, a loud retort rang out, and Eevee collapsed. As blood began to saturate her blouse, Flanker transmuted instantly and dashed toward the forest directly across the roadway.

"Oh, my God! Eevee! No! Please no!" Aiden captured her within his embrace before she could collapse the ground. "No, not now! No!"

Hercules kept his head and ran toward the parking lot, got his truck, and drove it over to where she lay. "In here now! It will take less time to bring her to the hospital ourselves. Move, Aiden! I will return for you, Aegis. You see what Flanker is up to." He tossed his cell phone to the overseer. "Here. Call the police!"

"I shall. Hurry, please?" Aegis caught a glance of Flanker carrying a man beneath one arm, a rifle beneath the other. The culprit writhed, terrified, begging for mercy, obviously fearing for his life.

The windowless waiting room was filled to capacity as the nurse entered. "Are any of you related to Eevee Smith?"

"We are cousins." Hercules stood and pointed to Aiden. "He is her betrothed."

"Yes. I am. Her, um. Oh, Lord! How is she?" Aiden shifted from foot to foot.

"In surgery. The doctors don't yet know what her prognosis is. Her vitals weren't too good. Has she been sick lately? The flu? A cold?"

"Ah, yes." Aiden offered. "She hasn't felt very good lately. She just wouldn't go to the doctors, no matter what I said." He improvised.

"Well, that would explain it. Oh, I almost forgot!" She reached into a large pocket. "I guess that since you're her fiancé, you'll want to hold onto these." She passed Aiden a clear baggy that held a childlike bracelet and necklace and what appeared to be a scrunchie shaped like an eye patch. "After she leaves recovery and is moved to a regular room, you can give those back to her."

"When will we know? When will we hear...anything?" Aiden was on the verge of collapse. He'd worried himself into such a state that the others feared that he would lose all control.

"It's going to be a while. I can't give you any more information than that. Sorry. Please help yourself to some coffee, or better yet, why don't you go down to the cafeteria and get something to eat? It will be closing soon."

"Thank you very much." Hercules stood at Aiden's side. "We shall."

"Bye now. I've got to get back to my other patients." She turned then hesitated. "The chapel is on the first floor, just as you come in."

"Again, thank you, nurse. We shall wait here."

Atlantis

"**M**Y LADY, DAME PUISSANT! YOU may not enter unannounced! Poseidon will have my head!" The page fretted.

"Step aside, I have no time for formalities!" She opened the door herself, walking into the same chamber that she and the others had spent several trying days. "I see that you still remain here in Atlantis. Are you awaiting the completion of [Miriam] Eevee's assignment?"

"Ah, Dame! Excuse me if I do not rise. You were not given permission to enter unannounced! I value my privacy." His gaze returned to the table before him. "Or would you care to see her perish from a gunshot wound? This is quite entertaining."

As she approached, Dame was able to see that the table had transformed into a televised accounting of Eevee's encounter at the old church.

"You are gloating. I think that you are entertained by the events that have taken place at the Sanctuary." She moved forward farther, clutching several scrolls closely to her breast.

"Ha! It is as I predicted! That mortal, that woman who thinks that she can beat me, has failed miserably!" He laughed as the three sentries transmuted. "I shall never again have to see her appear before my council prior to another life cycle that she does not deserve! She ceases here!"

"You think? And pray tell, why is that?"

"She did not heal a tenth child! She misused the last orb! She shall perish in that trauma center, with those fools at her side. Good riddance!"

"I think not." Dame placed one of the scrolls before him. "You may wish to refresh your memory. Read this scroll through."

He huffed. "What foolishness is this? I know what I decreed!"

"Read it!" Dame Puissant became angered.

"Who are you to speak to me in this fashion! I shall have you removed forthwith!"

"Oh, but you are in no position to do so. Here!" She tossed another scroll onto the table. "I will save you the effort. The Elders have asked that I oversee all council activities as well as selecting future participants. They have found that council activities, without censorship, can be very dangerous or unjust. Sitting and monitoring will keep me quite occupied."

"This is not so. There are those Elders that I count as close allies. They would not do such a thing without consulting me first." He was furious. With a shaking hand, he swept the offensive scrolls aside. "Eevee Smith is mine! She failed! There is naught that you can do to save her!"

"Again, back to your edict. You never once made mention of 'children.' It was her who chose to cure wee tykes who were terminally ill, not you. Now, as to the terminology, I believe that you said 'subject' repeatedly. Therefore, even Afleet was a subject, for he was filled with disease, with maledictions, nine to be exact! He consumed that which she discarded, filling him with malediction nine times over."

"No! No! I had her! I assigned a goal that was all but unattainable by a human, let alone a woman! She cannot do this to me! I will not allow it!" He stood suddenly, knocking over the ornate throne. "*You* cannot do this to me!"

Dame threw the final scroll on the floor. "That one seals your fate, Poseidon! Back to the sea with you! I hope that you find those creatures out there to be pleasant company. You shall not ever sit on a council again, let alone First Seat! You are evil and vindictive! Until you have learned some humility, you will get a good dose of your own medicine! You have been exiled!" She turned. "Page!"

The door opened. "Yes, my lady?"

"Please escort Poseidon to the nearest exit. He will not give you any trouble. You have my word."

Eevee knew that she'd had visitors earlier but was unable to surface from the darkness to acknowledge them. As she was about to surrender to the lingering effects of the anesthesia, she felt a light tug at the blanket over her breast. A sweet smile creased her parched lips. "Ah, Dame. Come to join me for one last cuddle?" The kitten purred. "Then come." Dame wore the red polka-dot eye cloth. "I always loved that patch above all." As the kitten made its way, it paused for a moment, licked Eevee's cheek once, and then settled under the blanket. Eevee shed a tear as she made certain that the kitten had settled into place and whispered, "Love you too, sweet cheeks."

Postscript

DAME PUISSANT SAT IN A garden amid apple blossoms that were in bloom. Their beauty reflected in the pristine glass that lined a path to the place where she would sit as First Chair for The Arthurian Council. The enchantress Morgan, Chief of Nine Sisters, was to share the chair along with her. No longer would there be just one, discouraging personal agendas.

Dame was visiting Avalon for the first time, and the organizers of this council determined that this would be for the best because the five other seats were to be occupied by Glitonea, Monroe, Thiten, Glitonia, and Thiton. She thanked her lucky stars that King Arthur was not one of the chosen, for she feared that his Highness might object to being surrounded by such strong-willed women. She expected Morgan to maintain order should the five sisters turn any disagreement into a sisterly squabble.

She inhaled the sweet scent, her mind wandering to Eevee. She missed the times when her alter-ego was able to set aside all responsibilities and simply curl beneath the blankets and cuddle. She had so enjoyed the bubble baths that Eevee prepared and the pains that she had taken to place a wonderfully soft sponge beneath her in order to prevent drowning or any discomfort the direct contact with the porcelain would cause. A whimsical smile reached her lips as she recalled the times that they spent selecting material amid the plethora of cloth scraps tucked away in her nightstand. Eevee had an affinity for the crimson dotted squares, while she herself preferred the soft hues of pink and yellow.

Dame had vowed not to visit her friend ever again, for that would cause both of them more pain and sorrow. However, she had weakened and visited her Eevee one more time, standing at the foot of the bed in the middle of the night. There she lay sound asleep while her husband watched a ball game in the living room.

When Eevee turned in her sleep, Dame saw that she wore a red polka-dotted eye patch wrapped around her left wrist.

"I am proud to have known you, my love. Live well!

About the Author

FOREST FOR THE TREES IS the first of several novels that Diane, a retired Insurance Agent, has decided to share with those who enjoy kicking back, and reading a good book. She enjoys time spent with her daughter's Lisa, Michelle, and of course granddaughter Trinity Lee. This former resident New Hampshire is now residing in South Carolina. She survives her loving husband Robert Raymond, and dedicates this first novel in his memory. Her day-to-day companions, Gyzmo and Sayge keep her entertained with their silly antics. These resurrected stories, that she began writing years ago, are now being molded into completed volumes. She welcomes you to a fantasy world of reincarnation, and invites everyone to meet a group of courageous characters, that understand what love and commitment are all about.

CPSIA information can be obtained
at www.ICGtesting.com
Printed in the USA
LVHW032341190721
693160LV00003B/310